THE KING'S ASSASSIN

THE HENCHMEN CHRONICLES

BOOK TWO

CRAIG HALLORAN

The King's Assassin

The Henchmen Chronicles - Book 2

by Craig Halloran

Copyright © 2018 by Craig Halloran

Amazon Edition

TWO-TEN BOOK PRESS

P.O. Box 4215, Charleston, WV 25364

ISBN eBook: 978-1-946218-45-2

ISBN PAPERBACK: 978-1-793081-21-6

ISBN HARDBACK: 978-1-94618-39-1

www.craighalloran.com

Publisher's Note

This book is a work of fiction. Names, characters, places, and incidents either are the product of the author's imagination or are used fictitiously, and any resemblance to actual persons, living or dead, events, or locales is entirely coincidental.

✵ Created with Vellum

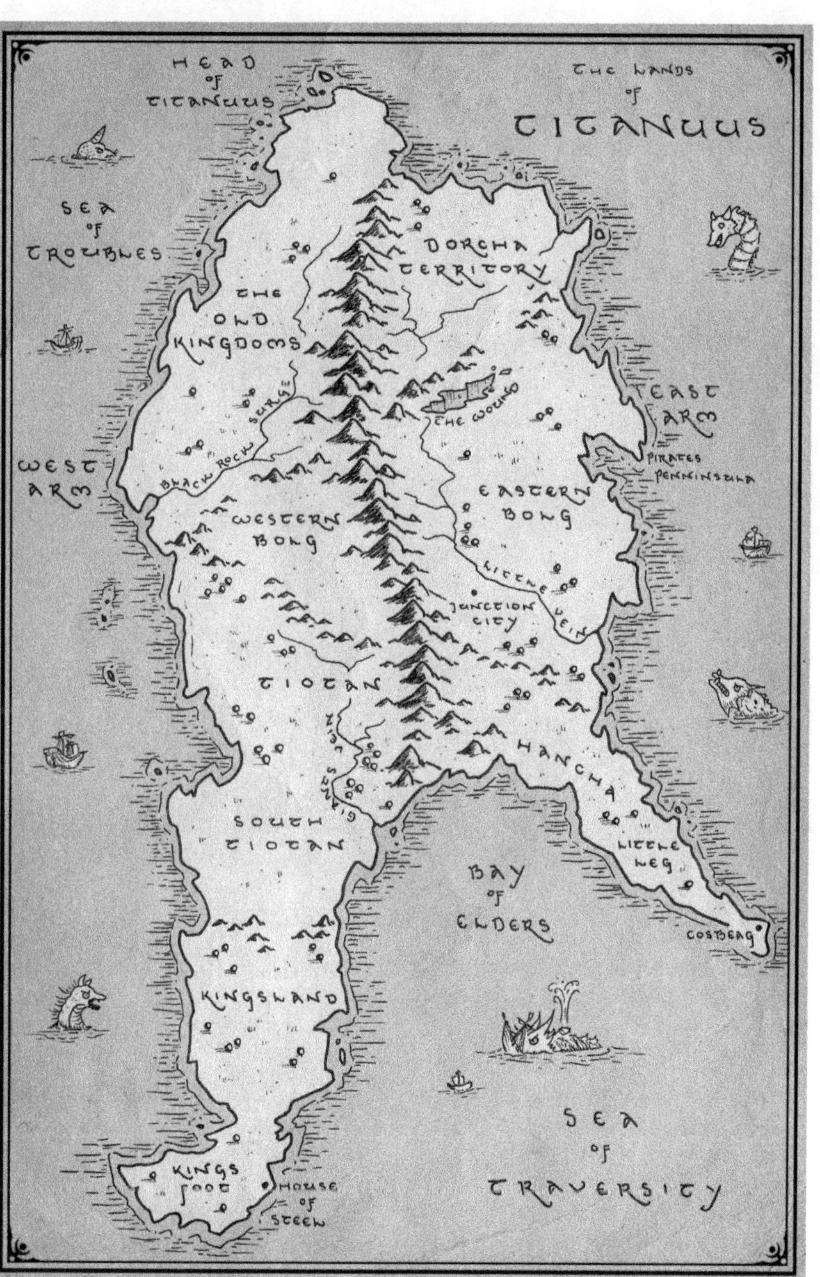

HEAD OF TITANUUS
THE LANDS OF TITANUUS
SEA OF TROUBLES
DORCHA TERRITORY
THE OLD KINGDOMS
EAST ARM
WEST ARM
THE WOUND
PIRATES PENNINSULA
EASTERN BONG
WESTERN BONG
LITTLE VEIN
JUNCTION CITY
TIOTAN
HANCHA
GIANTS VEIN
SOUTH TIOTAN
LITTLE LEG
BAY OF ELDERS
COSTBERG
KINGSLAND
KINGS FOOT
HOUSE OF STEEL
SEA OF TRAVERSITY

1

THE GREAT CRATER CALLED ELDER'S BIRTHING WAS AS NASTY A PLACE as a person would want to be. The muggy and humid climate had Abraham drenched with sweat. Steam rose from the bubbling tarpits as he and the Henchmen rode past. A fine mist swirled over the ground made of clay and mud that clung to the horses' hooves and made sucking sounds. The air stank of sulfur.

Abraham sucked down half his water skin and wiped his elbow across his brow. "Ah, nothing more refreshing than a swig of hot water."

He scanned the faces of the somber-faced company. Sweat dripped down Horace's bald head like rain. Sticks's damp ponytails clung to her neck. Solomon, the bigfoot, walked along with sticky strands of long hair and mud up to his ankles. No one else looked any better.

Abraham tried to keep the mood light. "It's not so bad once you learn to ignore the smell, humidity, and heat. Right, Horace?"

With his bearded chin sunk into his barrel chest, Horace

replied, "Aye, Captain." He spat out tobacco juice. "It's a fine place, better than the sands by the seas, if you were to ask me."

"No one asked," Vern said. His long flaxen locks were as wet as a mop. Sweat dripped off his chin onto his saddle.

The Henchmen had been following Solomon for hours through the crater, which seemed to have no end. They were surrounded by the oddly shaped columns of stone that stretched like stalagmites hundreds of feet in the air in some places. The rock formations were as smooth as river stone in some places and as jagged as broken rocks in others. Black-and-yellow moss grew on many of them. Trees and bushes grew with prickly leaves. Bugs the size of varmints flew and scurried over the ground. Some sort of cricket- or locust-like creatures were chirping constantly.

The insectoid chirping stopped. Some of the horses nickered. The group rode closer together, and not too far ahead, Solomon stopped. The aged eight-foot-tall sasquatch looked over his shoulder at Abraham.

"What is it?" Abraham whispered.

Solomon shrugged. "I don't have any idea."

Nothing seemed out of the ordinary. The terrain hadn't changed for miles. It had been one odd rock column, tar pit, and weird plant after the other. Every head in the group was slowly turning. Their eyes scanned the surrounding area, high and low. Swords and daggers scraped out of their sheaths.

Abraham's arm hair stood on end. He grabbed his crossbow and looked at Sticks, who was riding beside him. "Something's up," he said.

"That long-haired ape probably led us into a trap," Horace said as he slid his spear out of its saddle sleeve.

Dominga's horse reared up and let out a terrified neighing. The petite black woman clung to the saddle. Her horse went down. She leapt away and screamed.

Abraham turned his horse toward the commotion as the surrounding rocks and thatches came to life. A snapping turtle head the size of a man's burst out of a rocky shell and clamped down on Dominga's horse's leg. Similar attacks erupted all around.

"Holy crap!" Abraham yelled.

He fired his crossbow at a snapping turtle in a rock shell that scuttled toward his mount. The bolt skipped off the turtle-man's armored head. It snapped at his horse.

"Get the horses out of here!" he shouted.

Dominga dashed away from the turtle-men and jumped onto Vern's saddle. The strapping warrior unleashed his sword on a turtle-man running at him on two legs. The end of his sword split the hard shell-face right between the eyes.

The Henchmen turned their horses in every direction, only to face a swarm of attackers.

Abraham dropped his crossbow, which was tethered to his horse, and ripped his sword, Black Bane, from its sheath. The turtle-men's leathery skin was black, bright orange, and yellow. The irises of their eyes were large and bright. He hacked down at one that was biting at his horse with a fierce chop into its shell. A hunk of stone splintered off, but it kept coming.

"What in the seven hells are these things?" Abraham yelled.

"Terra-men, Captain! I've seen the likes on the shores of East Bolg," Horace bellowed. He jammed his spear into the rocky shell of his own attacker, but the spear skipped off the stony shell. "But they weren't so thick as this!" He gouged the terra-man again with his spear. "That shell is stone hard. Get away from my horse!" He gouged the terra-man in the eye with the tip of his spear.

The horse of the black-haired and broad-faced warrior, Bearclaw, went down to the ground. The well-built warrior landed on his feet. He chopped away at a yellow-eyed turtle-man with his two-headed Viking axe. Up on two legs, the terra-man came at

Bearclaw with its powerful stubby arms and clawed fingers slashing. It ripped open Bearclaw's tunic, and its neck stretched out of its shell. It snapped at Bearclaw and caught the warrior on the forearm.

Bearclaw cried out in pain and, with the axe in his free hand, whaled away on the terra-man. "Unleash me!"

The terra-men had the Henchmen walled off at every turn. The creatures weren't fast, but they were deliberate. They'd clamped down on the legs of half of the horses and brought them to the ground. Abraham jumped off his horse and smacked its flank with the flat of his sword, shouting, "Eee-yah!"

The horse bolted away. Two terra-men snapped at the beast, just missing it before it vanished beyond the columns.

Sticks slipped beside Abraham, holding short swords in her hands. Her busy eyes followed the approaching terra-men. "How do we kill these things?"

He sliced the stubby clawed hand off one terra-man. Its head ducked into its shell. It came at them both. He stabbed it through the hard plates of its chest. The sword sank in halfway to the hilt. The terra-man's head popped out. Its neck twisted side to side, and the creature flopped over and died.

"Like that," he said. "Just use your length."

"Easy for you. You have Black Bane." Sticks slipped away from a clawed, two-legged attacker and cut her sword into its hand, slicing one of its claws off. "I guess I can do it bit by bit."

The terra-man crept steadily toward her.

She clipped it in the nose, cracking off a piece of shell from its beak. "This is going to take all day."

Abraham unleashed a sword swing from the wrath guard position. The sword tore clean through the terra-man's midsection, sending its sloppy gray innards flying. "No pizza for you!"

Like a mudslide, the torrent of terra-men kept coming.
Fearlessly, the Henchmen fought on.

2

———

Solomon the troglin hoisted a terra-man up over his head and hurled it into another. The monsters' shells hit hard with a loud clack. The flying terra-man bowled the other over. Both of the fallen terra-men struggled to rise, having landed flat on their backs. Their scaled limbs writhed outside their shells.

"They struggle as mightily as any turtle I know!" Solomon shouted in well-spoken English.

Apollo and Prospero rushed the fallen terra-men, baring their long swords and scraggly beards. They pounced high and stabbed their blades into the soft necks of the terra-men with wroth force.

Using his length, Abraham sliced downward into the rushing terra-men from the high guard position. Their hardened rock shells were no match for Black Bane's dully glimmering steel. Turtle skulls were cleanly cut open, exposed necks clipped like ribbons. Black Bane sang with kisses of steel that sent the terra-men into eternal slumber.

Cudgel, the burly bald black man, cried out as a terra-man bit down on his ankle. He bludgeoned it with tremendous overhanded swings of his flail that busted the grit off its shell. "Get this thing off of me!"

His brother, the lean, long-limbed, athletic Tark, dashed through hordes of terrapin attackers. With two hands, he thrust his sword into the shell of his brother's attacker. The blade sank into the shell and went hilt deep.

The terra-man's mouth gaped open, making a raspy sigh.

Cudgel popped the terra-man's face with a fierce swing from his spiked flail. "Eat spike!" He hopped on one foot as his other ankle bled freely. "Elders' blood, it hurts!"

Tark slipped a shoulder underneath his brother's arm. "Can you walk?"

"Not if it's broke," Cudgel said.

Abraham hacked down every terra-man who got too close to him or Sticks. They were no match for his speed. The shelled bodies were piling up, but they kept coming.

He stabbed. "Take that, Raphael!" He sliced. "Eat steel, Donatello!"

"How do you know their names?" Sticks ducked a clawed terrapin swing and punched her dagger into her attacker's throat.

"I don't!" he said as he butchered a terra-man's head like a sliced-open melon. "It's a thing in my world."

He fought on, uncertain whether his fighting prowess came from Ruger or the sword, Black Bane. He had an uncanny awareness of his surroundings. He sensed his men, where they were fighting, and where the enemy was coming from, like a sixth sense of some sort. He tried to back away from their attackers, but the terra-men had them surrounded in all directions.

"We have to find a way out of here!" he said.

The ground shook. An odd sound like thunder followed.

Thooooooooooom!

"What in the hell was that?" he asked.

The terra-men stopped attacking. Instead, they scurried together, making a wall with their bodies.

The ground quaked as if stomped by giant footsteps.

Thooom! Thooom! Thooom!

"Captain!" Horace cried out. He thrust his spear in the air. "Look!"

The terra-man of all terra-men stepped out from behind the strange columns. It stood twelve feet tall, with burning orange eyes. Natural yellow moss and knotty rock-like ridges grew on its shell. In one claw, it dragged a dead horse by a rear leg. Its great neck stretched out of its shell. Its eyes narrowed and scanned them all.

Dominga fired a crossbow bolt at the monster. The bolt skipped off its winking eyelid.

It opened its mouth and spoke in a great, hollow voice. "Who dares to slaughter my children?"

Abraham wasn't sure what was more surprising—a twelve-foot-high juggernaut turtle or the fact that it spoke. His fingertips tingled as Black Bane burned in his grip. *This is madness.* He swallowed the growing lump in his throat and spoke up. "Your children attacked us, Bowser! We did not attack them!"

The giant terra-man swung its head toward Abraham. "My children hunger. Your flesh and bones will feed them. You are meals from the Elders. All living are meals from the Elders and their children."

Abraham glanced at the others and said, "We aren't meals. We're men. Just passing through. And since when do turtles eat flesh? I thought they were all vegetarians."

"You speak strange for a man of Titanuus. No matter." The giant terra-man opened its great jaws wide and bit the horse's head off. Its mighty jaws crunched the skull with tremendous cracking sounds.

Holding her belly, Dominga said, "I think I'm going to be sick."

The great terra-man tossed the horse's corpse at the feet of his children. "Eat, my sons. Eat the wild flesh." It causally wiped its stocky scaled arm across its mouth. "We don't have such succulent food in the crater of birth. The Elders must be thanked. But my children that have fallen must be avenged. For they are so very, very precious to me."

Abraham wasn't very keen on fighting the enormous terra-man and all his children. From his point of view, the odds were stacked against them. Lowering his bloody sword, he said, "I am Ruger Slade. Can I ask what your name is?"

The terra-man tilted his head, and with unblinking eyes, he said, "I am Barath the Ancient." He managed to show the slightest smile. "Thank you for asking."

"Barath, feed your children the horses. But these men must come with me. They are food for... the Fenix."

Barath's eyes enlarged. "Whaaaaat?" He blinked. "Whaaaaat?"

Rubbing the back of his neck, Abraham casually said, "Er... well, if you are thanking the Elders for the horses, then you better make a tribute in return. These men will do. I'm sure the Elders will understand your mistake when you attacked the bearers of their soon-to-be sacrifices." He was throwing all the baloney he could at Barath. "The sooner we depart, the better."

"I'm not aware of any sacrifices to the Elder spawn, Fenix." Barath's clawed fingers opened and closed. "I think you are lying to me, flesh and bones. Children... feast on them."

3

THE TERRA-MEN'S HEADS POPPED UP. OVER TWENTY OF THEM WERE still there, plus their father, Barath. The Henchmen backed into a defensive ring, brandishing their weapons.

His eyes fixed on Barath, Abraham asked, "Does anyone have any ideas?"

"We can take them, Captain," Horace said.

"Not without them taking some of us with them," he replied.

With Black Bane's handle hot in his grip, he felt more than confident to resume the fight. He wanted to fight, or at least Ruger did. But he didn't want to lose any men. Cudgel had a busted leg, and Bearclaw's arm might have been broken. He had to think of something.

He stepped forward and flashed his sword through the air. "Listen, Barath. You have our horses. Keep this up, and you'll have a fight on your hands that you don't want. I'll turn you and your boys into turtle stew. Or die trying."

Barath spread out his clawed hand, and his children halted. He eyes the sword. "That briar that you wield cannot hurt me. My shell is harder than steel... than iron of any kind." He thumbed his chest. "I'm indestructible."

"Maybe so, but your children aren't. How many more are you willing to lose? And do you really want to risk pissing off the Fenix?"

Barath rubbed his chin.

The Henchmen exchanged glances throughout the group. Every hard-eyed man and woman's knuckles were white from gripping their handles and pommels. They were ready to fight, every last one of them. Sticks twirled a dagger with one hand. Horace spat out brown juice. Vern's heavy stare was locked on the nearest terra-man to him.

"I adore my children. All are precious to me," Barath said. "You are bold, flesh and bones. I can honor that. Never let it be said that Barath cannot show compassion and mercy. My children will find your broken bodies soon enough in the crevices. Go on. Search for the Fenix. Greet death. We will dine on your bloody bones later."

"Grab what you can," Abraham said, as he picked up one of his packs that had fallen from the horses. "Thank you, Barath." He slung a heavy pack over his shoulder. "You wouldn't be able to point in the direction of the Fenix's lair, would you?"

Barath stretched out his arm and pointed a single finger. "You'll know it when you smell the breath of the Fenix. Keep walking as long and far as you can. Just put one foot in front of the other. In the end, it won't matter."

***

The Henchmen didn't waste any time distancing themselves from the terra-men. As soon as they were out of earshot, Horace sent Dominga and Tark out to search for surviving horses. They found three of them. Cudgel, with a broken right ankle, rode on one horse. The other two were loaded down with gear, which mostly consisted of water and rations. The rest of the Henchmen carried what they could, but that was it.

As for the head count, everyone was present and accounted for: Solomon, Sticks, Horace, Bearclaw, Vern, Iris the mystic, Prospero, Apollo, Cudgel, Tark, Dominga, and the last serving Red Tunic, the pie-faced Twila. Thirteen in all.

After making his head count again, Abraham muttered, "Long live the baker's dozen. Man, what I would do for a lox-and-cream-cheese bagel right now."

He had an aunt and uncle who used to own a bagel shop that he'd worked at one summer. It was hard work, baking in front of the bagel ovens, watching the rotisserie shelves roll over and over behind the glass shield of a five-hundred-degree oven. He'd thought that was hot, but it was nothing like the sweltering heat of Elder's Birthing. At the shop, he'd learned what a baker's dozen was. He'd learned bagels came in a voluminous variety of flavors, too. With sweat dripping in his eyes, he started naming them—anything to keep his mind off the madness. "Plain, onion, salt, poppy, sesame, everything, wheat, sourdough, cinnamon raisin, jalapeño cheese. Oh man, I loved those. Pumpernickel, blueberry, oh, and don't forget those bites with the cream-cheese frosting."

"What are you saying?" Sticks said. She had a small pack between her shoulders. Her brown hair was matted to her head. If she was as miserable as him, her expressionless face didn't show it.

"I'm thinking about the past. It was a lot friendlier than my present situation. I think I might have taken it for granted." Running his hand along the ledge of the path they walked, he noticed the corded muscles in his forearm. "Even though this body's much more fit than mine ever was. I almost feel like I can do anything in it."

Horace walked up from behind them and said, "You should have killed the turtle abomination with it, Captain."

"The answer to everything isn't always fighting. We all still live. We'll need every strong arm we have to face the Fenix, I figure," he said. "I can only imagine it's far worse than Barath."

"Aye," Horace brushed past him and Sticks. "If you say so."

4

———

THE COMPANY TOOK SHELTER LATE IN THE EVENING UNDERNEATH A large rocky overhang. A warm rain was coming down and splattering on the muddy ground. Abraham set his back against the rough stones, holding Jake's pack with his eyes closed. Sticks lay quietly with her head down by his legs.

Is all of this real or not?

He'd stayed so busy hauling through the crater with his nerves on edge that he'd only been thinking of finding the Fenix. So far, the king's quest turned out to be a mission in madness. The terra-men were an odd sort, as strong and violent as nature. Barath was an abomination that had bitten off a horse head with one bite. And the terra-men had talked, the same as any man.

He touched Sticks on the head. "Does everyone speak the same language?"

Without opening her eyes, she replied, "I don't understand."

"Well, everyone we've spoken to, man or monster, speaks the same."

"They all do, so far as I know. Perhaps there are other words that the secret societies and sects speak, but the kingdoms all share the same speech." She rolled her head toward him and asked, "Do you not speak one language in your world?"

"There are thousands."

"How do people get along?"

"It doesn't seem any different than this world. They still fight. And the more we understand each other, the worse it seems to get." Absentmindedly, he stroked her cheek. "I'm not sure if it's a good thing or not."

"That sounds confusing," she said.

"I think we made things too complicated where I'm from. As bad as this is, at least I feel like I know what to do and where I stand." He reached over, grabbed his waterskin, and drank. Out in the rain, Iris and Tark were filling up the waterskins. "Do you think I should have tried to kill Barath?"

"You've never lost a fight."

"He was huge. I'd have to stab him one hundred times before he went down. Besides, I don't think he is out to get us. It's his territory. We barged into it. But seeing turtles eat horsemeat like ravenous hounds... Well, that was creepy."

"How so?"

"In my world, turtles eat plants. Not meat or people, for that matter. They are smaller too."

"We have turtles but terra-men too." She laid her gentle fingers on his. "I think you did the right thing, not killing Barath. The old Ruger would have sent twenty Red Tunics to die before he would lend a hand."

"Yeah, well, with only one Red Tunic left, that just wasn't an option that I had." He eyed Twila, who had joined Iris and Tark in gathering the water. "Not that I would have used it."

Sticks didn't reply.

Abraham sorted through his thoughts. He wanted to get back

home. In order to do that, he'd need help. He might have found help from King Hector, if he could retrieve a Fenix egg and cure Queen Clarann. If not, perhaps Solomon could help. At least with Solomon, he didn't feel alone in this world. The hippie-turned-troglin gave him a sense of normalcy. Without Solomon, he'd have gone completely crazy. *I'd be locked up in an institution somewhere in a twisted version of the movie* Dream Team.

Sticks began to snore softly.

Solomon ducked into the overhang and squatted in front him. His gray fur was dripping wet. Mud was caked on his legs up to his knees. "How are you holding up?"

"I'm not turtle food."

"I've seen my share of oddities in this world, but that Barath character might have been the tops." He looked from side to side then set his eyes on Abraham. "I had no idea. But I don't think your Henchmen will believe me."

"I can't control what they think. They are a stern lot. Let's just find the Fenix egg and get this over with."

He offered Solomon his waterskin, but he waved it away. Abraham was glad because he wasn't very comfortable drinking after the old troglin.

"You said the Fenix is an abomination?" Abraham said. "Worse than Barath?"

"I didn't say. I said the troglin said. I have no idea what it is. I just know that it is supposed to reside in this crater. A thorough exploration should reveal the location to us, even if Barath didn't point us in the right direction. We'll have to keep our eyes open. I imagine it won't be too hard to find."

"What about his warning you mentioned about not having Elder Blood?" Abraham asked. "Do you care to elaborate on that?"

"I'm only passing on what I heard. When I first arrived, I ran with a pack of troglin. We traversed the hills of the spine for years." Solomon scratched the hairy whiskers covering his chin. "There were children troglin that ran with the pack. The elder troglin would teach them. I would listen in." His protruding eyebrows wiggled. "It was a strenuous time, to say the least. Adapting to this body. Pooping outside in broad daylight and not using leaves to wipe because the others didn't. Anyway, I used my silence as a guise for knowledge. I learned things. But do you know what I learned most?"

"What?"

"That I really wish I had a big bag of weed. Because this place is crazy." He laughed quietly, and his nose crinkled. "But the troglin were adamant to stay out of the crater. And yet, here we are."

"So, you haven't talked to anyone else like us?"

Solomon shook his head. "There aren't many people that are friendly with the troglin. I hoped to find a portal in these hills and had all but abandoned hope until you came along. If there is one portal, there has to be another. Something must have caused them."

"I agree, but what?"

"If we can figure that out, then maybe we can find our way home."

Abraham nodded.

Horace crept up behind Solomon with his eyes so wide that the whites were showing. He pointed his thick finger out into the darkness and said, "Something lurks out there."

5

"Let's get a fire going," Abraham suggested. "And get a head count too, Horace."

Sticks sat up and yawned. "What's happening?"

"We might have company." He came to his feet and walked the length of the overhang.

Cudgel was sleeping inside. Apollo and Prospero huddled nearby. Dominga and Vern were guarding the camp. On Horace's order, Iris and Tark started making a fire inside the overhang.

"What do you think is out there? The terra-men?" Abraham asked Solomon, who was shadowing him.

"This crater won't be void of its own critters. Lizards and big cats. Bugs as big as my feet. It's possible that your men might be jumpy."

"Jumpy? These guys? If they think something is wrong, then something is wrong. I trust them."

Solomon sniffed. "I have excellent senses, even for an old troglin. Let me wander." He stepped out into the rain and vanished into the night.

Horace returned a minute later. "They are all accounted for. Vern sent the word out. He's hunkered down thirty yards from Dominga. Something creeps through the brush, he says." He looked from side to side. "Where's the troglin?"

"Taking a look."

"It's probably his brood, waiting for our lids to get heavy so they can feast on our bones."

"I don't think he's something that we need to worry about. You have to trust me on this," Abraham said.

"You should trust your men. Once a troglin, always a troglin. They are hairy devils, I tell you." Horace moved to the group making the fire.

"I know," Abraham muttered.

He hoped he wasn't overlooking anything with Solomon. He was giving the man, allegedly from Pittsburgh, the benefit of the doubt. The Henchmen were a proven lot. They had instincts and had earned his trust. But until he saw something from Solomon that would change his mind, he wouldn't change course. He had a game plan and was going to stick to it.

After a few minutes of hard work, the fire, made from rotting limbs and gathered brush, crackled and glowed with orange light. The humid air was warm enough without the fire, but the glow offered security. Bearclaw stood over the flames. His right arm was bound in a sling Iris had made for him.

"You should rest," Iris said. Round-faced and well-built and curvy, she checked Bearclaw's sling and bandages. You're lucky that you didn't lose your arm."

"The king's ring mail saved me. It wouldn't be the first time it did," the broad-faced, flat-nosed Bearclaw said. "How long will the bone take to heal?"

"I don't know. Let the salve do its work. Everyone is different," she said.

With the new fire casting shadows into the overhang, the group spread out and stood out beyond the flames. The Henchmen's keen eyes searched the darkness, where night birds called out from time to time like squawking crows.

Abraham caught Prospero and Apollo yawning. The odd warriors said little if anything at all. They never seemed to have a care about anything. Apollo blew snot out of his nose. Prospero burped up something. They reminded him of a couple of guys he'd played baseball with. Cody and Roy Smith were brothers he'd played minor-league ball with. They were goofy and unkempt but could knock the cover off a ball whenever they got a hold of one. They never fit in. They never tried to, either. They just played ball with all they had in them.

Something approached from the darkness. It was Solomon, carrying a dead panther in his huge arms. He dropped it on the ground by the fire. The black cat had a silky black coat of white-splotched fur and must have weighed one hundred and fifty pounds. Its neck was broken.

"There's your invader. A black growler. I'm surprised you even heard it."

"And I'm surprised that you found it," Horace said. "We didn't hear so much as a scuffle out there. And we are supposed to believe that you caught this cat without a stir?"

"I got lucky." Solomon dropped to a knee. "It sprang at me. I grabbed that furball's neck and squeezed before it tore my heart from my chest."

Abraham took his eyes off the cat and looked at Solomon. Claws had raked his chest open. He bled freely.

"Solomon, you're wounded," he said.

"Only a flesh wound." The troglin teetered over and fell onto his side.

6

KNEELING, IRIS STITCHED UP THE DEEP CLAW MARKS IN SOLOMON'S chest. His fur was matted and bloody. Using a small knife, she cut the thread she carried and wound the remainder up on a spool. Solomon's chest gently rose and fell.

She patted his big face and said, "I guess he'll live. But those wounds were ghastly." She looked at her audience, composed of Horace, Sticks, Abraham, and Bearclaw. "I'd keep those claws of the black growler. They might come in handy."

Prospero and Apollo had begun skinning the beast. With the help of Tark, they cooked its flesh on a spit over the fire. The meat had a sweet savor to it, and Abraham's nostrils flared.

"That smells good," he said.

"Well, it should smell good," Horace said. "A black growler this big would fetch over one thousand shards of gold. The pelt alone is worth the most of that." He spat.

Iris frowned at him.

"What?"

Solomon's eye lids fluttered. He groaned and opened his eyes

21

then sat upright, grimaced, and clutched his chest. "Oh! Grateful Dead, my skin feels like it's on fire." His long fingers caressed the matted hairs on his breast. "Oh man, that thing sliced me open like a sheet of paper, didn't it?" He looked at Abraham.

Abraham took a knee and said, "At least your guts are still in you. I have to admit I didn't expect you to fall like a tree over a little scratch from a cat."

Solomon managed a smile. "Me either. I don't think it was the wound so much as the hunger." His nostrils widened as he sniffed the air and started to slaver. "The black growler smells like quite a feast."

Abraham hollered to the men by the fire. "Apollo, prepare our big hairy friend here something to eat. As well as the rest of us. We should have our bellies full when we head out tomorrow. Maybe this cat meat is just what we need." He frowned at Solomon. "That didn't sound right, did it?"

Solomon shrugged. "Meat is meat to me."

The Henchmen divided up the growler meat and gave the largest portion to Solomon. He devoured the growler's two back legs raw and licked the blood from his fingers.

Abraham delighted in his portion. The cooked slab he had was savory and as tender as any venison he'd ever had. Almost everyone in the company devoured the meat and licked their fingers with juice dripping down their chins. It awakened his senses, and the weariness in his limbs began to fade. For the rest of the night, the group rested. The rain stopped. The dawn came. A headcount was taken, then they broke camp and resumed the quest.

About one hour into the walk, the Henchmen passed between two columns and by a bubbling tar pit the size of an Olympic-sized pool. A wretched stink drifted through the air like a slap in the face. Half of the company covered their noses. All three of the horses began to whinny.

Solomon approached from the front of the line, his great arms swinging by his sides. He passed Cudgel, still riding on the horse. They were eyeball to eyeball.

He stopped in front of Abraham and said, "I think we found it or something that might be it."

"Are you serious? We haven't been walking an hour," Abraham said.

"Come look," Solomon turned and walked back in the direction he'd come.

Abraham told Sticks and Horace, "If we were that close to our destination, I'll be amazed."

"I'll be relieved," Sticks stated.

"The troglin probably needed the night to set the trap for us," Horace replied.

"Let it go, Horace," Abraham said. "That's an order."

"Let what go, Captain?" Horace replied with a befuddled look.

"Never mind."

The stench of tar, sulfur, and rot came out of a tremendous cave partially hidden behind the rock columns. Like a straight mouth, the cave entrance was at least one hundred yards wide and less than half as high. Tar oozed out of the cave in hot, sticky streams that filled the pools below it. Stalactites hung down from the inside of the cave like great teeth. It was a breathtaking and ominous sight that could pass for the entrance to hell.

Abraham breathed in the foul air. "That must be the breath of the Fenix."

All the Henchmen stood in a row, looking up into the massive cave entrance. Iris, Dominga, Tark, and Twila pinched their nostrils.

"Ew, this will be new," Vern said as he cast his lazy gaze at Abraham. "If there's an abomination to be found, then it's to be found in there. Might as well say your prayers, Henchmen. The end is near."

Abraham would rather have done nothing more than turn around and depart. That was him speaking. But inside was another man, harder than iron, who didn't fear anything. Ruger Slade would move forward, inch by inch, foot by foot, no matter what. He gave Abraham courage that even the toughest of ordinary men wouldn't have. He scanned the faces of his crew. They'd all come together that far. He wasn't about to tell them they could back out now. He knew they wouldn't do it anyway. He took a drink of water and mentally prepared his speech.

"Listen up," he said.

All eyes of the party fixed on him.

"I can't say for certain that this is where the Fenix dwells. But judging by the looks of it, if it's the worst place to go, then that's probably where we need to be going." He pointed. "We aren't going inside that cave, looking for a fight. We're looking for an egg. It's an extraction mission." Abraham hadn't done anything like this before, but he made it sound as though he'd done it one hundred times. It came naturally to him. "Cudgel and Twila, you'll both stay back with the horses. And if anyone else wants to stay back, that's fine. Probably, the smaller the group, the better. Besides, if we don't make it back, someone will need to tell our tale of how the King's Henchmen battled the Fenix."

The comment drew many smiles, even from Vern.

Abraham nodded. "All right, then. Grab your balls and cover your nose. Let's take this stinkhole."

7

THE HENCHMEN CLIMBED UP THE HILL LEADING TO THE CAVE'S entrance. They dipped torches in the stream of tar and lit them. The torches made black streamy smoke and cast a yellow-orange flame that crackled. Tark and Dominga scouted from the front, with Abraham, Horace, and Sticks not far behind them. They took their time entering the vastness of the cave. Abraham's eyes adjusted to the dim light. If the Fenix lived in the cave, he could only imagine it would be a massive birdlike thing.

"Everybody keep an eye on your neighbor. We don't need anyone getting lost," he said.

With a sour tone, Vern said, "This stink is almost blinding. It's worse than what comes out of Horace's butthole."

"Is not," Horace grumbled.

His comment brought forth a few dry laughs.

The cave sloped downward. They churned ahead slowly until the light from the cave mouth faded. The streams of tar that spilled out of the nostril-like orifices were gone. The cave ground was soft dirt with no signs of animals. No bats hung from the ceiling. Not a single cave bug crawled. The atmosphere was dead.

Holding a torch out in front of him, Tark said, "I can't see from one end to the other. It just goes."

Abraham expected the cave to narrow at some point, but it didn't. It stayed wide and continued long. "How deep are we in, Tark?"

"I'm over a thousand steps. That's pretty deep for a cave," Tark said. "I don't like it."

"Damn." Abraham had gone on a few hikes in his lifetime with his dad, Earl, who taught him how to count steps to keep track of his distance. It was all part of his father's pilot survival training, in case he was ever shot down in Vietnam. "A half a mile is pretty deep." He thought about the East River Mountain Tunnel, where he'd come through the portal. It was one mile long, but not nearly as deep and wide. He'd heard about caves that went on for miles and miles. This might well be another one of them. He looked down at his tracks in the ground. "Horace, make sure we don't lose our way out of here."

They moved on through the dark, murky stench, which continued as they walked downward. The rancid odor hung in the air like hot breath. The loose ground beneath their feet became slippery. Over one thousand steps into the trek, Abraham began to lose track of time as the pace ground on.

"Nothing could live down here," Vern muttered. "It's too foul for the living."

"They say the Elders can thrive anywhere," Iris said. She walked along with the hem of her robes pulled up. "But I have to admit I don't feel a thing. My own skills elude me, as if they've been sucked out of me."

"Don't anyone panic," Bearclaw said. "It's just a cave that smells like a bunghole."

"True, but something must be making that smell," Iris replied. "It's worse than rotting carcasses."

"Perhaps it's the bowels of Titanuus churning," Solomon suggested.

"Barath said that it was the breath of the Fenix that we smell," Sticks said. "Follow the breath—find the Fenix."

Horace clawed at his beard. "This is not a place for flesh and blood. That much I believe. But I agree. Follow the stink to the source."

Tark and Dominga shook their heads and carried on. Solomon followed behind them, drawing a curious look from Dominga. Solomon covered his nose.

Even Abraham had enough of the stench. His stomach turned, and he fought back the urge to wretch. The body of Ruger Slade seemed to have guts of iron, however. He had a steady hand that did not shake. As far as he could tell, the body that hosted him was unflappable.

"I see something," Solomon said. He stretched out his long hand and pointed his index finger. "Ruger, come and step beyond the torches."

Horace joined Abraham's advance. Far ahead, the slope took a steep incline into a wide channel cut in the rock, which had a green hue. "What is that?" Abraham said.

"An Elder's birth canal," Horace replied.

The group crept ahead. The stench worsened with every step. They made their way into the tunnel. The faint green glow came from tiny crystals in the channel's rock wall. The wide channel was still fifty feet wide but only twenty feet high. The light in the rock was very faint. The henchmen drew their weapons and walked through the channel of rock.

Sticks had her head down and was shaking it.

"What's wrong?" Abraham quietly asked her.

"I thought I could handle anything, but this place is turning my legs into noodles." Sticks swallowed. "All I want to do is vomit. This is awful."

"I don't think you're alone. Just stick together. No pun intended," he said.

Iris slipped in beside Sticks and took her by the hand. "I tremble within. Let's be strong together."

Sticks pulled away. "Let's just get it over with. If you want to hold hands, do it with Horace. This smells far worse than the tobacco on his breath."

Iris nodded. "You make a good point." She moved over to Horace. "Breathe on me."

"Er, certainly." He breathed in her face.

Iris smiled and held his hand. "As disgusting as I find your tobacco chewing, at the moment, I find it refreshing."

"Fresh enough to kiss?" Horace asked.

"Maybe, when we get out of here," Iris said with a playful smile.

Horace grinned from ear to ear.

Abraham's feet started to slide on the ground, and he fought to keep his footing. So did everyone else. The ground shifted beneath them like a living thing. One by one, with their arms flying outward, the Henchmen fell down. Abraham was the last to drop. He was sliding downward on a bed of black sand, and his hands desperately clawed through it. The slope suddenly steepened, and the slide increased in speed.

The Henchmen plunged deeper into the bowels of darkness.

8

THE HEAVY-SHOULDERED CUDGEL WAS SITTING IN THE SHADE, sipping on his waterskin when his nape hairs stood up. He cupped an ear and turned toward the cave. "Did you hear something?"

Twila was feeding one of the horses a handful of oats. She turned and said, "No. What did you hear?"

"It sounded like a scream." Using a stick for a cane, he tried to stand.

Twila hurried over and stopped him. "Be still and rest your leg. There is nothing you can do for them now. Besides, the wind howls through that opening. I think that is what you are hearing."

"No, it was a scream," he said.

"I've been riding a long time with the Henchmen for some time, and I've never heard them scream, aside from crying out in pain. Even that doesn't happen much." She took a cloth out of her belt and dabbed the sweat on his bald head with it. "You worry about your brother, don't you?"

"I'm the oldest, and we are the last, so yes, I worry about him."

"I worry too. You are very handsome men. I love your eyes—so light and, well, what is the word for it?"

"Spooky?" he said.

"Well no, that doesn't sound complimentary. Maybe they are haunting, but in a good way," she showed a toothy smile and put her hand on his thigh. "They are pretty."

Cudgel couldn't help but smile. "I think your eyes are pretty too. They are very soft and kind."

She continued rubbing his thigh and asked, "So, how does your leg feel?"

"Whatever Iris wrapped around it makes it tingle all of the time. I think it's strengthening."

"That's good." She eyed the loaded crossbow lying at his side. "Can I ask you a favor?"

"Of course."

"Since we have some time on our hands, I'd like to be productive. Could you tell me how to use the crossbow?" She reached across him and let her fingers caress the weapon. Her full breasts brushed across his knees. "I think it is fascinating."

Cudgel picked up the crossbow as she sat back on her knees.

He eyed her and said, "The first rule of the crossbow is to never toy with it when it's loaded." He removed the bolt and pulled the trigger so that the string made a loud *snap*. "I shouldn't do that either, but for the sake of training, I don't think it will hurt it." Using two fingers like a claw, he pulled the string back and locked it in place with a grimace. "Not many can do that."

"You are so strong," she said, elated and clapping quietly. "I'll never be able to do that."

As if by magic, Cudgel produced a clawlike key, which had two metal fingers and a handle. "Take this. Put the bow down headfirst and secure it with your foot." He pulled the trigger again. *Snap!*

"Use this to pull and lock the string back. You're a sturdy gal. If Sticks can do it, you can."

"Yes, she is very scrawny." She took the key and crossbow from Cudgel. She put the crossbow head on the ground and braced her foot against it. Using the key and both hands, she grunted and pulled the string back. Her arms trembled. "Ugh!" She locked the string in place. She panted. "Whoa, that was even more difficult than I imagined."

"It won't be so difficult when your life depends on it. You won't even think about it."

"I'd keep it loaded and ready just in case. I think I'd only be good for one shot if it was the last moment before melee." She aimed the crossbow at the columns. "So, can I load the bolt?"

He handed her the crossbow arrow and said, "Be my guest. Take a shot if you want. We have plenty."

She took the bolt and said, "I don't want to waste one."

Scratching behind an ear, he said, "I won't say anything, and I don't think anyone will notice."

She loaded the bolt into the crossbow slide and renewed her aim at the columns. "I wish I had something softer to shoot at so I could save the bolt."

"Again, don't worry about it. All you have to do is point and shoot. Hold in half a breath and aim the tip where you want it to go. Pull the trigger nice and easy." Cudgel pointed at a vine that had sprouted from the ground and grown around the rock column. "Try for that vine. It's pretty thick. You can do it."

She lowered the crossbow, looked at Cudgel, and said, "I want you to know that I appreciate this. Being a Red Tunic, I don't feel comfortable asking for help, seeing how I'm supposed to be the help."

"That's the military order of things. I started out as a Red Tunic too, and it wasn't easy, but I've made it this far. I figure after we get out of this fix, you'll probably be branded a Henchman too. Then the new Red Tunics can set up your tent for you. Heh heh."

"I'd be lying if I didn't admit that I daydreamed about it. But that's not all that I dream about." She looked him in the eyes and smiled. With her foot, she touched his leg. "I'd really like to be with you, and seeing how it's only the two of us, I think we can get away with it without anyone knowing."

Cudgel looked back into the cave and said, "You're right. But when I'm with a woman, I prefer to have her in a much more comfortable position."

"Listen, Cudgel, I'm a frisky woman, and right now, I'm feeling it for you." She started to set the crossbow down as she began unbuttoning her tunic with her other hand. "I don't care about the smell. I want you. Now, take those trousers off so I can take you."

"Heh. Why don't you take them off for me?"

She opened her tunic all the way, revealing her ample breasts clinging to a cotton jerkin. "As you wish," she said.

Cudgel made a smile as broad as a rainbow.

In a fluid cat-quick motion, Twila raised the crossbow, pulled the trigger, and shot him in the neck.

Making a gurgling sound, the wide-eyed Cudgel clutched at the bolt in his neck. His hot stare turned on her. He leapt at her legs, but she skipped away like a deer.

Laughing, she said, "Oh, Cudgel, what is the matter? You sound like you have something caught in your throat."

He limped at her and drew his sword. Through clenched and bloody teeth, he said, "Come here, you witch!"

Her warm and friendly voice had changed to a dark and deadly tone. "Now, why would I do that? You might try to hurt me."

Cudgel spat blood as he fought to catch his breath. He tripped and fell onto the ground then looked up into her face. He swung his sword at her feet, but she eased back out of range.

Twila squatted down. "I'll say this for the Henchmen. They all have a lot of fight in them. Too bad that just isn't enough." She pulled the sword free from his dying grip while he fought for his last breath. She leaned over and kissed him on the forehead. "If it's of any consequence, I really do find you very handsome. And if we ever had a moment, I'm sure we would have enjoyed it. Goodbye, Cudgel. Now the dirt will be your everlasting mistress. But her kisses will never be as sweet as mine."

Twila gathered the horses and rode away.

Cudgel sputtered his final breaths.

9

THE PAST - 2009

Beep. Beep. Beep. Beep. Beep.

Abraham woke with a sharp gasp. "Noooo," he moaned. A sharp pain lanced through his ribs. "Ugh." He blinked. His vision was blurry, and he thirsted.

Beep. Beep. Beep. Beep. Beep.

His heart pounded in his ears. He realized his body was immobilized. His legs had been lifted into the air and wrapped in casts. His arms were strapped down at his sides. He ached. His eyes drifted upward and to the side. He could see a heart monitor that he must have been hooked up to.

Beep. Beep. Beep. Beep. Beep.

"Jenny," he softly said, in a dry, cracking voice.

With a slight turn of his head, he realized he was alone in a hospital room. Faded green scrub-colored curtains hanging from the ceiling were half drawn around him. Flowers were everywhere in the room along with bright and colorful balloons that read Get Well Soon. Many of the flowers had begun to wilt in their faces. A few balloons hovered in the air, moving with the flow of the air conditioning. A dangling balloon string brushed across his chest. He tried to move his arms, but they wouldn't go.

He twisted his head left and right. "Jenny!"

Abraham's mind jumped back into the past. He was flying from Florida to meet his father, Earl, in West Virginia. The plane was a birthday gift for his dad, thanks to the big contract he'd just signed. From there, they were going back to Pittsburgh to sign autographs for the Pirates. It was him; his wife, Jenny; his young son, Jake; and his best friend and teammate slugger, Buddy Parker. Abraham was flying the plane. The flight was great. They started their descent above the mountain state. They'd dropped beneath the fluffy white clouds and cruised over the mighty hills of green when, from out of the rainless clouds, lightning struck the plane.

The instrument panel went crazy. A wing and the engine caught fire. Jenny and Jake were screaming. The plane descended quickly. Abraham did everything he could to keep the plane in the sky, but they were undoubtedly going to crash. The last thing he remembered yelling as he yanked on the plane's yoke was, "I love you, Jake! I love you, Jenny! I'm sorry, Buddy! Everyone hold on!"

Beep. Beep. Beep. Beep. Beep. Beep.

Tears streamed down Abraham's face. "Jake. Jenny." Fighting through the weakness, he managed to lift his voice. "Somebody help me!"

A black nurse peeked her head in the door. She was older, a little heavy, with kind eyes and wearing pink scrubs. She stared at him, and her eyes widened. "Oh my! You're awake!"

In a raspy voice, he asked, "Where's Jake? Where's Jenny?"

She hustled into the room, checked his vitals on the monitor, and said, "I'll be right back. Don't you go anywhere."

He caught her by the sleeve and said, "Where's my family?"

The nurse swallowed and gently pulled away. "I'll be right back, hon. Okay?" She vanished through the door.

Abraham's heart sank. He knew something was wrong. He'd seen it in the nurse's eyes. "Nooo."

His fingers found the remote connected to his hospital bed, and he blindly pressed the buttons. The bed lifted him until he rose far enough to see more of the room. A chair was in the corner, and Jake's Pirates backpack sat on it.

His lips trembled. "Please be alive. Please be alive. Nurse!"

The same nurse popped her head in the door and said, "Hon, it will be okay. The doctors are going to come to check on you. So be patient, please. I promise that we will do the best to take care of you."

"Can you tell me where my wife is?" he asked, but she'd already closed the door. "Please!"

10

THE PAST

THE DOCTOR WHO HAD COME INTO ABRAHAM'S ROOM WOULDN'T comment on his family. All the tired-eyed man said was, "I just did the surgery, that's all I did. Things look good. That's all I did." He departed, leaving Abraham alone in his thoughts, swarming inside his head like a hive of bees.

Shortly after the doctor left, Abraham's father came into the room. Earl was a rugged-looking man with angular features, clean-shaven with a buzz haircut. He always carried the presence of a military officer wherever he went. He wore a denim jacket and had a sad look in his gray eyes.

"Dad," Abraham said, his throat swelling. "Tell me. What happened? Where's Jake and Jenny?"

Earl walked over and put his warm callused hand on Abraham's head. His eyes watered. "Son, they didn't make it."

Abraham's body shook. He sobbed uncontrollably. "No, Dad. No, that can't be true!"

"You're going to have to be strong, Son. They are in a better place now."

"No!" Pain coursed through his body. He hurt everywhere. "No!" He looked right at his dad. "What about Buddy?"

"He's gone, too."

Tears streamed down Abraham's cheeks. He felt hollow inside. His entire life had been wiped out.

"Dad, I didn't do anything wrong. We were just flying. Coming in for a landing. There were clouds in the sky, but they were clear. The lightning... It-it came out of nowhere. I tried to land safely. I tried." He broke out in tears.

His father leaned over and hugged him. He was crying too. He held Abraham tightly and said, "I know, Son. I know. Nobody blames you. It was an accident. I'm just glad to have you back with us. You've been in a coma a long time."

Abraham stifled his tears. "What? A coma?" His lip quivered. "How long have I been in a coma?"

"Three months. You were all busted up when they drug you out of the plane. The doctors worked a day putting you back together. They got you stabilized, and the vitals were good, but you wouldn't wake up. Here." Earl grabbed a towel and wiped his son's face. "It's a miracle you made it, though. I'm glad you're alive."

"So, where are Jenny, Jake, and Buddy?"

"We waited as long as we could before we had the funeral services, hoping that you would wake, but when it didn't happen, we moved on." Earl rubbed his son's head. "No one blames you, Son. You have to know that. Jenny's parents understand. The investigation showed it was an accident. It's important that you understand this. It's going to be a tough rehabilitation for you."

"I don't want to rehab. I would rather I died with them. People are going to have to hate me. Buddy's family... They'd want to kill me. They loved him so much."

"Son, this might sound selfish of me to say, but I feel as selfish as you. You were bringing me a wonderful gift. Your intentions were good. I can't believe it turned into such a tragedy. Some things we just can't control in this world." Earl wiped his eyes on his denim jacket sleeve. "It's been hard on an old guy like me too."

Abraham had never seen his dad every cry before. Even when Earl accidentally cut the tip of his finger off with a skill saw, he didn't flinch. Seeing his dad cry made his heart tremble, and Abraham cried even more.

Earl patted him. "Let it out, Son. Let it out. Just let it all out."

Abraham had had everything he ever wanted: money, fame, and most importantly, a loving family. Now, all of it was gone. He had nothing left but guilt and emptiness. He cried continuously for minutes until his tear ducts went dry. "Poor Jake. He was so terrified when we were going down. I never saw anyone so scared before. Jenny was holding his hand, trying to keep him calm. She was so strong. So brave. I failed them. I shouldn't have been flying that thing."

"Son, you are a good pilot. I've flown with hundreds, and even the best have gone down because of bizarre circumstances and malfunctions. The important thing is that you don't blame yourself."

"They have to hate me, Dad. They have to. I was the pilot. They were my responsibility."

"It was a tragedy. It happens to the best of us. It happens to the worst of us."

He looked behind his father. "Hey, will you give me Jake's backpack?"

"Sure. Sure." Earl fetched the Pirates pack and set it on Abraham's chest. "One of the first responders fetched it out of the wreckage. It held up pretty well."

With pain running up his arms, he managed to lift his hands and grab the pack. He held onto it as if he was holding on for dear life. "Did you see them?" he asked. "Was it bad? Were they m-mangled?"

"I didn't see it for myself. The coroners told me. I wouldn't want to remember them any differently than the last time I saw them. The coroner said they died instantly, still strapped in their seats. It was a merciful way to go. They are with the Good Shepherd now, Son. You have to believe that."

He let out a shuddering sigh. "I know." Unlike his father, he didn't have the same final memory of his family's faces. What he saw was panic and fear. Jenny was strong, but the creases were deep in her face. Jake was a kid, scared to death. Buddy was bent over with his head between his knees, praying loudly.

But Jenny had said one thing he remembered. She said, "I love you, no matter what happens."

11

———

THE PRESENT - TITANUUS

THE LAST THING ABRAHAM REMEMBERED WAS SLIDING DOWN A slippery slope and into a void of darkness. He landed in a shallow puddle of tar that must have knocked him out. He was on top of someone and crawled off. His eyes adjusted to the tiny green lights illuminating the rocks. He was in yet another massive cavern. He hooked his arm around who he thought was Horace and dragged the man out of the tar and onto a sandy bank.

The Henchmen's fall had caused them to pile up on one another. Most of them were crawling out of the sludge. Abraham waded in knee deep and helped some of the others out. Most of them were coated in black, but it began to ooze off.

He found Sticks and pulled her to the bank. "Pretty sticky, huh?"

She looked up toward mouth of the tunnel they'd slid out of. "What happened? The ground just gave."

Iris was on her hands and knees, crawling out of the muck. She flipped her sticky hair from her eyes and said, "Something made it move. I felt it, like a living thing. I thought we were being swallowed."

Tark wiped his nose and sniffed the air. "It is foul like the innards of a belly. I think we were swallowed by the Fenix."

"That's preposterous," Horace said. "We're in a cave. Not that I know that much about caves, but we are in one. Not a stomach of some Elder beast."

"You don't know that," Tark said. He slung muck off his hands. "Titanuus still churns in his bowels. They say it's not dead yet. His heart beats beneath us. Who is to say that his spawn are not as tremendous as he is."

"She is," Dominga added.

Tark turned and looked at her and asked, "Are you saying that Titanuus is a woman?" He let out a gusty laugh. "Only a woman would believe that Titanuus is a woman."

"And only a man would believe that it is a man," Dominga replied.

"Because he is a man!" Vern said.

"If that is true, then how can a man give birth to the Elders," Dominga fired back.

Tark and Vern exchanged looks. Even Prospero scratched his head.

Bearclaw waded out of the sludge and said, "It doesn't matter because no one has ever seen an Elder. It's all legend."

"It's not legend," Iris stated. "And Titanuus is a man. That's how it's always been taught. Sorry, Dominga."

"You believe what you will. I'll believe what I will."

"We're here to find an egg, not identify Titanuus's gender. But judging by the smell, I'm pretty sure he's a man," Abraham said. "So, as long as we are here, let the search begin. Solomon, Tark, Dominga, lead the way. Keep following the smell."

"You heard the Captain," Horace said. "Let's find the egg."

Abraham wanted to get moving again. He didn't like the idle time. It made him think of his past, and looking back hurt too much. He'd thought he was over what had happened to Jenny and Jake, but when he dreamed about it when he was knocked out, it all came back. It was awful, worse than any stink he'd ever smelled. Anything was better than reliving his past.

The deeper inside the cavern they went, the worse the smell became. Tarlike pits were scattered like pools along the cavern floor. They bubbled, burbled, and popped. The Henchmen used the natural light emitted by the crystals in the caverns for direction. The cavern wasn't like a normal cave. It was different. The ground had a thin coat of slippery slime and wasn't hard as rock either. It was weird.

"I can't imagine anything thriving down here," Sticks said. "There is nothing to eat or drink. Not even the bugs have meat. It's barren."

"Something makes that foul odor," Horace commented. "Something must live down here."

"Yes, us," Vern said. "For now."

The company walked through the tunnels for a long time until they came to piles of petrified muck as tall as a man. Apollo scraped at one of the piles with his dagger. He sniffed the foul flakes on his blade and said, "It looks like excrement and smells like it, too." He wiped the blade off on his trousers. "Something lives down here, for certain."

"Captain, we still have some torches. Shall we light them and get a better view of our situation?" Horace asked.

"No. I don't want to alert whatever might be in here. Besides, that tar is oily. It might ignite if we aren't careful."

"Aye."

Ahead, Solomon drew deep breaths into his nostrils. His nose crinkled. "I think we are close to something." He lumbered forward with his long arms slowly swinging. He stopped in front of a moat of tar and oil that guarded a huge, long stone shelf. He pointed at it. "Look."

Sitting on the shelf of rock and partially hanging over the rim was a massive bird nest made of tree limbs, packed mud, and vines. It must have been over fifty feet wide.

Abraham couldn't believe his eyes. "I'll be. It is a nest."

Everyone stood at the ledge of the moat with their eyes fixed on the nest. The moat was ten feet across.

"I can jump it," Dominga said. She backed up twenty feet, set her feet, and sprinted ahead.

Vern stepped into her path and grabbed her.

"Let go of me, you idiot!"

"Oh, no you don't. Don't you remember what happened with those fire worms?" Vern warned. "We don't know what's in that moat."

"Good call," Abraham said. He picked up a branch that lay on the ground nearby. "Let's take a poke at it, shall we?"

He stuck the branch out over the waters. A globular tar man popped up out of the waters and snatched the branches from his fingers.

"Gah!"

Suddenly, the moat and the surrounding pools of tar began to gurgle angrily. Slimy, sloppy tar men emerged from them and came forward.

12

———

LEWIS

Days had passed since the Henchmen departed. The handsome and well-knit leader of the King's Guardians, Prince Lewis, slipped out of the House of Steel in the wee hours of the morning, unescorted by his men. Cloaked head to toe, he snaked his way into Burgess, where the bald and chinless Viceroy Leodor waited for him in one of the smaller but oldest cathedrals. Alone in the grand stone building, Leodor secured the entrance doors and led Lewis into the stony vault below the cathedral's sanctuary. Ancient crypts lining that were stacked one on top of the other. Leodor knocked aside thick cobwebs with his torch.

"I take it that you weren't followed," the complacent Leodor said.

"I've been slipping out of the castle since I was five years old. No one caught me then, and no one will catch me now." Lewis ducked underneath an archway and tore off the cobwebs that stuck to his hood. He pulled the hood off. "If there was one Elder I wished were dead, it would be the Elder of Insects. I hate these things."

"Don't blaspheme. You are in the House of the Elders," Leodor warned.

"They aren't listening. And no one has ever seen an Elder, anyway. Just a bunch of fairy tales told to frighten children."

Leodor spun around, halting Lewis's advance. The placid viceroy looked him dead in the eye and said, "You don't believe in the Elders? Where do you think my powers are granted from?'

Lewis looked down at the viceroy and said, "I don't know, and I don't care. For all I know, they come out of your bung hole. Good for you. Now, let's get this over with so you can brag about your sorcerous powers to some big-eyed enchantress want-to-be later."

The viceroy snorted and led Lewis to the back end of the crypt. A large sarcophagus there had images of wild dogs carved into the stone lid. He stepped around it where a sheet of brown canvas covered something over ten feet tall. Together, they pulled the canvas down. An ornately designed bronze frame, ten feet tall and just as wide, was mounted to a blank stone wall. Demonic skulls with horns and fangs were woven into the frame, with shiny stones set in the eyes.

"Creepy." Lewis stretched his hand toward the frame.

Leodor smacked his hand away. "Don't touch it. It could kill you instantly."

"I have my gloves on."

"Your pretty little leather gloves won't save you from the Underlord's wrath. Now, step aside."

Leodor handed Lewis the torch and picked up the candle-stands lying on the floor. Three of them were there, with three candles each. Each stand was as tall as a man, fashioned in twisted bronze the same as the frame mounted to the wall. The candle bases were small skull faces holding chubby black candles mounted in the skull. He made a triangle in front of the bronze frame and stood within the triangle of candlestands.

"Join me," Leodor said. After Lewis stepped inside the triangle, he said, "Light one candle and cast the torch aside."

"This isn't my first time. I know the routine."

Using the torch, he lit one of the small candles in the middle. A green flame burned. He tossed the torch outside the triangle. The flickering flames took the form of a tiny flaming demon. It hopped from candle to candle, lighting all of them one at a time before settling back into its burning place of origin. An icy chill went down Lewis's spine. The torch lying on the ground extinguished.

"Aren't you going to chant something?" Lewis asked.

"I will if you are silent. Be sure to stay—"

"I know—the protection of the triangle."

"Just be silent." Leodor closed his eyes, clasped his fingers together, and began to chant.

Lewis gripped his sword as icy arcane words spewed forth from Leodor's small mouth. The air left the room. The wall and frame before him warped and wobbled. A pinwheel of dark colors twisted inside the bronze frame. The spinning image slowed and took form. His heart thumped hard in his chest.

A man with blue eyes like burning crystals, wearing dark robes, his hands crossed over his chest, stood in the background. His head was bald and tattooed with black rings, the skin bluish, with a pewter pendant hanging from his neck with a demonic dog face on it. His iron-hard stare locked on Leodor. His words echoed loudly in the chamber. "What news do you bring forth, servants?"

"Oh worshipful Underlord, we humbly come to serve your needs," Leodor said with a bow. "It has come to our knowledge that Ruger Slade has changed personalities again. But in a more direct manner. He revealed himself fully, claiming that he was Abraham Jenkins, a man from another world."

The Underlord walked closer until the sunken leathery features of his stern face filled the frame. "And you killed him?"

"No. Not directly." Perspiration broke out on Leodor's forehead. "The king, well, put faith in the man. We sent them to the Spine on a suicide mission to fetch the Fenix egg and save the queen. We won't be seeing them again, ever. Ruger Slade, for all intents and purposes, is dead."

"Let's hope so, for your sake." The Underlord stepped back until he showed head to toe but still in a dominating size. He toyed with the pendant hanging from his neck. "The Elders have a way of meddling in my affairs. One never knows how or when they will show up. Be wary. The portals have unpredictable qualities, drawing in strange personalities and unique artifacts to this world. If they don't serve the Sect's intentions, continue to do away with the baubles that you find. We can't have King Hector gaining allies similar to our own. The portals are designed to give us an edge over him."

"None of that will matter once I am the King," Lewis said. "I'll rule the kingdom, and the rest of the lands will be yours, Master Underlord."

"Don't be overconfident, pampered Prince. Only a greedy coward would betray his own father, so I have little faith in you. But, to your fortune, your seed will be needed to feed the future, otherwise, I would do away with you." The Overlord moved away, and the image began to fade. "Keep me apprised." His picture in the mirror went blank.

"'Pampered Prince'?" Lewis scoffed. "Who does the Underlord think that he is? Wretched old fart. I'm way ahead of him."

13

ABRAHAM SNAKED BLACK BANE OUT OF HIS SHEATH AND CUT A TAR creature's neckless head from its shoulders. The swampy body of the monster sagged into the ground.

"They are coming from everywhere, Captain!" Horace roared. He stabbed his spear into another tar creature's chest, and it went through one side and out of the other. "I felt bones in it! Bone and sludge for blood!" Horace ripped his spear out as the creature kept advancing with its muddy tar arms outstretched. "It doesn't know it's dead!"

The Henchmen cut into the sludge men with unfettered vigor. Hard and heavy blades sliced through the tar-bodied monsters. The slow creatures fell under the cuts of steel. Others kept advancing.

Abraham swung his blade like a windmill and sawed away at them.

Bearclaw's double-bladed axe busted open face after face.

Apollo and Prospero swung their longswords with wroth force, splitting some of the creatures from the pits in half. Tar-coated limbs went flying. The battle turned into a bloodbath.

"There's too many!" Sticks said. Her short swords whittled away at her closest attacker as another slunk in from her flank. "Will our numbers ever find greater favor?"

"Just keep swinging!" Vern said. A tar creature drove its body into his legs. He went down to the ground. With his legs pinned, he chopped into it with two hands. "Get this thing off of me!"

The sludge monsters created a chain with their bodies, the last one standing inside the pit. Working as one, the sludge monsters dragged Vern toward it.

Seeing Vern scraping over the stone painted a horrific picture in Abraham's mind. Perhaps it was Ruger who told him what was happening. He didn't know, but his skin began to crawl. He noticed the bones of the dead at his feet emerging from some of the sludge men he'd slain. They were adventurers just like them, slain and turned into the living dead to serve as guardians of the Fenix and its egg.

"This sucks," Abraham said.

Vern was being dragged closer to the pit. "Somebody help me!"

Iris rushed to Vern's aid with her eyes glowing like stars. She chanted in a powerful voice. "Elders of Fire, bless these hands with flames that burn both the living and the dead!" Bright green-and-yellow flames engulfed her hands. She plunged them into the sludge monster holding onto Vern. The flames spread over the monster's body and spread to the others. They let out mind-jarring shrieks.

"Horace, get out those torches!" Abraham yelled as he chopped another monster down. "Iris, light them up!"

The spear-wielding bear of a warrior hustled away from the outstretched grip of his attackers and pulled the torches out of his pack. "Iris, set these torches aflame the same as you do my heart," Horace said.

"You have the worst timing when it comes to sharing your affection." Iris grabbed the torches by their heads and set them on fire. "But I like it. Maybe we'll share a kiss later if we make it."

"Ho ho ho!" Horace roared. He stuck his torches in the belly of his nearest attacker. "Merry kisses!"

The sludge man caught on fire. Horace tossed one of the torches to Dominga, who lit one sludge monster after the other.

The tar-dripping fiends retreated back toward their black pools.

"It's working," Abraham said. "Try lighting the pools."

Horace stuck his torch in the oily pit of tar, but the flame extinguished. Like a living thing, the oily tar tugged against Horace's iron grip. He braced his foot against the ledge.

"It's strong as a blacksmith," he said, grunting.

"Let it go," Abraham said, and Horace did. "We need to cross that moat. Use those flames to keep those things at bay. I have a feeling that fire won't keep them away forever." He approached the moat, looked at Iris and Dominga, and said, "Keep those flames above the waters. I don't think they'll come out if they sense the flame. We'll see." In a single bound, he jumped the moat and landed on the ledge of the other side. The moat didn't stir.

"Captain," Iris said, "my flames won't burn forever."

"I understand. Do your best."

Sticks jumped the moat next. She was followed by Bearclaw, Tark, Apollo, and Prospero.

Abraham started climbing the bed of rock that the great nest lay upon. Nearing the top, he grabbed hold of the nest's dangling vines. The nest was at least ten feet high. Like a squirrel, he slowly climbed it. *I can't believe how strong my hands are. I'm loaded down with armor and caked in tar, yet I can still climb this like a monkey.* He peeked over the rim of the nest, fully expecting to see a gargantuan bird ready to swallow him whole. Instead, he saw something else. Inside the nest was another swampy, gooey pit, with white foaming pus-like formations growing on top. It stank to high heaven.

The others climbed up by his side and beheld the foul sight within.

Sticks pointed toward the center of the Olympic-sized pool of goo. "I hope those aren't the eggs."

14

THE HOUSE OF STEEL - LEWIS

ON THE MORNING AFTER HE HAD MET WITH VICEROY LEODOR AND the Underlord, Prince Lewis was summoned to meet his father on the castle patio overlooking the Bay of Elders. He hadn't cared for the Underlord's undermining comments about him. He'd wrestled with them in his sleep most of the night. Yawning, he ran his fingers through his feathery locks of black hair. He was suited up in his suit of blackened chain-mail armor, covered by his emblematic maroon tunic, which showed the lion's face with wings coming out of it, the symbol of Kingsland. He marched down the grand halls of the castle, paying no mind to the subjects who bowed as he passed through.

I don't need Leodor or the Underlord. They are the ones that hesitate. When I'm king, I'll fix the both of them. Treating me like a pawn in some grand game... I am the game.

He met his father and Viceroy Leodor on the patio. King Hector stood by the wall, wearing a flattering suit of emerald and golden robes. The Crown of Stones hung over his brow. He was feeding the birds crumbs that he tossed into the air. Leodor stood near the king. The viceroy of the Sect had soft eyes with bags under them, looking as if he never slept at all. He didn't appear any different than he had hours before, when Lewis met him in the cathedral. Leodor was the one who had recruited him into the Sect as a young boy, and that was a secret they'd kept from his father ever since.

Lewis bowed. "Good morning, Father." He gave an irritated look to Leodor. "Viceroy."

King Hector gave his son a firm hug. "Good morning, Lewis. Have you had breakfast yet?"

"No. I'll pass through the kitchens later."

With the warm, goofy smile of a gentleman, the wavy-haired king said, "It's a sad thing when your mother is unable to force us to the tables. She always valued our time at breakfast. She would say it was the only time that she could round us all up before we all ran away from one another." He clucked and sighed. "We should keep with tradition."

"I agree. So, how is Lady Clarann? Her circumstance hasn't worsened, has it?"

"You would know if you would check on her once in a while."

"Father, forgive my detachment, but she's not my real mother though I am fond of her. She's been a good mate for you."

King Hector's brows buckled. "She has raised you like a mother since you were a boy. You bathed with her as a boy, for Elder's sake, and giggled all of the time. Shame on you and this twisted distance that you put between the two of you. Do you even remember your real mother?"

"Of course I do."

"Really, then what does she look like?"

"Beautiful. Curls of raven hair. A pointed nose and chin. She was a true aristocrat and not built with the broad face of a commoner."

"You disappoint me, Son. Clarann is not some commoner. Even your real mother would approve of her. She was a very understanding woman." Hector wagged his finger at his son. "She'd be disappointed with you if she saw how you were acting. It's neither princely nor knightly."

Lewis frowned and asked, "Did you summon me to lecture me on my estranged relationship with your wife, or am I called for a higher reason?"

"Funny that you should mention estranged relationships," Hector said. "I have a mission for you. Leodor informed me this morning that your half-sister, Clarice, has wandered from the castle. Apparently, she caught word that another expedition is underway to fetch the Fenix egg. If you'll recall, she tried to join the campaigns before, and we wouldn't allow it. Now your bull-headed sister has departed with her Guardian Maidens on her own personal quest. I need *you* to track her down and bring her back."

Lewis huffed. "Father," he whined. "That is a waste of my time. Send some of the Guardians after her. I'm certain they'll be able to track down that sawed-off little runt in no time. I have more important matters to attend too."

Hector poked him in the chest. "This is where you need a life lesson. There is nothing more important that family."

"She's not family. She's my half-sister."

"Listen to me, Lewis. She shares my blood the same as you do. That makes her whole blood. Do you understand me?"

Lewis looked down into his father's eyes and gave him a disappointed "Yes."

"Clarann doesn't know that Clarice slipped out. It would break her heart, so I want you to retrieve your sister and all of her maidens with all haste. We can't let anything happen to them. Do you understand?"

"I understand."

"Good. Now, you take twelve of your best Guardians and the fastest horses, catch up with her, and bring her back." Hector patted his stomach. "I need some milk. This news has my belly burning." He looked Lewis dead in the eye. "I'm counting on you to handle this, Lewis. Elder speed, Son. Elder speed." He headed back into the castle, leaving Lewis and Leodor all alone.

Lewis looked at Leodor and said, "Let me guess. You let the secret slip to Clarice, didn't you?"

Leodor replied, "It's possible my tongue might have slipped in front of one of the Guardian Maidens."

He smiled. "Good."

15

———

THE SPINE - ELDER'S BIRTHING

"WHAT IS IT, CAPTAIN?" HORACE SHOUTED FROM BELOW THE NEST. "Is there an egg? Yes?"

"There's something." Abraham had seen his share of eggs before. He used to eat them like candy when he was in training camp. He even tried drinking them raw like the boxer did in *Rocky*. But what he had his eyes fixed upon was different. Floating in the muck near the middle of the nest were three slimy green eggs the size of traveling trunks. "Man, that Fenix must be awfully big. I don't even think dinosaurs made eggs that big."

"What's a dinosaur?" Sticks asked.

"A giant lizard," he replied.

He scanned the nest and the surrounding area. On the other side of the nest was the cavern wall. He saw no sign of any creature or Fenix or any other monster that was living. Only the gooey bubbling waters remained. He looked down into the nest. The slimy waters filled up half the nest.

"That's still deep," he said.

Tark's smoky eyes were glued on the eggs. "Captain, how are we going to get one of those eggs out of there? They are huge."

"Probably heavy too," Apollo said.

"We'll figure it out." Abraham pointed around the nest's ring. "Bearclaw, you guys walk the perimeter. Make sure we don't run into any more surprises." He looked down at the others, who were standing on the other side of the moat. "Horace, do we have any rope?"

"We always have rope, Captain." Horace spat on the ground. His face clenched. "What do you need rope for?"

"These eggs are pretty big. We might have to tow them out if that can be done."

"I'll get the rope ready," Horace said.

Abraham sat down on the rim of the nest, facing inward. Sticks joined him. Bearclaw walked clockwise around the nest. Tark and Dominga walked the rim counterclockwise. Abraham kept his eyes on the eggs. They were lumpy things, coated in grit and grime, with little craters coating the shell. All of them were different sizes. The stinking waters bubbled around them.

"Any ideas?" he asked Sticks.

"Do we take one, or do we take them all?"

"A good question. I don't see us getting all of them out of here. Not to mention that it's going to be harder getting out than it was getting in. Unless there is another way out of here." He glanced up at the ceiling. "It would really suck to die down here. A pretty smelly place for a funeral."

Bearclaw, Tark, and Dominga made it to the other side of the nest.

"Do you see anything?" he asked them.

Tark shrugged. Bearclaw ran his hands over the back wall. Dominga stared down into the pool. Bearclaw's hands froze, and he muttered something. Tark and Dominga turned. Both of them kneeled beside Bearclaw, and they looked at the wall. Both of them jerked their hands back.

Abraham stood up. "What is it?"

"Not sure," Bearclaw said, "but it looks like this wall has eyes."

"Let me take a look."

Abraham and Sticks hustled over to the other side of the nest. He took a knee by Bearclaw. Sure enough, a reptilian eyeball bigger than his head stared right back at him. It was one of many. He waved his hand in front of it. It didn't blink.

Quietly he said, "Whatever it is, I think it sleeps."

"How do you know that?" Sticks asked.

"Did you ever see *Conan the Barbarian*? You know, when he drips sweat onto that giant snake's eye and its lens opens?" he asked.

They gave Abraham blank stares.

"Never mind. Wrong world. Wrong time. The point, if it's sleeping, don't jostle it."

"Do you think that it's the Fenix?" Tark asked.

"Probably."

"Maybe we should kill it," Bearclaw said.

"No, I don't think you want to wake a sleeping giant. Let's leave it alone and go. We're going to have a hard enough time getting the eggs out of here. Tark, you and Dominga keep an eye on, well, those eyes. We'll figure out how to get that egg out."

Sploosh! Sploosh!

Everyone's heads snapped around toward the center of the nest. Prospero and Apollo were wading chest deep through the pool of sticky slime.

"Are you guys crazy?" Abraham said in a hushed whisper.

The older Henchmen approached the eggs.

"They are crazy," Bearclaw said. "One should never be surprised by what they try and do. Better them than us."

"How's the water?" Abraham asked.

"Smelly and warm. A fine mud bath. No doubt that the swine would like it," Apollo said.

"I think the swine do like it," Dominga said with a smile.

Apollo and Prospero made their way to the eggs and pushed on them. "Captain, which one should we take?" Apollo asked.

"Let's start light. Try the smallest." He looked at the others behind him and shrugged. "Does anyone know anything about the incubation cycle of an Elder-spawn egg? If you do, speak up now or forever hold your peace."

Each one in the company gave him a stiff shake of the head.

"Is everything going well up there, Captain?" Horace shouted.

"Good Lord. Sticks, get over there and shut him up. Eventually, he's going to wake something up. Fetch the rope, too." He looked at Dominga and Tark, who were eyeing the eyes in the wall. "Did it blink?"

Dominga shook her head.

Apollo and Prospero pushed on the smallest egg. It wobbled in its floating perch. The bearded men huffed and puffed as they put their backs into it.

"Our feet are sliding. The egg clings to a perch of goo. Very stable." Apollo pulled out a dagger. "I'll try to saw it free."

On the other size of the nest, Sticks grabbed a rope. She started back around the nest. Abraham lifted a hand, and she stopped in her tracks.

"We'll try to reel it in from your side once Apollo frees the egg," Abraham said.

In the pool, Apollo—with his hands under the waters—sawed away with vigor.

"Any luck, Apollo?"

"My king's steel is sharp, but the effort is slow. I think it will come along eventually," Apollo replied.

"The sooner the better," he said.

"Captain," Dominga said with tightness in her voice.

"Yeah?"

"I think one of the eyes just blinked."

16

As far as Abraham could see, the eyes hadn't moved at all. But the muggy atmosphere was becoming more prickly.

"Saw faster, Apollo!" he said.

"I am. Maybe that skinner you carry would fare better, seeing how it can cut anything," Apollo said.

Abraham's hand fell to the handle of Black Bane. He didn't know if there was any truth to Apollo's statement or not, but perhaps Black Bane's razor-sharp metal would do the trick. After all, as far as he knew, the sword was magic. He pulled the sword and climbed down into the pool. "Ew. I already regret this."

"Nice, isn't it?" Apollo said with a smile showing all beard and no teeth.

"Not unless you like living in a latrine. This is awful," he said of the warm, sticky sensation. He stuck his sword under the egg and started cutting. "This better work."

"It will. Black Bane cuts anything," Apollo said.

With one hand braced on the egg, he started sawing at the

tendon-like objects below, which clung to the egg. "Sorry about this, Black Bane. Dominga, is anything winking up there?"

The petite Henchman squatted in front of the eye. She turned her head and said, "No."

"It winked," Tark blurted. He pointed his finger at one of the eyes. "That one. I saw it." He pulled a dagger. "It lives."

"Are you certain?" Abraham said.

"I saw it," Tark said.

"I don't know. I didn't see it," Dominga replied. "Just hurry up."

He sawed faster. The egg broke free of the cords that held it. The surrounding murky waters wobbled. The ground under the pool shifted. Apollo and Prospero's eyes grew big.

"Move!" Abraham yelled.

With the egg floating in the water, they pushed it toward Sticks.

She tossed one end of the rope into the pool. "You can't tie a rope around that egg?"

"No, we just need it to climb out," he said. "Bearclaw, get over here."

Bearclaw secured the rope over his shoulders. "Climb up."

The waters started to churn and bubble. Their gooey warmth was heating up.

Abraham took the rope and climbed out of the pool. "Hurry up!"

Prospero got on Apollo's shoulders. Apollo rolled the egg up the side of the nest. Prospero rolled it up the rest of the way to the nest's edge.

Abraham rolled it onto the rim. "Get up here!"

The old knights climbed the rope hand over hand and out of the pool. Both of them climbed down over the other side, in front of the moat.

"Drop it down to us, Captain," Apollo said.

Abraham picked up the egg. The massive thing filled his arms and must have weighed two hundred pounds. "I can't drop it over the ledge. It's too heavy."

"Is that the egg, Captain?" Horace said.

"It's either that or an awful-looking paperweight." The ground trembled. "Crapola!"

He could see where Iris had managed to make fires by the pools, which seemed to keep the sludge men at bay. Those fires appeared to be dimming.

"We need to move!" he yelled.

Prospero climbed back onto Apollo's shoulders.

Abraham rolled the burdensome egg down the side of the nest into Apollo's arms. Straining, Apollos lowered it to Prospero. The egg sank into Prospero's arms, and he lowered it with a grunt.

Tark and Dominga jumped off the nest to the ledge behind the moat. "All of that thing's eyes are moving," she said. "It's awake, Captain. The Fenix is awake!"

They still had ten feet of tar- and sludge-filled moat that they needed to cross with the egg. Jumping it would be impossible with the egg in tow.

"We need to toss it across," he said.

"I'll catch it!" Horace bellowed from the other side of the moat.

The ground shifted under their feet.

"Can you throw it that far?" Abraham asked Prospero and Apollo.

"Prospero is the strongest of us, and you are far stronger than me, Captain," Apollo said.

The egg was the size of one of the round stones in a World's Strongest Man contest. Even getting one's arms around it was a handful. Prospero waddled as he tried to walk with it. He grabbed one side of the egg as Prospero held the other. They started swinging it. It slipped in Prospero's grip and dropped to the ground. Everyone gasped.

"Whoops," Prospero said.

Apollo slapped his face and dragged his fingers down his beard.

The egg lay on the ground, unscathed. No crack showed on its exterior.

"Captain, you're the strongest. See if you can throw it over," Tark suggested.

"I am." He lifted his brow. "Of course I am."

Abraham had yet to test his limits on anything. He had no idea how strong he really was. From what he saw of his muscular self, he could have been as strong as a bull. But he certainly didn't feel herculean by any means. He squatted down and picked the egg up. He rolled it up onto his shoulder with a "Hurk!" Back in college, he'd participated in a hay-bale tossing contest. He had pretty good idea of what he was doing by launching it from his shoulder. Testing the weight, he twisted at the hips.

Put your legs and shoulders into it, he told himself. *Use all of your body.*

"You can do it, Captain. Toss it right to me!" Horace thumped his chest with his fist and opened his arms, waiting for the catch. "I could throw it, so I know you can throw it."

Abraham bent at the knees, said, "Here it comes!" and gave it a heave.

The egg sailed up two feet high in a gentle arc. It landed in Horace's awaiting arms and bowled him over. He pushed it up in the air, from the bench-press position. "I caught the egg!"

The Henchmen let out a rousing cheer. No one was more surprised than Abraham. *Dang, I am strong as a bear!*

The ground quaked. Something on the other side of the nest started moving.

17

ABRAHAM, STICKS, DOMINGA, TARK, BEARCLAW, PROSPERO, AND Apollo leapt over the moat, which was shielded by Iris's fire. Once they made it across, the lingering flames on her fingers extinguished.

"That took all I had left," she said.

"You did well," Abraham said. He was still marveling at his great strength. The minor herculean feat enthused him, but the awakening Fenix kept his senses level. "We need to find a way out of here. Horace, I need you and another strong back to carry the egg. I'll do it if I have to."

"Let me try to help," Solomon said. He stood over Horace, who was still on his back hoisting the egg up. Solomon plucked the egg out of Horace's hands and lifted it to his body like an egg carton. "I think I can handle it."

"Why didn't you do that before?" Abraham asked. "You could have probably jumped the moat with it."

"You didn't ask, and I really wasn't that sure myself."

Horace popped up from the ground. "Give me the egg. I'll carry it, you filthy troglin. You'll probably try to eat it."

"Be my guest." Solomon stuffed the egg in Horace's awaiting arms.

"Oof!" Horace said as the egg sank against his belly. He waddled as he walked away from Solomon. Puffing for breath, he said, "Don't worry, Captain. I have it. I'm the strongest bull in the valley."

Abraham wasn't sure about that. He knew Horace had the iron strength that matched his girth but figured he himself was a match for him. As for Solomon, the bigfoot man was part animal and eight feet tall. He might have been aging, but he was no doubt formidable.

"If you carry that egg, then Solomon will have to carry your spear," Abraham said.

Horace growled and gave the egg back to Solomon. "Fine, but he better not drop it or eat it."

"Ruger!" Sticks said. "We need to go!"

As a single unit, the Henchmen headed back in the direction they'd come from, leaving the nest and the sludge pools behind. They didn't stop until they arrived back where they'd started. Thirty feet above them, the tunnel they'd fallen through awaited.

"How do we get up and out of there without slipping?" he asked.

"We didn't have the rope ready the last time. I can climb up and secure it," Sticks said. She slung the coil of rope over her shoulder. The gritty woman started to scale the wall that led up to the opening.

"I'll go with her," Dominga said. When Vern tossed her a small pack, she snatched it and carried it on her shoulder. "Thanks."

A bone-chilling moaning carried throughout the massive cavern. It was part animal, part sub-human.

"It sounds angry," Iris said. The homely woman kept looking back over her shoulder. "I never imagined that I would have to face an Elder before. At least, not until I was dead."

"And you never would have had to until the new Ruger came along," Vern said. "Before, the Red Tunics handled the dirty work." He brushed the back of his hands over his grimy armor. "Now, we are the dirt. We didn't chase after monsters like this, either. It was men against men, not a bunch of adventuring monster hunters."

"Becoming a Henchman never promised any of us otherwise," Horace said. He spat out tobacco juice. "So, quit your belly aching, Vern."

"Can't help it. It's how I like to pass the time," the salty flaxen-haired warrior replied.

Abraham didn't pay him any mind. He'd been around his share of complainers. He watched Sticks and Dominga disappear into the tunnel.

The sound of rock cracking echoed throughout the cavern. Iris jumped and clung to Horace. He put his arm over her shoulder.

Skrreeeeeee. Skreeeeeee. Skreeeeee.

The weird animalistic sound was followed by a tight burst of huffing and snorting.

It was the weirdest, most mind-grating sound Abraham had ever heard. A power behind it filled up the cavern. Abraham had hoped that when they found the Fenix, it would be dormant or in some sort of deep hibernation. A reason must have existed that it had lain in silence for so long. No one had disturbed it. He could still see the huge, glaring eyes in his mind. No mortal saw the Fenix and lived. They were about to test that theory. He cupped his hands over his mouth and called up into the tunnel. "Uh... Sticks? How's that rope coming along?"

No one answered. The seconds went by like minutes.

"I'm sure she has it," he said in a reassuring fashion.

"Something comes," Tark said.

A loud hufflike bark started, followed by that mind-jarring *skreeee* sound. Iris and Vern plugged their ears with their fingers. Everyone that had a weapon had it drawn. Judging by the size of the Fenix's eyeballs, its head must have been the size of an elephant. Its body would fill half the cave. They would not be able to get around it.

"Sticks?" Abraham said. "Dominga?"

With his head twisting back and forth on his shoulders, Vern shouted, "Will you two dirty little whores hurry up?"

"I don't think your character assassination is going to spur their efforts," Solomon said.

"What do you know, ape?" Vern replied.

A long and loud sniffing sound began, following by a hungry sigh.

"The Fenix probably hasn't eaten in a very long time. I bet it's hungry," Horace commented.

Far back in the cave, a tremendous hulking body blacked out the twinkling green crystals that decorated the walls. It approached slowly and became bigger. The sniffing and screeching became louder.

"Start climbing," Abraham said. He shoved Horace and Iris forward.

The Fenix head appeared in the dim light. It was one of the most hideous things he'd ever seen.

"Go, everyone. Go, go, go!"

18

A ROPE DROPPED OUT OF THE TUNNEL ABOVE. STICKS POPPED HER head out from over the rim. "It's secured!" she said. She cast a daring look toward the commotion coming from the cavern, and her face turned ashen. Her little chin hung.

Iris, with the help of Horace, was the first person to climb from the cavern floor into the tunnel.

"Climb," Sticks told the mystic. "Climb!"

"I am," Iris said. She started to look back over her shoulder.

Sticks pushed her face away and said, "Climb."

Horace hustled into the tunnel after Iris. He clung to Sticks's side, and both of them assisted everyone else. Tark came up, followed by Apollo, Prospero, and Bearclaw. Solomon navigated the climb while carrying the egg with little difficulty. Vern and Abraham were still on the ground.

"Get up there." Abraham was holding Black Bane. "You'll only die if you stick around."

"You're the Captain. You should go first," Vern argued.

Abraham shoved him. "Get up there. That's an order!"

Vern sheathed his sword and hustled to the wall and started his climb.

Am I mad? Abraham thought. His feet were firmly on the ground. He held his sword out in front of him in the high point position. The battle would be like fighting a rhinoceros with a toothpick. The Fenix was huge. It was a hideous creature with a hammer-shaped head and four sets of enormous eyes. Its four nasal canals were hairy caverns. It had whiskers like a cat that probed the ground. The Fenix slunk forward on claws like a great bird. The monstrous wings folded alongside the spiny ridges on its back were leathery. Saliva dripped from huge fangs in its mouth and sizzled on the cavern floor. *Why am I still standing here?*

"Captain, run now while there is still time!" Horace shouted.

Abraham didn't understand what was happening. His feet were glued to the floor. He should have been the first one out of the tunnel and still running. Any normal man would have done that. Instead, he stood firm. He didn't want to fight the Fenix. Apparently, Ruger did. The flames of battle burned inside him. Ruger wanted this, not him.

"Captain! Get up here!" Horace shouted.

"Take the rope now!" Sticks added.

"Ruger," Abraham said to himself. "This is madness. Let me go. We can't fight this thing. It will swallow us whole!"

The Fenix crept forward. It was only one hundred feet away.

The tail end of the rope hit Abraham in the face. "Grab on!" Horace said.

Ruger's body gave in. Abraham entwined his free arm in the rope. "Pull me up! Pull me up!"

The Fenix came faster. Its great jaws opened wide as all its eyes locked on Abraham. It sped up as it scurried forward.

"Faster, dammit! Faster!" Abraham said.

Horace and Sticks reeled him in like a fish.

With its mouth spread wide, the Fenix lunged and snapped its jaws.

Abraham tucked his legs up to his chest.

The Fenix's teeth clacked loudly together. *Chomp!*

Aided by his companions, Abraham climbed inside the tunnel by the skin of his teeth. They started climbing up the slippery slope by using the rope hand over hand.

"Move it, Horace, move it!" Abraham said.

Led by Sticks, the trio traversed the tunnel. Horace's feet kept slipping on the slick ground.

Abraham put his shoulder into him. "We are almost there! Go!"

He stole a glance behind his shoulder. The Fenix had begun stuffing its head into the tunnel. Like a rat, it was squeezing its great body into the gap, which should have been too small for it. It was coming. Abraham could see that in its eyes. It would have them all dead in minutes.

"Go! Go! Go! Go!"

Finally, the last three Henchmen emerged out of the tunnel and onto the firmness of the cavern's ground. Every one of them was panting for breath. The rest of the Henchmen were waiting. Iris carried the lone torch.

"Is it trapped down there?" Tark asked.

"No, it's snaking its way up that wormhole," Horace said. "We must go."

"Agreed." Tark beckoned for the others to follow him. "I know the way."

"Hold on," Abraham said. "I'm staying."

Half the dumbfounded group said in unison, "What?"

"Listen. Get that egg out of here," he continued. "But that thing's coming, and our best chance of stopping it is fighting it once it climbs out of that hole. I don't know if we have the mettle to do it, but if we don't, well, I'm pretty sure we are all dead men... and women."

A savage growl came up out of the tunnel.

Iris covered her ears and cringed.

Horace tapped the butt of his spear on the ground. "It's a sound plan. I'm staying."

Bearclaw stepped forward. "No horse is going to be able to run that fast. We must fight it one way or the other." He spun his axe and kissed each blade. "I'm taking two eyes before I go."

"You do realize you are fighting the spawn of an Elder," Iris said. "Mortals don't kill them. They kill mortals."

"Perhaps the time for change has come," Solomon said. "For only the ridiculous achieve the impossible."

"Where'd you hear that?" Abraham said. "Woodstock?"

"No, I read it in a bathroom stall," the troglin replied.

"Just get that egg out of here. Tark, you, Iris, and Dominga get out of here. We'll buy you all of the time we can."

"Aren't you going to send me out?" Sticks said plainly.

"No, I thought you'd rather stick with me. No pun intended," he said.

"Actually, I'd rather go, but my knees are knocking so bad, I don't think I can move. You'll need me anyway," she said.

Tark and Solomon led the others away.

The Henchmen formed a semicircle in front of the tunnel entrance. Abraham stood in the middle of the pack. Horace stood on his right, with Apollo and Prospero. Sticks and Bearclaw were on his left, with Vern beside them. Horace spat. Shaking his sword, Vern cursed.

The Fenix squeezed up the tunnel. Its eyes glowed like blue

ice. Its hot, rancid breath carried up the tunnel, coating them in stinky steam.

With a twist of his wrist, Abraham flipped Black Bane end over end. "This is it," he said. "Who wants to kill the spawn of an Elder today?"

As one, the Henchmen shouted at the top of their lungs, "Death before failure!"

19

Abraham led his robust group of fighters into the mouth of the tunnel. The fearless knot of Henchmen charged through the hot, steamy breath of the Fenix as it squeezed its hulking body up through the tunnel.

"Die, beast!" Horace bellowed. He jammed the tip of his spear in the monster's nose.

Horace hacked at its eyes with his axe. Vern clipped at the Fenix's face with his sword while Apollo and Prospero chopped into the beast's skull with hard overhead chops.

"Taste the king's metal, foul, malodorous thing!" Apollo roared.

Steel sliced into the thick leathery hide and hard knotty ridges of the Fenix. Its great neck twisted from side to side. Steam continued to spew from its mouth, smelling like garbage. It let out an earsplitting *skreeeeeeeeeeee!*

Using Black Bane like a butcher's blade, Abraham turned the Fenix's nose into hamburger. It pushed forward, not slowing its sluggish charge. He hoped the sting of steel would push it back. If anything, it just made the monster mad. It was coming out of that hole.

"The spawn feels no pain!" Bearclaw said as he landed a two-handed chop into onto of the monster's eyes.

"Everything can die!" Sticks said. She tossed a dagger at its neck. The blade ricocheted into the ground. "Or not."

Its eyelid closed a split second in time, and Bearclaw's axe skipped off it. "Madness! Its eyelids are iron gates!"

"Keep at it!" Vern cried out. The swordsman was sticking his sword between the hard plates that covered the Fenix's skull in some places. "Everything has a weakness." He spun around and jabbed his sword at another of the monster's eyes. His blade bit home, plunging deep into its eyeball. "See, you need to aim better!"

The Fenix's eyelid closed down on the Vern's sword. With a shake of its thick neck, it ripped the sword out of Vern's grip.

"Ballocks!" Vern cried out. "That eyelid is as strong as a blacksmith's hand!" He kicked the monster with his boot. "Elder freak! Return my blade."

Bearclaw laughed while he was chopping. "It wouldn't be the first time that something dumber than you disarmed you."

Vern looked into the monster's eyes and replied, "I don't think it's dumb. I just need to start carrying more swords." He pulled his daggers, darted in, and started stabbing away.

Foot by foot, yard by yard, the abominable Fenix came forward, unslowed by the Henchmen's valiant efforts. It surged onward, its great jaws snapping at them. The Henchmen were in a slow retreat.

"Captain, this thing is not flesh and blood," Horace bellowed. He thrust his spear into the monster's cheek. "It does not bleed. Our strikes don't slow it. I'm putting everything I have into my blows. If it does not bleed, how can it die?"

"Something has to give!" Abraham rained down a two-handed chop on the bridge of the monster's snout. The steel hacked off a hunk of flesh, and blood spurted out. "It bleeds! It's hide's thick, but it bleeds. Put your backs into it, men!"

"Aye! Slay the spawn!" Horace roared.

The Henchmen's redoubled efforts were futile. The Fenix kept coming. They were backpedaling.

Abraham yawned. Out of the corner of his eye, he caught the others yawning too. *What is happening now?* He wasn't the only one yawning. Horace's jaws were wide open. Vern rubbed his eyes. Sticks rubbed her sleepy eyes. Prospero wandered away from the beast, found a spot along the wall, and lay down like a baby.

"Horace, do you feel sleepy?" Abraham shouted.

"My lids become heavy," Horace replied. "I'll keep fighting in my sleep, Captain. I promise."

"Crap!"

No wonder the Fenix wasn't trying to fight them. It had already sprayed them with its steamy breath, which must have been some sort of toxin. Abraham's limbs became heavy, his strikes slow and futile. He looked the monster in the eyes. A deep intelligence lurked in those massive orbs. It knew it had them. It knew it all along. It didn't have to fight because it had already won.

"Well played, monster."

Vern stumbled away from the Fenix and dropped to a knee. He started crawling away, out of the tunnel.

"Horace, we have to get out of here! Everyone, get out! Get out!" he said.

Apollo hustled to Prospero and started dragging him out of the tunnel. Bearclaw helped Vern and Horace stumble out of the mouth. All of them escaped the mouth of the cave with the Fenix right on their tail.

"What is this?" Horace said as he stumbled around in a circle, blinking his eyes and using his spear like a walking stick.

Vern sat down and fell backward with his arms spread out like wings.

Bearclaw swayed and dropped to his knees. He tried to prop himself up with his axe.

The Fenix's head popped out from the tunnel as it let out a victorious *skreeeeeeee!*

Abraham fought to keep his head up and his eyes open. He looked at the Fenix's widening, slavering jaws. He looked at his sword, Black Bane. The pommel burned in his hand. The sensation kept him awake. The arcane etchings on the blade above the crossguard started to glow like campfire coals.

He turned his head and gazed upon the Fenix and said, "Black Bane, this is it. I just need one strike to kill it. Whatever you have, whatever you are trying to tell me, just do it." He lifted his sword and cocked its burning steel back behind the shoulder and screamed, "Death before failure!"

The Fenix opened its mouth wide. Abraham rushed into the jaws of death.

The Fenix lashed out and swallowed him whole.

20

Sticks, Solomon, Tark, Dominga, and Iris cleared the cave. All of them except for Solomon were puffing for breath. The troglin set the giant egg down. All of them looked back as the Fenix's screeching carried out of the cave.

"Ah, my poor Horace, I don't think he's going to make it," Iris said.

"I don't think any of them are," Dominga added.

"We need to keep moving. That's what Ruger wanted," Tark said.

"Let's go," Sticks said. She felt awful saying it, but she'd seen the Fenix. With or without Ruger Slade, she didn't figure they stood a chance against it. That would take a miracle. "There is nothing that we can do for them now. We need to keep moving."

Solomon picked the egg back up and cradled it in his lengthy arms. "May fortune favor the foolish."

"Where are the horses?" Tark asked, turning his head left and right. "Where's my brother? Where's Twila and the horses?" He cupped his hands to his mouth and meandered forward. "Cudgel! Where are you, brother? Cudgel!"

"Strange," Solomon said.

"Maybe the terra-men got them," Dominga said.

"Don't say that," Iris said.

"Well, either that or they had enough good sense to flee," the young black woman said.

"Don't say that! My brother is a Henchman. He wouldn't ever run, and certainly he'd never abandon me. Besides, his leg was brok—" Tark's eyes grew big as moons, fixed on a figure lying down on the ground at the shadowy rim of the cave. He scrambled over to the man, screaming, "Cudgel! Cudgel!"

Sticks rushed to Tark's side. He was on his knees, cradling Cudgel in his arms. Cudgel's eyes were wide open. He was dead, a crossbow bolt protruding from his neck. Tark rocked back and forth, tears flowing down his cheeks. "No! Nooo! This can't be. What has happened to you, Brother? Come back to me!"

Sticks stopped grinding her teeth and said, "Twila. She must have done this. I'm sorry, Tark." She laid a gentle hand on his shoulder.

"You really don't think that little woman would have done this, do you?" Iris said. "She seemed so sweet. So simple. I can't imagine."

"I always thought she was squirrely," Dominga said. "But she seemed harmless. It would make sense that she might have been the one causing all of the trouble. Nobody would know it."

"Regardless, we must go," Solomon said. "We'll have to sort this out later."

Skreeeeeeeeeeeeeee!

"I'm not leaving without my brother." Tark wiped his eyes. "The rest of you go. He's all I have left. I don't care anymore."

"This isn't what Cudgel would want," Sticks said. "He'd want retribution. He'd do the same for you too."

"I don't care."

Thunder rumbled in the sky. Everyone but Tark looked up. A lone cloud started to build in the air in front of the columns. It hovered one hundred feet above them, a storm of energy brewing inside it.

Sticks's nose tingled.

Solomon set down the egg and stretched out his furry, grimy arms. The hair on his body was standing straight up all over. "It's like static electricity." He looked at the cloud. "Oh my." He dropped to the ground. "Get down!"

A huge bolt of lightning burst out of the cloud just as Sticks flattened on the ground. The bright stream of flickering light was thicker than a man's arm. It streaked into the cave in a crooked white-hot cord of fire. It lit up the cavern with scintillating light and kept going. She shook. The cave trembled. The bowels of Titanuus exploded.

Abraham charged. He didn't anticipate the Fenix moving so quickly. Its neck stretched out suddenly, and its jaws were wide enough to engulf him. He leapt into its great maw and stabbed Black Bane into the roof of its mouth. Grunting with tremendous effort, he pushed the blade in as far as he could, hoping to pierce its brain.

The Fenix's jaws started to close. Its tongue pushed Abraham back toward its throat.

He hung on to his sword as the suffocating blackness closed all around him. With slime oozing into his face, he twisted his blade one last time, saying, "Man, it can't end like this."

Suddenly, the inside of the Fenix's mouth lit up like the Fourth of July. A bolt of energy blasted out the Fenix's teeth and latched onto Black Bane. Wroth mystic power surged through Abraham's fingertips and coursed through the sword and into the skull of the Fenix. The body of the Elder spawn quaked. Its fleshy mouth dried up and sizzled. Out of its jaws came a mind-jarring screech.

Abraham didn't have any idea what was going on. But he liked it. He pushed the sword in deeper and yelled, "Eeeeeeeeeee-yaaargh!"

The Fenix sputtered and smoked. Its body crackled and popped. It bucked, twisted, and writhed.

The lightning faded.

The Fenix let out a foul, throaty sigh and died.

Abraham pulled the sword free of the roof of the monster's mouth. His limbs trembled as he walked out of the Fenix's gaping mouth. He looked back and saw the Elder spawn's eyes were burnt to a crisp in their sockets. Smoke streamed out of all its orifices. Hunks of burning flesh dripped off its body.

He scratched his head. He was alive. It was dead. That was nothing short of a miracle, and he had no idea how it had happened. He yawned. He was tired. He'd never felt so tired. All he wanted to do was sleep. In his shaking hand, the engravings on Black Bane had started to cool. Wispy fingers of smoke drifted from the tip of the steel.

All he could think to say was, "Thank you, Black Bane."

You're welcome.

"Huh," he said just before his eyes closed, as he fell down and fell asleep.

21

ABRAHAM WOKE. HE WAS OUTSIDE THE FENIX'S CAVERN. THE SUN had set behind the columns in the crater, covering him in partial darkness. Someone nearby snored loudly. He propped himself up on his elbows to see Horace, lying on Iris's lap. She was stroking the stalwart man's beard. Her eyes grew when she looked up and saw Abraham.

"You awaken?" Iris said with relief. "Finally. This one sleeps like a hibernating bear. I don't think he'll wake."

"Probably not, so long as he's lying on those comfy thighs of yours," Abraham said out of nowhere, not sure where it had come from. "Sorry."

Iris broke out in a smile. "No need to apologize."

The group was down and away from the mouth of the cave, below the ledge they'd climbed up earlier to enter. Sticks made her way over from a small campfire. Her creaseless face showed elation behind a rail-thin smile. She helped Abraham to his feet and said, "So glad that you could join us. How was your nap?"

"Fitting," he said, pinching the bridge of his nose. He had a migraine. "I just feel like both sides of my brain are on one side of my head." He scanned the area to see that all the Henchmen who had fought the Fenix were lying about on the ground. "I take it we all made it?"

"Not all," Sticks said.

She pointed at Tark. He'd set himself apart from the rest of the group and was leaning over Cudgel's body. He was on his knees, rocking back and forth and singing quietly.

"Cudgel is dead."

"Dead? What happened?"

"We think Twila killed him."

"What?" He pictured the young pie-faced woman with dimpled cheeks and freckles—she was a hard worker but seemed ordinary. "How?"

"She shot him in the neck with your crossbow," Sticks said.

"That doesn't sound right. Even with a broken leg, Cudgel wouldn't be caught off guard. Was he asleep?'

"No, it didn't look like it. There was a scuffle in the dirt. She got him. Pinned the bolt in his throat. He fought her with the bolt sticking out of his neck." She shrugged. "He bled out trying to crawl back into the cave."

Tark's shoulders were heaving.

Abraham's heart sank. Every one of them had been through hell. They were coated head to toe in gory, nasty grime. But none of them had lost a brother. Tark was the last one of them all. Abraham thought of his best friend, Buddy Parker. That loss felt as bad as losing his own brother. The grief in the faces of Buddy's family, when he finally faced them, had almost killed him. "I better go talk to him."

Sticks put her hand on his shoulder and pushed him back down. "I wouldn't." She glanced side to side. "The last time one of their brothers died, they were very emotional about it. Do you remember?"

He shook his head. "So, Twila took all of the horses and gear?"

"All of it."

"Damn. She's a little wolf in sheep's clothing, isn't she?"

"I guess."

Abraham suddenly realized that Jake's backpack was on those horses. It was his only connection to home. *No, I can't have this. I have to get it back. We have to get the egg back.* "Well, how far of a head start could she have?" He stood, and pain shot through his eyes. "We need to catch up. A handful of us can go."

"She's on horseback. It will be tough to catch up on foot," Sticks said. "And we need to be at full strength. There is no telling what other terrors we might face."

"She might have to face them too. She'll have to go through the terra-men."

"Only if she goes back that way." Sticks took out a dagger and spun it inside the palm of her hand. "Twila is clever. A saboteur, spy, or assassin. I don't know, but I'm pretty sure she's also a survivor." She spun her dagger one last time and slid it into her sheath. "But it's your call, Captain."

"I'm getting my gear, and we're taking the egg back to King Hector. I'm not staying in this hellhole any longer. Everybody get up!" he said. "Now!"

Iris patted Horace's face. "Wake up, ox. It's time to go."

Dominga shook Vern and Bearclaw from their slumber. Apollo and Prospero finally stirred. All of them were yawning and stretching, with Horace the last to come around.

"I dreamed I slept in a field of lilies, only to wake up in the field of my dreams," he said to Iris. "Do I live? What happened to the Fenix?"

"A lightning bolt blew it up," Abraham said. "Now get your ass up. Let's go."

"Oh," Horace said as he slowly came to his feet. "Where did the lightning come from, Captain?"

"I don't know," he said, unable to hide his irritation. Losing his backpack had shaken him. He felt that if he lost it, he would lose everything he knew. As for where the lightning bolt had come from, he'd have to sort that out later. And he thought that he'd heard his sword talk too—that lingered. "Let's get a move on. We have a mission to complete and a murderer to track down."

Solomon approached. "I don't think navigating this crater at night would be wise."

"Well, we can't catch up with Twila if we don't march day and night either. We have to do this, Solomon." He moved to Tark. "I'm sorry about Cudgel, my friend, but we have to go. He'd understand. Let's grab some rocks and give him a proper burial."

Tark stopped singing and began to shake his head. "Grab some rocks? And bury him out here like some wild coyote? We've abandoned enough of my brothers to the dirt. I'll not let it happen to another. I'll dig him a proper grave with the skin of my fingers. Go away, Ruger. Go away. The only thing you care about is your mission. So, go. Complete it! Kill me right here if you must. I don't want to be a Henchman!"

Vern hurried over to Abraham and Tark. "Cudgel is dead?"

"Twila did it," Dominga said.

"And you fools thought I was the trouble all along. I hope your heads are clear now! Sorry, Tark. Cudgel was a good man. All of you were." Vern's heavy stare landed on Abraham. "You aren't going to say a few words, Captain? Are we just going to leave him in a shallow grave and let the vultures pick him clean?"

"We have to track down Twila," Abraham said. "She can't get away." His guts were twisting inside. He needed Jake's pack.

"Bearclaw, you and Dominga find the tracks. Start leading us out of here. Tark, you can stay, but at some point, you'll have to move on."

"I'll stay with you, Tark," Vern said.

Abraham grabbed Vern by the back of the neck and slung him down to the ground. "No, you'll go!"

Sitting on his backside, Vern said, "Sure, Captain, sure, but aren't you going to say a few words?"

Abraham found all eyes on him, even Tark's. All of them had been through hell, and they looked like it too. They were weary. Even Horace's chin was dipped. One and all of them had been fighting their guts out for him for days. They followed him like sheep. They deserved better than what he was giving them. He looked at Solomon, who stood behind the group, holding the egg in his hands. That might be the key to him getting home. He moved over to where he could get a better look at Cudgel. Cudgel had a caked-up hole in his neck. His dying must have been awful. He was betrayed by one of his own. Abraham sighed. Tark's distraught face changed his heart. *My backpack can wait.*

"I have a few words to say. Solomon, bring over that egg and plant it right here by Cudgel."

Solomon set the egg down where he was asked.

"We aren't going to kill ourselves over an egg that might not do anything. We're going to find out if it works first." He looked at Iris. "Can the dead be brought back to life?"

"The essence of the dead lingers in the body until it is buried or it's consumed by one element or another. It is well known that it can happen," Iris said. "Why?"

"Because I'm going to tap this egg and find out if it has any healing powers at all before any more of us get killed." He drew his sword, jammed it into the top of the egg, and twisted. A hole in the top cracked open.

"Captain, what are you doing? That is for the queen!" Horace said.

He withdrew his blade and pulled the goo-caked hunks of shell away. A sweet aroma drifted into his nostrils. After all the reeking smell they'd been through, nothing ever smelled better.

"I swear, that smells like vanilla ice cream and cherries," Abraham said.

"What are you going to do, Captain? Drink it?" Horace said.

"No." He picked up the egg and tilted it over Cudgel. "I'm going to give our brother a bath with it." He poured.

A syrupy white goo came out and splattered all over Cudgel's body. It filled the shallow grave the dead man lay in.

Tark's smoky eyes were glued to his brother. He looked up at Abraham. "You did that for me? For Cudgel? But the queen..." Tark said, his jaw hanging.

"Right now, Cudgel needed it more than her." Abraham nodded. "We all came to this dance together, and we're going to leave together if at all possible. I'm sorry, Tark, if it doesn't work. Cudgel is a good man. He deserved better."

"I just wish I could have told him goodbye. But thank you for trying," Tark said. "It brings me peace."

Iris knelt beside Tark. She dipped two fingers in the strange egg yolk and applied it to a deep laceration on Tark's arm. The wound quickly started to mend. "It might not bring back the dead, but it certainly regenerates the flesh. And quickly." She rubbed her fingers together. The egg yolk started flaking. "But I fear those properties won't last without remaining fresh in a seal. Captain, may I?"

Abraham nodded.

Iris started applying the yolk like a salve to everyone's wounds. While she did that, the yolk started caking around Cudgel.

Abraham put his hand on Tark's shoulder. "I really am sorry. I tried. Let's give him a burial that you like."

"What about Twila and the queen?" Tark said.

"We'll figure something out," Abraham said.

"Yes, we'll figure something out 'cause I'm going to find that pie-faced witch."

Abraham was looking at Tark, and his lips weren't moving. Tark was looking at him, and his lips weren't moving either. They both looked down. Cudgel's eyes were wide open. He was smiling.

22

Thanks to the Fenix egg yolk and Cudgel's revival, the Henchmen had a spring back in their step. They had a problem too. Without anything to seal the egg, the yolk quickly dried up, and its healing properties were ruined. They could all blame that on Twila, who'd stolen all their gear. In the meantime, Abraham was thankful they were all alive even though he was concerned he'd lose touch with all reality without his pack.

You know who you are. Don't forget it. You're Abraham Jenkins. A Pittsburgh Pirate turned beer-truck driver. Turned super swordsman. Ah man, this is nuts.

He led the group back into the cavern where the Fenix was lodged inside the tunnel. Using their weapons, they chopped the monster up. They had no other choice because they had to go back for another egg to return to Kingsland. It turned out to be a rigorous task, but at least no one complained about the stink.

They tied the ropes to the bones of the Fenix's carcass and shimmied back down into the cave. They took more fire with them and placed it by all the black pools to keep the sludge monsters at bay. With all things appearing to be in order, Abraham led Apollo, Prospero, Bearclaw, and Sticks across the moat. Solomon and Horace waited on the other side. Apollo and Prospero were the first to scurry up the nest and disappear over the rim with a *sploosh.*

Abraham looked over at Sticks and said, "Better them than me."

"Once odd, always odd," she said.

He climbed the nest with Sticks and Bearclaw bringing up the rear. Apollo and Prospero were wading chest deep through the pool of goo. "Are you coming, Captain?" Apollo asked. "The water is fine. Warm and reviving."

Abraham sighed through his clenched teeth. He'd just gotten out of the muck pit, and now he had to go in again. He considered passing his sword over to Apollo and letting them saw away. He shook his head and said, "I'm coming." He dropped into the pool, and his face drew up tight. "This is awful."

"Feels good, aye!" Apollo splashed the nasty waters at Prospero.

Prospero stiffened and splashed Apollo back. The exchange heated up. Both men started wrestling like pigs wallowing in mud.

Shaking his head, Abraham said, "Such fine company I keep."

"It looks like fun, Captain," Sticks said. She actually had a smile on her face.

"Yes, why don't you join me?"

"No, thank you," she replied.

Abraham took out Black Bane. "Sorry about this," he said to the sword, hoping it would reply, but it didn't. He reached underneath another egg and sawed at the strange cords that fastened the egg to its perch. He was working on the smaller of the two as the last one was much bigger. As he sawed away, he noticed a crack in the bigger egg. He stopped sawing. "Wait a minute."

Prospero dunked Apollo under the murk and let out a gusty laugh. Apollo's arms flailed above the waters.

Abraham made his way around to the other side of the bigger egg. A hole was in the egg. Hunks of the eggshell floated in the waters. He rose up on tiptoe. Nothing was in the egg. "Holy crap, this thing hatched."

Sticks called out to him. "What did you say?"

"This thing hatched!" he hollered as he scanned the water left and right. "Prospero, Apollo, cut it out!"

Prospero let Apollo out of the murk.

Apollo gasped for air and punched Prospero in the chest with both hands. "Don't do that again!" He pushed the hair out of his eyes. "Something wrong, Captain?"

"One of the eggs hatched. Be wary. Let's get this other egg out of here... fast." He hurried back to the egg that he was sawing on and started cutting again.

Apollo and Prospero put their hands on the egg and rocked it back and forth. With a snap, the roots underneath the egg finally came free.

"Let's go," said Abraham. "Go, go, go!"

They pushed the floating egg across the pool to where a rope waited to help them climb. Brandishing his sword, Abraham guarded their backsides. The only thing that moved in the waters was them. He saw no sign of a fledgling Fenix.

"Sticks, holler at Solomon," Abraham said. "We need to get this thing out of here fast."

Solomon climbed up on the nest. "Did you call?"

"Grab the egg."

Prospero climbed on Apollo's shoulders. Working in tandem, they rolled the egg up the inner wall of the nest, the same way they had before. With some heavy grunting, they pushed the egg up to the top, where Solomon was able to secure it with his big paws and roll it up on the rim.

Solomon picked up the egg. "Hmm, it's a tad heavier." He shook the egg, and something sloshed around inside. "A good fifty pounds, but my back can take it." He lifted it onto his shoulder and hopped up off the nest.

"All right, Tweedle-Dee and Tweedle-Dum, get out of there," he said to Apollo and Prospero.

The men grabbed the rope and climbed, leaving Abraham in the pool all alone.

Without looking up at Sticks, he asked, "You don't see anything, do you?"

"No. I'm certain that the little monster hides. Even if we encounter it, no doubt we can kill it. It's just a baby."

"Yeah, well, babies can grow up and become vengeful. One never knows." He reached back and grabbed the rope.

"Come on. I'm ready to get out of this place. I think I'm getting used to the smell," she said.

"Agreed," Bearclaw added. He climbed down off the nest. Sticks followed after him.

Abraham started to sheath his sword. The waters bubbled up behind him. He froze. The waters continued to bubble. Abraham jabbed his sword into the bubbles but hit nothing. He stabbed his sword in a few times. The pool bubbled in more than one spot. It appeared to be a natural occurrence.

He let out a breath and sheathed his sword. "Let's get out of here."

Abraham turned around and grabbed the rope with both hands. He felt eyes on him. His blood froze as he turned his head left and found himself almost nose to nose with the eight-eyed baby Fenix nestled in a cleft.

23

———

ABRAHAM'S EYES WERE LOCKED ON THE FENIX. THE FENIX'S EYES were locked on his. It was an ugly thing, like an eight-eyed hammer-head bat with a soft pelt of fur all over it. It was big, too, for a baby, possibly one hundred pounds and as big as a kid. Abraham slid his hand down to the dagger on his belt. He needed to kill it. One pair of eyes, the two rows at the top, stayed on him, and the other two sets followed his hand. He pulled the dagger free.

Sticks popped her head over the top of the nest and said, "Are you coming?"

"Quiet," he said. "I found the baby Fenix. It's right here, in the nest."

"Well, kill it."

"I'm getting there," he said, stealing a glance at her before dropping his eyes back on the Fenix, but it was gone. "What? Where did it go?" He jabbed his dagger into the spot where the Fenix had been nestled. "Sonuvagun, it's gone!"

"Are you sure that you saw it?"

"As sure as I can see you right now." He looked about with probing eyes. His keen senses could pick up anything most of the time, but the Fenix had vanished. "Damn. Let's just get the heck out of here." He put the dagger in his mouth and started to climb. Up and out of the nest he went and joined Sticks down by the moat.

"Maybe we should burn the nest," Sticks said.

Standing on the other side of the nest, Horace waved a torch back and forth. "Just say the word, Captain."

Abraham hopped over the moat, looked up at the nest, and said, "It's probably not going to survive very long without its mother or father or whatever. I think we've done enough damage. Let's just leave well enough alone. After all, we came after it. It didn't come after us."

"If you say so, Captain." Carrying the torch high, Horace led the way back out of the tunnel.

Finally, all the Henchmen were out of the caverns, and on foot, they resumed their trek out of Elder's Birthing.

Cudgel and Tark were all smiles that day. Both of them thanked Abraham at least one hundred times. Cudgel talked long about Twila. "She's a clever one, that one. She acted all innocent and stupid. She even offered to have a toss with me, and well, given the situation, I was tempted." He shook his head. "Mmm... mmm... mmm, that flowery voice of hers and sweet demeanor turned from one side of the hand to the other. She became cold and devilish. She shot that crossbow at me like she'd shot it one hundred times before. It hit, but I didn't feel it. I just wanted to kill her."

"We are going to get her, Brother," Tark promised. "You will be avenged."

Cudgel nodded. "That's kind of a funny notion now. How I can I be avenged when I'm still living?" He chuckled. "I'm just so happy to be alive, I could almost move on, but she betrayed the Henchmen, and she must pay."

Dominga walked close by with her hands on the hilts of the daggers. Her hips had a nice natural sway when she walked. "She'll pay, all right. For all that we know, she's the one that caused all of the misfortune that we'd run into. She caused the deaths of more of our brethren. I bet she let those frights loose that almost killed all of us. I knew we shouldn't trust her."

"Yes, well, the bigger question is, 'Why did she do it?'" Sticks asked.

"It sounds like someone is setting us up to fall," Abraham said. "There couldn't be a better explanation for it. The king has his enemies, and they can be within just as well as without. Someone doesn't want the king to win. They don't want the queen to survive. For all we know, they've poisoned her." He thought of Viceroy Leodor. The man was odd and very close to the king. It only made sense that a creepy man like that fit the bill. That was almost always the cause.

"Captain, we've never seen the king's servants. You would know better than anyone if that was the case," Vern suggested. "You bring in the new Red Tunics. You meet with Prince Lewis and Leodor. You make the decisions. You are as responsible for our calamities as any."

"What are you getting at, Vern?" Abraham said.

Vern stopped his march. Everyone stopped along with him. He walked up on Abraham. "I'll tell you what I'm getting at. Years ago, I was one of the King's Guardians. Most of us were. You were the captain, and we'd follow you to hell and back." He slid his eyes over Horace, Bearclaw, Apollo, and Prospero. "Then, you deserted. Many of us followed. Our lives have been chaos ever since. The man I followed, that we all followed, is gone. I don't what happened to the real Ruger, who stood with a spine filled with iron. But he's been gone a long time." He pointed a finger in Abraham's face. "You are possessed, and you need to hang!"

"You need to watch how you address the Captain, Vern," Horace warned. His voice was strong. "He has the right to cut you down if he likes. We gave an oath to follow Ruger Slade and serve the King. Possessed or not. It is what has been and what it will be."

"Horace, you are as blind as you are bearded," Vern said. "He could tell you to chop your own leg off, and you would."

"And you'd better, too, if he gave the order," Horace replied.

"He's crazy!" Vern shouted. "I know I'm not alone in my thinking. We've all had doubts. We've seen our brothers and sisters die. How much longer are we going to follow a man whose spirit changes with the wind? How many more of us have to die?"

"None of us have died," Sticks said. "We all still live. When's the last time we had a mission when someone didn't die?"

"Well, the mission ain't over yet," Vern replied.

Cudgel stepped forward, put a hand on Abraham's shoulder, and said, "I haven't been around long enough to understand all of the changes, but I'll tell you this. I like this man better than the last. His actions speak for themselves. I'll always follow him. Whatever changed, it's a good thing."

"I stand by Ruger and my brother as well," Tark said.

All the Henchmen surrounded Abraham, leaving Vern standing alone.

He shook his head and looked Abraham dead in the eye. "Who are you? Just tell me the truth."

Abraham couldn't help it when he replied, "You can't handle the truth."

24

"YOU DO A LOT OF TALKING THESE DAYS," VERN SAID WITH A SNEER. "I ought to knock your head off."

Several of the henchmen laughed.

"Vern, you're the worst brawler here. Iris could take you," Sticks said, stepping toward him. "But you can take a shot at me if you want."

"I'd like to see this," Tark said.

"Me too," added Cudgel. "My money is on Sticks."

"All right, that's enough," Abraham said. "Man, you guys want to scrap all of the time, don't you? Haven't we lost enough skin from our necks these past few days?"

No one said a word. Horace rubbed the back of his neck.

"As for my comment about Vern not being able to handle the truth, well, that was a joke from where I come from."

"I've never heard that expression before," Dominga said, "And I'm usually on top of things in Kingsland."

"It's from a movie," he said, fully anticipating the next question.

"What's a movie?" Iris asked.

"It's like a play or a puppet show. You have those sorts of things in the theaters, don't you?"

Many among the group nodded.

"Anyway, where I come from, the show is projected on a wall." He pinched the bridge of his nose. His migraine was still nagging at him. "Here is what I am trying to get at." He saw Solomon give him a concerned look. "Vern's suspicions are right, and I want to clear the air. I'm not Ruger as many of you had known him. I'm sure most have you have seen the changes. But you're faithful to your word, so you don't comment on it. All of you are good soldiers. As for me, well, I guess in order for you to understand it, we'll have to talk about possession. My spirit, or essence, is from another world, and somehow I wound up in Ruger's body. I can't explain how it happened any better than you could. But it happened. I came from another place and time. And now, I'm here, leading the Henchmen."

Abraham's words were met with stone cold silence. The company exchanged nervous glances with one another. Vern's hand went to his sword. Bearclaw's tight grip creaked on the leather bindings on his axe. Prospero and Apollo reached toward the swords crossed over their backs.

As Iris stepped behind Horace, he lifted his spear, pointed it at Abraham, and said, "You are saying that you are possessed?"

Horace didn't say *Captain.* That made Abraham's fingertips tingle. He'd tried to get Horace to stop saying it before, but he never did, until then.

Lifting his hands, palms up and outward, Abraham said, "I'm not possessed. Ruger Slade is possessed by me. But not by my choice."

"I told you," Vern said with haughty victory in his voice. "He is one of those otherworlders. The king and the Sect kill them. They are trouble. They are a curse upon all of Kingsland."

"King Hector knows," Abraham said.

"Lies!" Vern blurted. "If King Hector knew, he would have killed you."

Abraham reminded himself that none of this could be real. If it was a dream, he would have nothing to lose. If it wasn't, well, he had become one of the most incredible warriors who ever lived. He kind of liked it, but he didn't want to die either. "But he didn't. I'm a Henchman, on the same side as the rest of you, serving the kingdom. It's up to you whether or not you believe it. Personally, I have a hard time believing it myself, but I'm using the cards I was dealt." His stare grazed over the fingers fidgeting on the handles of their weapons. "So, what are all of you going to do, try to kill me?"

The Henchmen exchanged several looks amongst themselves. Finally, Horace spoke up and said, "Why no, Captain. We weren't going to kill you. We were going to kill Vern."

Vern's jaw dropped.

The company shared a jovial outburst of laughter. Even Abraham was nervously laughing.

Sticks slipped in beside him, and while the others were laughing, she said, "I think they like the new Ruger."

"Yeah, well, I'm glad. I started to think that they were going to run me through."

"Maybe Vern, but I think he's learned his lesson."

Vern walked away with a long face, his head down and shoulders slumped.

Abraham gave Sticks a pat on the rump. "I better go talk to him."

"Good luck with that," she said.

He caught up to Vern and said, "You don't have to like me, but we still need to work together and see this thing through. King

Hector said that he may release us from our bonds of servitude. We've made it this far. Let's finish it together as one."

"I'm not very comfortable following a man with changing personalities. I need someone I can count on. You used to be rock solid, then you became a worm, and now, well, you're brazenly unpredictable." Vern took a deep breath and looked him in the eye. "You were my mentor. My trainer. A father or dear uncle I never had. Then you went away. Or Ruger went away. I don't understand it. I want Ruger back. Not something else. Not some impostor." He poked his finger into Abraham's chest. "Where is he?"

"I can't answer that. And I can't say for sure that Ruger is gone, either," he said. "Some of the things I do, I'm not doing—he's doing it. It's as if we are two personalities in one. I control the mind, but he still has the body." Abraham clutched his fingers in and out. "When I stood in front of the Fenix the first time, I wanted to run. Ruger wouldn't let me. He wanted to fight. He's fearless."

"You're damn right he is." Vern's hard expression softened. He studied Abraham's eyes and said, "Ruger, are you in there?"

Without thinking, Abraham placed his right hand on Vern's left shoulder and tapped Vern twice with his middle and index finger. Vern's eyes grew.

"I didn't do that," Abraham said.

"I know," Vern replied with astonishment. "He did."

25

LEWIS

On horseback, Lewis led a train of his men up the coastline of Southern Tiotan. He was chasing after his half-sister, Clarice, and her Guardian Maidens. It was the last thing on earth that he wanted to do, but it had to be done. The sea breeze blew his feathered black hair into his eyes. He brushed it away. A flock of seagulls flew overhead. One of them pooped on his shoulder.

He took out a handkerchief, wiped the crap from his shoulder, and tossed the cloth away. "I hate birds. I hate the sea. I have much better things to do than this. We all do."

"Agreed," said the man riding beside him. His name was Pratt, Lewis's right-hand man. He was a big fellow, dark complected and heavy eyed, with very short brown hair, sideburns down to his ears, broad features, thick lips, and a lantern jaw. He was the biggest man in the group, by far. The King's Guardians no longer donned the customary full-plate armor and lion helmets. The group of twelve wore leather armor underneath traveling cloaks. Pratt had a gruff, ballsy way when he spoke. "We'll catch them soon. The Guardian Maidens know little about hard riding. They are birds that belong in the castle. We'll get them."

"Yes, well, we haven't caught up with them yet, have we?" Lewis said.

"No. But we will. I can feel it."

Pratt's eyes narrowed. Two riders were approaching, two more knights, dressed the same as the others. They'd been scouting ahead.

Pratt leaned over his saddle horn. "What have you found, Derik?"

All the guardians were well-knit men, and Derik was no exception. "Plenty of fishermen saw them pass no more than a day ago. By the sound of it, they are only half a day's ride, if that, and heading straight for the crotch of Titanuus. I'm not sure where they will enter the Spine, but it shouldn't be difficult to find out."

"Why do you say that?" Lewis asked.

Derik showed a pearly white smile and flipped Lewis a coin. It was a silver shard with Kingsland's marking. "Your sister is showing off her generosity. Apparently, the fishermen are doing a lousy job catching fish, and she gave them money for food. Oh, and she gave them a pack pony too. According to the fishermen, she said, and I quote, 'For you, your wives, your children. Let the king's grace be upon you.' She's so very kind. I admit I'm looking forward to seeing her again, as well as the maidens."

"She is an idiot." Lewis looked at the coin pinched between his thumb and finger. He flicked it away into the sand. "Only Clarice would prance up the shores of southern Tiotan and spew on about the king's grace. She'll have her throat cut if she parts her lips in front of the wrong people."

"We won't let that happen." Pratt took a slug of water out of his skin. "If anyone lays a hand on the princess, we'll butcher them."

Staring out to sea, Lewis absentmindedly replied, "Yes. Yes, of course."

He couldn't have cared less about Clarice, but he was in a tough spot. The King's Guardians were good men who would die trying to bring her back. None of them were aware of the game he played with Leodor and the Underlord. That was his secret that he kept to himself. Ultimately, the guardians served the crown, and they wouldn't go against the king, even on his own orders. That would be dishonor, and they would rather die first.

"We could catch up with them by nightfall, or at least Gravely and I could," Derik suggested. He slapped a shoulder of the rider beside him. "You don't have two faster riders than us. Right, Gravely?"

Gravely, stone faced and straight backed, nodded.

"Go on, then. We'll ride hard the rest of the day," Lewis said. He waved them on. "Go!"

"Off we go, then. See you tonight." Derik turned his horse and galloped off with Gravely.

"We'll have them by evening, then we can head back to Kingsland," Pratt said. "I have to admit I've enjoyed the trot along the shoreline. When my time is done, I'll live near the shore. It's peaceful."

"Pratt, I don't care." He dug his heels into his horse. "Let's get this over with."

"Just making conversation," Pratt added.

Pratt had a strong tendency to ramble on about mundane things. He wouldn't shut up unless Lewis ordered it. But Lewis respected the elder enough to let him ramble. Pratt had been a Guardian Knight for over twenty years. He'd ridden with Ruger Slade. He knew things.

"It will be a stone cottage set against the hillside, blending in with the rocks, one with natural light shining in from the morning sun. I'll keep goats and chickens and keep a shepherd on hand," Pratt said as he rode alongside Lewis. "It will be nice. I may even take a wife and have sons and daughters. They too could become Guardians, at least the boys."

Lewis blocked him out. He wanted to delay tracking down Clarice, but that wasn't happening. They were too close now. He'd hoped that misfortune would befall her. That would rid him of the pesky little menace. As much as he wanted to delay the quest, he couldn't any longer. He was just hoping she would make it into the mountains at least. That would increase her chances of encountering a fatality. But the last thing he needed was her being captured by the king's enemies. If that happened, he would be the one sent to rescue her. He couldn't let that happen either. He had to be the good son and play along.

Oh please, let her be dead by the time I catch her.

Lewis and the King's Guardians caught up with Derik and Gravely at the base of the Spine just before nightfall. Derik was on foot, checking horse tracks in the ground.

Squatting on one knee with his hand in the dirt, he said, "They were here, but they went up there." He pointed at the foreboding gargantuan mountains of the Spine.

"How long since they entered the Spine?" Lewis asked.

"A few hours at most. I can't imagine them traveling far at all at night," Derik said. "Are we going after them?" Thunder rumbled overhead. Dark clouds were rolling in from the sea. "I'm not going be able to track if that rain comes down. What do you say?"

Lewis studied the dreaded mountains and felt insignificant in their midst. This was the place he'd sent other expeditions to die. Now, he had to enter it himself. It started to sprinkle.

With a sigh, he said, "Ready the torches. We can't let them get too far. Let's go."

26

L ED BY D ERIK AND G RAVELY, THE G UARDIANS SNAKED THEIR WAY UP into the rigid mountains. The rough terrain was even more daunting to navigate at night, with strange trees and rocky outcroppings. Weird birds and critters made wild calls in the night that echoed through the channels. The sounds sent chills down Lewis's spine.

Pratt rode beside Lewis, carrying a torch and squinting.

"Perhaps you can settle down in the Spine," Lewis said.

"I'm curious to see what the Spine has to offer. I'm not beyond taking a journey through it. They say there are lost cities and civilizations unlike anything that lies beside the sea," Pratt commented. "I wish I could have been on those other campaigns."

"No, you don't. They didn't make it back."

"That doesn't mean they are dead just because we haven't seen them," Pratt said.

"You're annoying."

"I'm only being positive," Pratt replied.

He rolled his eyes.

Pratt stopped his horse and set his eyes on the rocky ledges above them. "Something moves above." He reached down and grabbed a light crossbow hanging from the saddle, and the other guardians followed suit.

Lewis squinted and followed Pratt's line of sight. One of the rocks had the look of a person on one knee. He couldn't tell whether it was real or not.

"Do you see a man or something else?" Lewis asked.

"I see a man," Pratt said under his breath.

Lewis started to slide his sword out of its scabbard. He saw no signs of Derik and Gravely, who were scouting ahead.

"You don't think—"

The distinctive sound of a bowstring snapping interrupted the silence.

Pratt rocked backward. "Argh!" A feathered shaft protruded out of his shoulder. "Bloody burdens, this is what I get for not wearing the king's armor!" He grabbed the shaft and ripped it out with a grunt. He eyeballed the arrow. "That's one of our feathers!"

The hidden archer fell out of their perch, and the person tumbled down the side of the hill and landed sprawled out on the path.

Lewis jumped off his horse and ran toward the archer, who was standing up. He tackled the archer and drove them hard to the ground. He pinned down the person's arms. It was a woman.

"Leah?"

"Prince Lewis?" she asked. She had beautiful round eyes and a long braided ponytail. She wore a bronze cuirass that enhanced her figure. She was one of the Guardian Maidens, one of Clarice's personal escorts. "What are you doing here?"

"Tracking down Clarice and you." He helped her to her feet. "Care to explain why you shot my Pratt?"

"I was only standing watch. Something startled me," she said.

Derik and Gravely climbed down from the spot where Leah was perched. "We slipped up on her, and just before I grabbed a hold of her, she fired," Derik said.

"You could have said something," Leah said. "I wouldn't have fired." She looked at Pratt. "Sorry. Is it bad?"

From his saddle, Pratt tossed the arrow at her. "It broke the skin. You'll have to pull the bowstring back farther if you want to do any real damage."

"I didn't have it fully drawn. Like I said, I was startled." She snatched the arrow from the ground. "I'm sure it would have killed you if it hit you in the throat."

The Guardians erupted in chuckles.

Lewis arched his brow and said, "Leah, I take it that Clarice isn't far away."

"No." She wiped her muddy hands on her britches. "You're going to take her home, aren't you?"

"Yes."

"Well, she won't like it."

He glowered at her. "Do I look like someone that cares what she likes?"

"No, Prince."

He took his horse by the reins. "Lead the way."

27

"YOU ARE COMING WITH ME!" LEWIS YELLED. HE'D BEEN ARGUING openly with Clarice for over thirty minutes. They were at her camp, and she wouldn't budge. Her Maidens wouldn't either.

"I'm not going anywhere until I find that egg!" she shouted back. Clarice was a fifteen-year-old who thought she was thirty. She was short and shapely, with wide hips, a small waist, broad shoulders, long chestnut hair, and gorgeous fiery green eyes. She carried a rapier on her hip and two daggers. "Go home. Go home or join me because my quest has just begun." As pretty as Clarice was, she was stubborn as a bull.

Lewis shook his head. "You're leaving one way or the other." He grabbed her arm.

The Maidens slid their curved short swords out of their scabbards, all ten of them. Each was a tall athlete with pretty features, wearing a bronze cuirass that accented her sensual figures. Their braided ponytails were uniform, and the stern looks in their eyes meant business.

Clarice twisted out of Lewis's grip. "Don't you dare touch me again."

He looked at his open hand and said, "You're a strong little varmint, aren't you?"

She pulled her sword free. "I've warned you enough about calling me a varmint, critter, rodent—"

"Badger-face," he added.

She stabbed at him.

He jumped out of the way and pulled his sword free. "You better put that blade back where it belongs, or I'm going to teach you a very regrettable lesson."

"For you," she said. She sliced her rapier back and forth in quick flashes. "Let's have a go at it, Lewis the Lewd. Or are you afraid that I'll embarrass you?"

"I'm the best sword in Kingsland, child. Now, put your toy away before I throttle you." He poked his sword at her chest. He had superior reach and was glad to show it. "I mean it."

In a flash of steel, Clarice batted his sword aside with her blade, back spun her body into his, and put a dagger to his throat.

His eyebrows lifted. "Clever, little ferret."

"What did I tell you about comparing me to varmints?" she said.

"You might be fast, but you're far from fearsome." Quick as a cobra, he grabbed her wrist and bent it backward. She cried out and dropped to one knee. He applied more pressure, and the dagger fell free of her fingers. "If you're going to put an edge on someone's neck, then you better finish the job!" He pushed her down into the mud. "How's that for fast?"

Surrounded by the Guardians and the Maidens, with a steady rain coming down out of the night sky, Clarice said, "I'm still not coming with you. You'll have to fight all of us first. This cause is just. It is noble. It is for my mother, and I won't be turned away."

The rain came down harder.

Lewis looked into the sky. "Find shelter. We're going back home tomorrow. Pratt, make sure the Maidens don't scamper off in the middle of the night. If you need me, I'll be underneath that overhang."

"We'll leave in the morning. You can't stop us!" Clarice said.

"See you in the morning." He walked away.

Morning came. The rains stopped. The Guardians blocked Clarice and her Maidens from the slippery, muddy passage. Clarice's cheeks were rosy when she made her demands again. "Lewis, only a coward would prevent this noble expedition. Are you a coward? Or are you heartless?"

"Coward, no. Heartless, possibly." He yawned. "We can stand here all day, night, and day again, like monster bait, or we can go home, where you and I both belong."

"Why do you hate me and mother so?" she asked.

"You aren't from the proper lineage. Haven't you figured that out by now?"

"I share the same blood as you do," she said.

"No, your blood is tainted," he said. Clarice's frown deepened. Hurt showed in her pretty eyes. He combed his fingers through his hair and decided to try the nice-brother act. "Listen, it's not that I don't care about you or the queen. You're both, well, tolerable, but you need to understand that I miss my own mother. And I never found your mother to be a suitable replacement. Let me ask you: what if you were in my shoes? Would you just accept a new mother so willingly?"

"If she was my mother, yes. Mother is good and pure and

strong. She abounds in love and grace. What child would not want a mother like that?"

Lewis caught Pratt looking at him with an arched brow. The hardened Guardian looked away.

Lewis sighed and said, "I'll make a deal with you. You come home with me, and I'll treat you and your mother much better."

"Our mother."

He shrugged his eyebrows and said, "All right, our mother."

Clarice's eyes brightened. She gave him a smug look, crossed her arms over her chest, and said, "I don't believe you. You've promised that before, remember? I'm not some stupid child that is going to believe you like I did the first time. I'm a woman now. Like my mother. I know better."

"You're a haughty little brat. That's what you are. If you march into those mountains, it will be to your doom. Just like the other expeditions that journeyed only to never return."

"I don't care. I have nothing to live for without mother."

"I wish I could let you go. I really do!" He threw his hands up. "Fine! You give me no choice. I'll disarm you and your Maidens and drag the lot of you home by your roots."

"You wouldn't dare!"

"You give me no choice. Pratt, take them!"

The Maidens drew their weapons and circled the princess. With their weapons drawn, the Guardians closed in. The knights, one and all, towered over the women even though some of the women were fairly tall. The Maidens were well-trained fighters and more than capable defenders. Not one woman batted an eye at the men who towered over them.

Pratt squared off with Leah and said, "No bloodshed. We use the cheeks of the steel only. Fair enough, Maiden?"

"Agreed," Leah said.

"You know," Pratt said in his slow rugged drawl, "I've never fought a beautiful woman before. It's awkward, but I won't insult you by going easy either."

"You're a true knight." Leah smiled. "En garde!"

Derik shouted from the top of the path, "Someone approaches!"

"A someone or something?" Lewis asked.

Derik rose on his toes and peeked around the bend. "A woman with horses. She's walking a trio of them."

Lewis lifted two fingers and said to Clarice, "This can wait, yes?"

"Lucky for you, it can."

"Well thanks to the Elder of Luck," he replied. Lewis immediately recognized the pie-faced woman in the red tunic. His throat tightened. He approached her and said, "Aren't you one of Ruger's retainers? Where do you come from?"

"Yes, I am Twila." She had scrapes all over her face, and the knees and elbows of her clothing were torn. "I came from a place called Elder's Birthing. A man named Solomon we met in a fisher town called Hackles led us there. He said that he would aid us in finding the Fenix's Egg. All that we found was our doom." She sagged to the ground.

"Get her some water," Lewis said.

Pratt put a water skin to Twila's lips and helped her drink.

Lewis kneeled beside her. "You said *us*. Where are the others?"

Twila guzzled the water, wiped her mouth, and said, "Thank you. I ran out of water over a day ago. As for Ruger and the Henchmen, they are all dead, and I want to get my arse off this mountain as fast as I can."

"Why?" Lewis asked.

"Because the terra-men and troglin are coming."

"How many?"

Twila shrugged. "The hills are filled with them. At least three for every man and woman."

"Saddle up," Lewis said. "We're going." He looked at Clarice. "Are you convinced?"

"I'll go, but at the bottom of the hill, I want the whole story. Maidens, let's ride."

28

THE GUARDIANS AND MAIDENS MADE CAMP A MILE AWAY FROM THE bottom of the hills.

Fifteen-year-old Clarice grilled Twila with questions. "Tell me how they died, all of them."

"Go easy, girl, this retainer is traumatized," Lewis said.

Twila sat by the fire, shivering underneath a blanket. She nodded and said, "I can talk." She closed her eyes and took a breath. "We started with thirteen, and I'm the only one left. We didn't enter the Spine from this avenue. We started our trek above Hackles. We crossed a stream of lava and lost two Red Tunics. The guide took us to a massive crater called Elder's Birthing. He said it was the home of the Fenix. It's a wild place of tar pits and prickly vegetation. We encountered terra-men, fought through them, lost many horses, and fled to a cavern where our guide took us." Her nose crinkled. "The air was foul, rotting like refuse in a dung heap. I waited with the horses, with Cudgel. Led by Ruger, the Henchmen went into the cavern. There were screams. Weapons against bone clamored." She stared deep into the fire as she spoke.

"I heard a sound so horrifying that my teeth clacked together. There was screaming. Yelling. All coming from the blackness. The screams fell silent.

"Deep in the cave, something massive dragged its great belly over the stones. Cudgel told me to run. I said no, but he forced me. When I looked back, I saw him standing like a tiny tooth in the mouth of the great cave. A creature with a head wide as three barns slithered out of the darkness and devoured him whole." Her fingers trembled. "In the daylight, I fled, praying that the creature would not dare the daylight, praying that it did not see me. I pray still now that it's not coming after me. For if that was the Fenix, then no one that sees it can live." She looked up at Lewis and Clarice as well. "I'm sorry. I was terrified. I failed the queen."

"This is not on your shoulders, Twila," he said, putting his hand on her shoulder. "We are grateful that you live. Now you can tell the tale of how the Henchmen valiantly battled the Fenix to their bitter ends. There is nothing but glory in that." He gazed at Clarice. "Don't you agree?"

Clarice nodded. "Don't fret, Twila. Your bravery may find you a place among my Maidens. Would you like that?"

"It would be an honor, of course. I just hope that I can stop shaking," Twila said.

"Get some rest," Clarice said. "We'll return to the House of Steel and inform my father. With this news, he can send a formidable force, defeat this beast, and take its egg."

"Are you mad?" Lewis said. "That might not have been the Fenix she saw. No one knows what it was."

"No, but it devours people whole. Horses whole. Father isn't going to send more men to their doom without knowing for certain where the egg is."

Lewis shook his hands. "You'll just have to have faith in the Elders that the Sect will come up with something."

Clarice shook her head. "We are going to find that egg. I know it's there. I'll be able to convince Father, and we will see this through. Whatever that beast is, Fenix or not, we will slay it."

"You're going to have to slay a lot," Twila said. She wiped the grime from her face with a damp rag. "Those jagged hills aren't meant for men."

"You made it out," Clarice said.

"Because the Elder of Luck was with me. That's the only way that I can explain it," Twila said. She rubbed her neck and grimaced. "Like the seers say, no matter the tragedy, like a scurrying rat, a remnant always survives."

Rolling her neck, Clarice said to Lewis, "Then that means that the other campaigns must have survivors, too. So, there is hope."

Lewis walked up to his half-sister, looked down at her, and said, "Just because they survived doesn't mean that they aren't imprisoned. Or worse."

29

———

ABRAHAM WOKE FROM DREAMING ABOUT HIS PAST. HE'D SEEN Mandi, from Woody's Grill. The gorgeous brunette who he'd shunned one too many times was holding hands with another man. A man in uniform. Colonel Drew Dexter. He had a thick moustache, like a young Sam Elliot. They had seemed happy. For some reason, it left him feeling empty, angry.

He yawned. He was underneath a rock bluff, lying on a bed of stone as something warm nuzzled against his backside. He was pretty sure that was Sticks. He peered outward. Dawn began to break. A fog lifted around the ugly, leafless trees. They'd been marching for two straight days, not stopping until they had to. All they wanted was out of that crater.

"Looks like another crappy day on Titanuus," he said to himself. "At least we have the egg." He yawned again and stretched his arms over his head. Then he reached down and jostled Sticks. "Come on. Early bird gets the worm. Let's get going." He ran his hands over her body. Her tunic felt soft and furry. He blinked and looked down at her. "What in the—*guh!*" He jumped up off the ground, grabbed his scabbard, and ripped his sword free.

The creature lying beside him popped up. It was an ugly eight-eyed bat-like creature, a small version of the Fenix about half the size of Abraham. It stood on little clawed feet. The small arms on the tips of its wings were spread out like Abraham's.

"Great googly-moogly!" he said. "Stay back!"

Abraham cocked his elbow back, preparing to thrust and end the thing. The baby Fenix mimicked his movement.

Horace, Bearclaw, Sticks, and more of the Henchmen rushed over. They had their weapons in hand and surrounded the Fenix.

"Let's gore the foul spawn of the beast," Horace said as he poked his spear at it.

The baby Fenix hissed at Horace and clacked its teeth at him.

"That's one ugly creature," Cudgel said. "It should not live. It should be burned."

"That's what we fought to save you brother," Tark added. "But it was one hundred times bigger."

"I don't know. It's sort of cute in an ugly way," Dominga said. "Look at that soft pelt. It gives the monster charm."

"Are you going to finish it, Captain?" Horace asked. He shuffled closed to the baby Fenix. "Say the word, and I'll end it."

The baby Fenix let out an earsplitting shriek that sounded like claws tearing across metal. The Henchmen winced and covered their ears.

"Back off!" Abraham shouted over the noise.

Horace backed up, and the shrieking ceased. The baby Fenix closed its mouth. Its wet nostrils flared, and it tilted his head from side to side like a bird.

"All right everyone, just calm down. Don't be so jumpy," Abraham said. "I'm going to try something." He slid his sword back into the scabbard. "I don't think this thing came to kill us. I do think it followed us. I saw it in the nest, back in the cavern."

He lifted both his arms. The baby Fenix did the same thing. He put his hands on top of his head. So did the baby Fenix. Abraham hopped on one leg, and the Fenix did too.

"It's dances!" Cudgel said with elation.

"The thing mocks you, Captain," Horace added. "I say we kill it."

Abraham stopped hopping on one foot. "It's not mocking me. It's imitating me. I think, when I saw it—"

"It imprinted on you!" Solomon said. "Ha! That is a wonder. A spawn of the Elders has become your hound."

Narrowing an eye at Solomon, Horace asked, "What is the troglin babbling about? It's not a hound, it's a–a bat or bird."

"A dragon," Iris said.

"It's not a dragon. It doesn't have scales," Sticks said. She sheathed her daggers. "Dragons have scales."

"Be still, everyone." Abraham stepped toward the creature. It stepped toward him. He stretched his hand out. It did the same. "It's like a baby duck. It bonds with the first person it sees. It thinks that I'm its mother. At least, I think that is what is going on." He was almost touching its creepy little hand. He spread his fingers out and locked fingers with it. The creature's grip was strong and warm as toast. "It's not a lizard. He's warm as baked bread."

Bearclaw flipped his axe up on his shoulder and asked, "How do you know it's a he?"

"I don't know. It just looks like a he to me." Abraham scratched the back of his head. "The question is now what do we do with him?"

Vern slipped alongside Bearclaw and said, "I'm with Horace—kill it. It's Elder Spawn. It will turn on us. Devour us." His lips twisted. "Look at it. We killed its mother. It will eat us. It might destroy all of Kingsland."

"Don't listen to him," Iris said, twisting her hair on a finger and staring at the baby Fenix. "Showing mercy to the Elder Spawn can garner Elder favor. And it was us that invaded its home. It was not the other way around. Are we pillagers that destroy families? And if this is the last of the Fenixes, a guardian of Elder's Birthing, what will replace it? All creatures have a purpose. So does this one." She walked up, stretched out her fingers and placed her hand on its head.

The baby Fenix's throat rumbled.

Iris made a big smile. "It purrs. Dominga, come, feel this."

Dominga eased up to the baby Fenix and started stroking its pelt. "My, it's warm. Ugly... but cute."

"Women don't make any sense," Horace said with a frown.

"Agreed," Vern replied.

Rubbing his chin with his great hand, Solomon said, "I think the Henchmen have a mascot." He chuckled. "I think you need to give it a name, Abraham."

"What do you call an ugly bat with eight eyes?" He shook his head. "Man, that sounds like a joke, doesn't it?"

Apollo perked up and said, "Horace's mother!"

Horace jabbed a finger at Apollo. "Don't you talk about my mother! Your mother's a... well... bearded lady!"

"How about Felix the Fenix?" Solomon suggested.

"That's not very imposing. Seeing how this thing is going to get very big," he said. "Man, he really does look like a hammerhead bat."

"You sound like someone that knows bats," Solomon said.

"I did a book report on them in grade school. It was one of the few projects that I enjoyed." Abraham unlocked his grip from the Fenix. "They mostly feed on insects. I hope that's the case with him." He patted its snout and cracked a smile as he remembered one of his favorite movies. "How about Simon?" He grinned. "Like Simon Phoenix."

"Short and sweet," Solomon said with a nod. "I take it there is a deeper meaning behind it?"

"You could say that." He scratched behind the Fenix's ears. "It's the name of a real bad dude from the movie *Demolition Man*. My dad and I loved it."

"Fitting. I'm sure it will come back to kill us one day." Solomon tilted his head and looked at the Fenix. "This should be interesting."

"What will be interesting?" he said. "Having two best buds named Solomon and Simon?"

Solomon chuckled. "Watching you teach it how to fly."

"Ha ha! I suppose it will be, but just so you know, I do know a little something about flying." Abraham's stomach knotted up as he thought about his dreams and the accident. He rubbed his aching forehead. "Henchmen, the king is waiting. Let's move out."

In a single column line, the company resumed their journey. The Fenix, Simon, walked behind Abraham like a man.

Sticks, walking right in front of him, looked back and said, "You attract interesting company."

"Yeah, don't remind me." He stepped over some stones, turned, and watched Simon climb over them. "I'm going to have a fine time teaching him how to ride a horse."

Sticks broke out in laughter. He'd never seen so much emotion from her.

"Somebody's feeling spry today."

"Perhaps," she said.

The column stopped. Word came from the front, where Tark and Dominga led, back to Horace, who turned to Ruger and said, "We have company ahead. Bad company."

"I wish," Abraham said.

He marched to the front. Down the hillside of the spine, dozens of terra-men had gathered.

"Great."

Barath the Ancient stood in the middle of the group. The giant snapping turtle stood like a man with his thick black-and-yellow scaled arms crossed over his shell chest. His bright orange eyes burned like suns. Towering at twelve feet tall, he glared at Abraham and said, "Children, take them."

30

THE NEXT MORNING, LEWIS RODE ALONG THE COAST IN THE BACK OF the group, accompanying Twila. Both of them were on horseback, and she was leading the other two surviving horses of the Henchmen. One of the horses was Ruger's. The strange backpack hung from the saddle.

He cleared his throat and asked Twila, "Are you certain they are dead?"

"You doubt me?" she said.

"You spin a convincing tale, but you've left out many details. You might have sold Clarice, but you didn't sell me."

Twila cracked her neck from side to side. A cross look started on her round face that seemed unnatural. "You hired me to do a job. I've done it. I've sabotaged every mission they've undertaken since I joined the group. Dozens of men and women dead because of me. And now, you doubt me?"

"It might help if I'd seen the bodies."

"You didn't see any of the other bodies. Why do you need to see them now?" She glanced back at Ruger's pack. "That cherished item. Do you think that he would part with it? And if they lived, no doubt they would be coming after my head." She tilted her head to one side twice, like a nervous tic. "I can't wait to get out of this disguise. It's been too long. It's irritating."

"I admit I dearly miss your splendid figure. That one is a bit... lumpy."

"These lumps and curves made the job easier for me. No one would ever expect a rotund woman to be one of the king's assassins." She reached underneath her tunic to massage her bosom then straightened her back. "These things aren't your friend on a long ride, but they make for excellent distraction. I can't wait to get back into my natural form."

"Me either," he said quietly, "Raschel."

"I like the way you said that. I missed you too, Lewis." She reached over and patted his hand. "It's been too long, hasn't it?"

"Far too long," Lewis replied.

When Lewis came of age and was sworn into the King's Guardians, he began sitting in the king's war room. King Hector proved to be willing to protect his kingdom by any means necessary. In addition to his vast army and fleet of ships, he hired mercenaries, spies, saboteurs and assassins, something like the Henchmen, to do his dirty work. The assorted lot of folk proved to be unreliable. However, because Lewis and Leodor held court with the kings, they were a part of the scheme that got their hands dirty. That was how he met Raschel. She was an assassin. The pair hit it off so well that they became as close as lovers. With the help of Leodor, they hatched up a scheme to put an end to the Henchmen, who— unlike the mercenaries and other ilk—would faithfully serve the king.

"What are you thinking?" she asked. "Your fingers are massaging the air."

He gave an absentminded look to his fingers. "Oh, well, I'm curious. Did you see what you said you saw?"

"No. But I'll tell you what I felt. I felt fear. And the smell was a muggy, putrid death. Nothing that ventured far into the cavern was coming out alive. It was the Fenix. And I believe the lore. No man who sees the Fenix will live to tell about it." She parted her lips and took a breath. "Out of all of my missions, nothing... nothing at all was scarier than that."

"But if you didn't see it, then how do you know it was the Fenix?"

She quickly shared the story about rescuing Solomon the troglin, the encounter with Barath the Ancient terra-man, and how Barath sent them to the Fenix's cavern. "My skin chills just thinking about it. I shouldn't be alive, but here I am. And lucky for you because if you ventured where we were, you'd all be dead too."

"No, we'd never be stupid enough to face the Fenix. The terra-men and troglin... Well, I'm certain we could hold our own if we had to battle. The King's Guardians are stalwart and formidable."

"Yes, but I'll tell you this, those Henchmen... They had true grit," she said. "I can't believe they had the guts to go into that cavern that smelled the way that it did. I wanted to puke, but somehow, they went in. I really don't understand how they did it. I couldn't have done it. Not with my knees knocking like they did."

Lewis gave her a curious look and said, "It's the brand."

"What?"

"The King's Brand. Leodor says that it has power. It gives the Henchmen inner strength. Fortitude. I never bought into it, but based off what you say, that is the only sense I can make out of it."

"Well, I agree that they have spines of steel, but why wouldn't such a thing be used on the Guardians?"

"The Guardians and the Maidens have other practices, and I know that my men are as brave as any."

"So, you think that you could march into the lair of the Fenix?" she said with a smirk.

"If I had to, I would." He arched a brow. "You don't believe me?"

"I think it's more than the brand. I think it's the man they follow. Ruger Slade, well, he changed up north when we encountered the frights. He's different now. The Henchmen like him. They follow him. He turned the tables."

"Yes, but he's dead now, right?"

"Of course. No one can look upon the spawn of an Elder and live. Trust me, he's dead, and all of the Henchmen with him. Nothing's ever come out of that lair alive except the Fenix."

Lewis shifted in his saddle and said, "I feel giddy and guilty."

"Why is that?"

"I'm finally rid of Ruger and the Henchmen." He smiled. "A thorn has been plucked from my side. But I feel bad for my father. He has no one he can turn to, and his wife is about to die."

31

Lewis and Clarice returned to the House of Steel to deliver King Hector the news. The king met with them on the outside terrace that overlooked the Bay of Elders. Leodor and two of his personal Guardians were with him. He was flipping bread crumbs to the sea birds when Leodor announced Lewis and Clarice's arrival. When Hector's eyes fell on Clarice, he sighed with relief, rushed over to her, and gave her a hug.

In his gentle voice, he said, "My sweet little dove, I am so glad you have returned. My heart was twisting inside my chest." He squeezed her hard. "Promise me that you won't do something so foolish again."

"I'm sorry, Father," she said as she hugged him tightly. "I can't promise that. I want to go back and find the egg. We can beat the Fenix. I know it."

Hector pushed her an arm's length away and said, "You won't be leaving this castle, period."

"But Father!" she whined.

"You might have slipped me once, but you won't slip me

again." His voice became strong as iron. "You'll remain in the House of Steel, where you belong, by your mother's side and mine. Do you understand?"

"We need to save her," Clarice said. "The cause is noble, and I'll give my life for hers. You must resume the quest, Father. I know the egg can be found."

"No," the king said. He looked at Lewis. "You've done well with your charge, Son. You and your men. And I am grateful. This family doesn't need to lose another one of our own. In times like this, we should stay together, be by your mother's side, to the very end."

Lewis nodded. "Has Clarann had a setback? I thought she was on the rebound before I departed."

"She has," Hector said with a frown. His gaze landed on Clarice. "And it has not helped that her one and only daughter is missing. Her heart broke the moment she learned that you left on her account."

"You told her?" Clarice said.

"I cannot lie to her. And what, did you not think that she would notice if you were missing? You abandoned her. You need to go to her now and apologize for what you put her through," Hector said.

Clarice's eyes watered, and her chin sagged. "I'm-I'm sorry, Father."

"Don't apologize to me." Hector squeezed her hands and kissed her on the forehead. "Apologize to your mother. And don't think she'll go easy on you, either."

"Yes, Father." Clarice gave a quick bow and hurried inside through the patio doors.

Hector let out a long sigh. "Lewis, I can't tell you how relieved I am that Clarice is back. You and your men deserve a feast." He glanced over his shoulder at Leodor. "Have the kitchen make arrangements.

The saggy-cheeked viceroy nodded and said, "Certainly, Your Majesty."

"You really don't need to prepare a feast. It wasn't so difficult a task," Lewis said. "But if it is your wish... And I'm sorry about Clarann. I wish that something could be done for her. Um... I fear I have more bad tidings to share as well."

"Oh," King Hector said. "Let's have a seat. I feel so exhausted." He moved to the chairs on the upper terrace as if his robes weighed a ton and sat down. "Ah... sit, Son, sit. Let's try to enjoy the shade. What other news do you have? Did you lose Guardians or Maidens?"

Lewis sat as Leodor stood behind them with his hands tucked inside the sleeves of his robes and frowning. Lewis eyeballed the pitcher of water sitting on the table then reached over and poured a glass. "No, all of the king's men and women are in good order." He drank deeply. "Ah."

"Well, tell me. What troubles you?" the king asked.

"It's Ruger... or Abraham. The King's Henchmen. All save one are dead." He gave his father a sad look. He pulled Ruger's backpack out of a sack he'd carried and gave it to the king. "I'm sorry."

Leodor's eyes widened.

The king held the backpack in his hands and deflated in his chair and said, "I knew that this attempt would be in vain, but I put hope in it." He looked Lewis in the eye. "How do you know this?"

Lewis thoroughly recounted his encounter and discussion with the Red Tunic, Twila. The king sat on the end of his chair, nodding, not missing a single word. Neither Hector nor Leodor asked a single question or tried to stop him. Sharing the entire tale took close to an hour. "Again, I'm sorry."

Aghast, Hector asked, "All of my Henchmen are gone now? I–I can't believe it."

"I would not fret, my king. Ruger was slated for execution," Leodor said. "At least he and his rabble died trying to fulfill a noble mission."

King Hector stroked the backpack. "I thought we might have turned a corner. That we might have an edge. Now, I have less than I had before."

"Sometimes, less is more." Lewis reached over and squeezed his father's knee. "They are one less burden to carry. Remember you have your armies and me. We'll do better. We can be more efficient."

Hector looked as though he'd lost his own son or a close family member, like a brother. He absentmindedly petted the backpack. "Ruger and I went so far back. I never thought it possible that he would die so soon. Then, these strange happenings. Possessions. Portals. Strange baubles." He gave Lewis a blank look. "What is happening to my world?"

Lewis gave Hector a polite smile and said, "It's changing."

32

RASCHEL WAITED IN HER APARTMENT FOR LEWIS TO ARRIVE. THE windowless apartment was located in the city of Burgess. It was a nicely decorated studio, small and quaint, with a double-sized bed against a wall, a sofa, a round table with two chairs, a cupboard, and a vanity. She sat in front of the vanity's mirror, looking at Twila's face. Twila was a cute but pudgy woman she'd met in the city's marketplace. Twila was a wholesome fruit vendor with a knack for selling customers more than they needed. Raschel had ordered several bushels of apples. Then she had Twila deliver them to her apartment and killed her.

"Oh Twila, you were such a nice person, too. I really hated to do this to you, but it served my purpose quite well," she said to herself. She twisted a ring on the ring finger of her right hand. It was quite ordinary to the naked eye, made out of onyx with diamond-shaped ivory teeth inlaid. She turned it on her finger until two small teeth, like a small snake's fangs, popped out. It was called the Ring of Tarsus. "Fascinating that it works so well."

After she'd lured Twila into her apartment, she struck quickly.

Using the fangs in the ring, she grabbed Twila by the neck with the palm of her hand. The fangs sank into the innocent woman's neck and hooked on. The fangs drained Twila's blood and pumped it into Raschel's body. Magic and flesh worked as one. Second after second passed as Twila's dying eyes watched Raschel transform into herself. Drained to a husk, Twila felt her heartbeat fade. Her flesh and bone became brittle and turned to dust. Raschel turned into Twila. She spoke with Twila's voice and not her own.

With a smirk, she said to herself, "Bye-bye, Twila, and thanks for all of the good times." She took off the ring and the image in the mirror wobbled. Her face twisted and contorted. Twila's pie-faced features slimmed. A narrow chin formed. Her eyes turned dark and seductive. Once her pleasing lips formed, the rest of her body lengthened. She cried out and slapped her hands on the table with a painful shout. Arching her back, she opened her eyes wide and watched her sensuous hair lengthen. She shuddered. A film of sweat dressed her high cheekbones. Her full lips parted, and she let out a sigh. "Oh, I'm so glad that is over. I felt like a buffalo before."

She removed the clothing that was hanging from her body and checked herself in the mirror. Her stomach was flat, hips narrow, and breasts firm. She'd returned to her well-toned athletic form. "That's so much better, not that pleasantly plump was so awful. It had its advantages." She donned a black silk gown, stuffed the old clothing into a cloth sack, and tossed it into the corner by her door. She put the Ring of Tarsus back on and flopped back-first onto the bed. "That was miserable, but at least I'm going to be paid a lot of money for this."

Lying on a green satin pillow, she reminisced about all she'd done. In her travels with the Henchmen, she'd served as a spy for Lewis. Together, they doctored maps and plans and sent them on suicide missions. She turned Henchmen and Red Tunics against one another. She ruined food supplies and created faulty equipment. She made failures look like accidents. Men and women who battled back from the brink of death, she finished off. Raschel shook her head. "I can't believe I pulled all of that off. Ha. I'm even better than I realized. Lewis will owe me a fortune for all that I sacrificed. I'll be so rich I'll start my own kingdom." She yawned and took a nap.

Raschel had slept well the night before and spent the morning cleaning herself and disposing of all remnants of Twila's identity. That afternoon, a soft knocking came to her door. She opened it and found herself looking into Lewis's handsome face.

"What a nice surprise," she said. "I wasn't expecting you so soon."

She stepped aside, and he slipped in and closed the door behind him.

Lewis took her in his arms and kissed her passionately. He scooped her up and carried her to the bed. "I've missed you! You look ravishing!" He kissed her neck. "Don't ever change again. You can do your bidding without all of that changing."

She wiggled out of his grasp and from her knees held him at a distance with her hands. "Let's talk business first. I've been through sheer hell. Now, it's finished. I want to be paid."

"When you are my queen, you'll have all of the money you want, but"—he reached behind his back and produced a satin purse—"this is yours. Just as you requested."

She pulled the purse's drawstrings and spilled the contents into her hand. Large diamonds, rubies, and emeralds, fell out. The bright gems glinted in her eyes. "This is marvelous!" She hugged him. "This makes it all worth it. So, how did the king take the news?"

"He looks like a lost puppy. I almost feel sorry for him, but that's how one should feel about someone that is old and weak."

"Don't underestimate the elderly. They can surprise you," she said as she counted the gems in her hand. "I have to be honest. I'm not so sure that what I did was worth it, now that I have it. I almost died several times. I think I'll resort to straight-up assassination. Long missions like that... Never again."

Lewis pushed her down on the bed and said, "You don't need to kill anymore. You have plenty. There will be more."

"I enjoy the game. I'm young and not retiring. I'll only become weak without a challenge."

"Don't be crazy. There is nothing easy about being the queen. There are countless demanding duties." He pushed her down and straddled her and removed his jerkin. "The first one is pleasing your husband."

He bent down and kissed her all over. She kissed him and worked off his trousers. They made love on and off for hours.

Knock. Knock. Knock. Knock.

Lewis and Raschel's heads popped up. They exchanged a look. She grabbed a dagger hanging from a scabbard on her bedpost.

Quietly, he asked, "Are you expecting someone?"

"You are the only one that knows about this place. It might be a mistake," she said.

A parchment of paper was slipped underneath the door. They heard feet scampering away. Lewis swung his feet over the bed. Raschel picked the note up from the floor.

"It has your name on it," she said. "Shall I open it?"

He swiped at the note, but she deftly pulled it out of reach. "You'll have to be faster than that."

"There's no time for toying around. Hand it over."

Raschel gave him the note. It had a green wax seal with an elegant *L* stamped in it.

"It's Leodor. I should have known he'd know where I was. He doesn't miss anything." Lewis lifted a brow. "Unless he's been here?"

"No," she said. "Never."

He opened the triple-folded parchment and read. His jaw dropped to his chest, then he swallowed.

"What is it?" she asked.

Lewis's forehead creased. His nostrils flared as he held the note in front of her face and said, "It says, 'Ruger has arrived at the House of Steel. He brought the Fenix egg. Get your arse back here.'" He took the note and stuffed it in Raschel's mouth. "We'll talk about this later!"

33

THE HOUSE OF STEEL

ABRAHAM SAT OUTSIDE ON THE KING'S TERRACE, WHICH overlooked the Bay of Elders. He was behind a large table with a buffet of food, drinking the finest wine he ever tasted. Everything —the meats, cheeses, bread, fruits, and vegetables—was succulent and exquisite. He licked his fingers and wiped his mouth. At the moment, he was eating alone, waiting for the king to return. They'd already had a long conversation about everything that had happened. The only other people that were there were four of the King's Guardians. They were in full-plate armor and wearing their lion-faced helmets. He could feel their eyes on him. At one time, he must have known all of them, but he did not know them now.

He sipped his wine. "Ah."

King Hector hustled through the terrace patio doors and joined him at the table. The soft-eyed king had a hopeful smile on his face. He wore forest-green robes with golden trim. The golden Crown of Stone was cockeyed on his head. He put a napkin on his lap and raised a wine glass. "Leodor has informed me that the queen is bathing in the yolk of the Fenix." He fanned himself with his hand. "I feel giddy. I never imagined this would happen. In all truth, I thought the mission was futile. But nothing ventured, nothing gained, eh?"

"I couldn't agree more, Your Majesty," Abraham said. "Sometimes I feel as if I am dreaming."

Hector smiled and motioned for the Guardians to move away. The soldiers backed toward the terrace's outer walls. The dropping sun shone off the metal of their armor.

"Out of the sun. Into the shade," the king said. "Blend in, my Guardians."

The Guardians moved into the shadows cast by the sun setting west of the castle.

Abraham and King Hector were already in the shade that came at the end of the day. "I hope the ocean breeze is taking my foulness away from you, King Hector. When I came with the egg, I came with all haste."

King Hector, who sat at the head of the table but within one seat of him, leaned forward and said, "And you did the right thing. Now, please continue telling me about your second encounter with Barath the Ancient."

"Certainly." Abraham refilled his wine glass and offered to do so for the king.

The king shook his head, his light-green eyes intent on him. Abraham had already told the king about everything that had happened from their first encounter with Barath and the terra-men and how they slew the Fenix and retrieved the eggs. He even mentioned the baby Fenix that imprinted on him, and that led him up to that last encounter with Barath.

"So, we are trying to make our way back off of the Spine when we run smack into Barath. There he is, twelve feet tall and surrounded by what must have been fifty more terra-men that we could see. Barath says, 'Children, take them.'" Abraham leaned his chair back on two legs. "All of us drew our weapons, figuring to engage in the fight of all fights. Instead, Barath opens up his scaly paws, and he says, 'No, you misunderstand. My children will lead you off of the Spine with haste. They know a shorter way.'" He looked at the king, and said, "Naturally, I had to ask why."

"And what did he say," King Hector asked.

"Barath said that no one had ever faced the Fenix and lived. He said that was a sign. When he saw the baby Fenix, his eyes grew the size of boulders, and he knelt down. 'Just go. Go with all haste,' he said, 'and give King Hector my best.' Then he looked me dead in the eye and added, 'The tide turns. The Elders awaken. Tell that to the king.'"

King Hector leaned back in his chair, crossed his arms over his chest, and quietly restated, "The tide turns. The Elders awaken."

"I'm not sure what that means, but do you know?" Abraham asked.

"Long ago, the Elders walked among the world of men. Well, some of them, for there are so many. Most thrive in the seas. But perhaps the Elders will start to reappear." The king shrugged. "I don't know. But what I do know is that you killed the spawn of the Elders. You killed a Fenix. This is a godlike creature. It's quite possible that there might be repercussions, and what Barath said is a warning." He gave Abraham a curious look. "Where is the baby Fenix?"

"Before I came here, I had to stop by my stronghold and cage Simon. At the stronghold, we prepared the egg in a wagon loaded with hay and covered it up to keep prying eyes away."

Hector patted his knees and rubbed them. "Yes, yes. So, in all truth, the yolk of the egg brought a man back from the dead? Your Henchman, eh… What was his name?"

"Cudgel. And yes, he's bright eyed and bushy tailed."

"He has a tail? Like a squirrel?" the king asked.

"No, it's an expression from my world. It means 'ready to go.' Sorry."

"No Ruger, er, Abraham... I forget that we are dealing with an otherworldly personality. It's going to take some getting used to. But my hope for my dearest Clarann is growing. I feel that it is going to heal her fully." He slapped a knee and pointed at Abraham. "And if it does, you and your Henchmen will have your reputations reinstated."

Abraham arched an eyebrow. "And if it doesn't?"

Hector propped an elbow up on the table and said, "I like you, Abraham. I liked Ruger. I think in a way, you are one and the same, men with a strong sense of duty. But if the queen is not healed, I have no way of verifying your story. For all that I know, the entire tale is a well-fabricated lie. And given the daily climate that I face, I can't afford to take any chances. I'll have to execute your sentence."

34

THE FRONT TWO LEGS OF ABRAHAM'S CHAIR HIT THE TERRACE FLOOR. "What? You're still going to kill me?"

"Easy, Abraham. We want to be hopeful in this situation. If all that you said is true, then you won't have anything to worry about," the king said. "But I can't put all of my faith in a man who rolls up to my castle door with a wagon and a boulder in the back of it. I saw the ugly rock, and though it is unique and I do have hope, only a fool would believe the entire tale that you've woven."

Abraham's jaw dropped. After all he'd been through, he couldn't believe Hector doubted him. And he'd been feeling pretty good about himself.

"Now," the king continued. "Lift your chin up from the floor and enjoy the fine meal that has been prepared for you. I'm sure Leodor will bring word to us soon."

Abraham clamped his mouth shut. Butterflies fluttered in his stomach. He'd never considered that the egg yolk might not work on the queen. That increased his worries. He didn't have much faith in Viceroy Leodor, either. The aloof mystic seemed like someone the king put too much trust in. *He could be with the queen, doing anything.* "Shouldn't you be there, to make sure that the yolk is properly applied? It dries up fast, like I said."

"No, I can trust Leodor. He heard what you said."

I don't know if he heard me, but he definitely saw me. When I showed up at the castle with the egg, he looked like he saw a ghost. Abraham swallowed more wine. It seemed as if, despite his efforts, the guillotine was descending slowly toward his neck again. *All of this time, I've been thinking I'm dreaming. The truth is it's a nightmare.* "It doesn't seem fair. I've... We've given all that we had."

"And all of you returned unscathed. That's miraculous," Hector said. "Ruger, I can see your disappointment. Put yourself on my throne. What would you do? The enemy closes in from all directions. The numbers dwindle. The expeditions fail. I have to be a king who is a king of his word. You were given a second chance, thanks to the queen. But if she dies, you die." He pointed at his Guardians. "I cannot lead men if I cannot enforce the law. A lawless society cannot survive. It will quickly die. The tall pines of the forest always start dying from the top. If my word fails, the kingdom falls. Do you understand?"

Abraham nodded. He had no desire to argue with King Hector. He had such a pleasant and likeable demeanor. Like a great oak, he wouldn't be shaken, either.

"I suppose," Abraham said. "But you are the king, and you could change the law."

"And bend eons of rules just to serve myself? Or you? If a law was truly unjust, I could understand it. But that isn't the case. You are a deserter. You abandoned your station. Many men died from it." King Hector took a goblet of wine in hand and drank. "You should be dead. However, I showed mercy and gave you the King's Brand. If you break your oath, you'll die from it. It was the best choice I had. We live and we die by our choices.

Right or wrong, there are consequences. The law must enforce it."

"You know, you're a real hard-ass, but in a nice way." Abraham finished his wine. If it was possible that he was going to die soon, he might as well enjoy himself. "In my world, you'd make a fine president."

"Don't they have kings in your country?"

"Some countries do, but lately, they haven't worked out so well."

King Hector sniffed. "Interesting. So, the royal bloodlines aren't strong in your world?"

"Well, think about it. It isn't exactly a merit-based system when someone is born into it. And then the oldest male inherits the crown." He sniffed his wine's bouquet. "What happens if the oldest is wicked, pugnacious, spoiled, or depraved? He'll become a foul leader, his subjects enslaved or miserable. The country is not productive, and it is soon conquered by another."

"You are singing a familiar song. This is the dilemma the House of Steel has faced every day for centuries." The king grabbed a golden hunk of cheese and started to nibble at it. "What form of government does your country impose?"

"It's a republic, where the citizens elect their leaders by voting for them on a ballot."

King Hector spat out his cheese. "That's the most insane thing that I've ever heard. Let the people decide for themselves? It's preposterous!"

"And prosperous. You see—"

Prince Lewis burst through the doors onto the terrace. "Father, I came as soon as I heard the news." He eyeballed Abraham and clenched his jaws. "Ruger, it is surprising to see you again."

"I bet it is," Abraham replied. He was getting used to being called Ruger. He set down his goblet and drummed his fingers on the table. "So, Twila said that we were dead, did she? It's no wonder you look like you saw a ghost. Where is she?"

Lewis shrugged. His face was clammy, and his feathery hair dripped sweat down his cheeks. He dabbed it with a cloth napkin. "I haven't seen her since we departed the other day. I naturally assumed that she would return to the stronghold and bear the news to your hirelings."

Abraham shook his head. He'd already discussed with the king what Lewis had told him about Twila. "Oh, she wasn't anywhere to be found, but that wasn't any surprise to you."

"I beg your pardon?" Lewis said. "What are you saying?"

"Yes, what are you saying?" the king asked.

"I'll tell you what I am saying. I'm saying that Twila has been sabotaging our missions for quite some time. And someone that wanted us to fail planted her with the Henchmen. She made a fine job of it until I came around."

"Father, this man is insane." Lewis gave Abraham an appalled look. He poured a goblet of wine. "I don't know this Twila any better than a pig's elbow. And I don't pick his retainers, hirelings, or henchmen. He does."

"My son makes a valid point," Hector said. "You are allowed to pick your men. Not us. I've given you the freedom to do that."

"Why would I sabotage my own missions?" he said. "Twila killed Cudgel. She stole our horse and gear and abandoned us to the Fenix."

The king lifted a finger. "Ah, but we haven't been able to validate your story, have we? We only have your words, and we await Clarann's revival to verify it."

Lewis's eyes widened, and his tight expression eased. "Yes, you come telling tall tales, but you can't prove any of it."

The moment he saw Lewis's stiff expression ease, Abraham knew in his heart that the prince was in on it. Proving it would be another matter. He cleared his throat. "Your Majesty, I have a dozen men that can bear witness to my story. And don't forget: I have the Fenix."

"You have the Fenix?" Lewis said. "I don't understand. What sort of preposterous tale is this? Father, what sort of lies has he been feeding you?"

"Ruger says that he has a baby Fenix, in a cage, back inside his stronghold."

"Ha. I'll believe it when I see it," Lewis said. "I shall send my Guardians to fetch it. How does that sound to you, Ruger?"

Abraham got up from the table. "I'd be more than happy to show you the way."

"That won't be necessary," someone else said.

All the men turned toward the source of the voice. The king gasped. Queen Clarann was standing in the doorway.

35

Queen Clarann was a fair-haired lioness with ice-blue eyes. Her wrinkly skin had been restored. Her lips were full and red. She wore a golden terry-cloth robe that caressed the firm curves of her body.

King Hector rose out of his seat, knocking his chair over. "My love!" he gasped. His hands trembled when he touched her face. "You've never looked so beautiful." He wrapped her in his arms, his body still shaking. "How do you feel?"

Clarann nestled her head in the king's shoulder and stroked his hair with her hand. "I've never felt better, Hector." She kissed his cheek and looked at Abraham. "Never better."

Abraham slid out of his chair and took a knee. His heart pounded inside his chest. He wasn't really sure what was happening. Clarann was a vision, but no more so than his wife, Jenny, or Mandi. But his body wanted hers. *Ruger! Oh no.* Something was going on. Apparently, a deeper connection existed between Ruger and the queen that he hadn't picked up on before. Perhaps it was Ruger's boldness that pushed them through to conquer the Fenix.

You old dog, what have you been up to? He parted his lips and started to speak, but Prince Lewis beat him to the punch.

"Clarann, so glad to see that you are well." Lewis walked over to the queen and the king and gave them both a rigid hug. "It's cause for celebration."

"Indeed," Hector said. "We will have a great celebration, for Kingsland has its queen back."

Leodor walked out onto the terrace. His heavy eyes sought Lewis's. Abraham caught the uncomfortable glances between the two.

"You have done well, Leodor," Hector said. "I thank you!"

Clarann broke from Hector's embrace and said, "I don't think it is Leodor that deserves the credit. All he did was prepare a bath. Ruger is the one that brought the egg to us. Did he not?"

"Oh, well, of course, dearest. I'm sorry, but I'm simply giddy seeing you in your full glory. I only wanted to give credit where credit is due." Hector kissed her hands. "It was Leodor that made the suggestion. His idea bore great fruit." He turned his head toward Abraham. "Abraham, I doubted your word, but today you have proven yourself."

With a tilt of her head, Clarann asked, "Abraham? Who is Abraham?"

"Er, well..." Hector brushed a hand over his chest as if trying to wipe a mistake away. "Just a slip of the tongue."

"Hector, don't start fibbing to me now," she said. "Why did you call him Abraham?"

"Queen Clarann, I think that you should rest. Let me prepare a bed for you," Leodor suggested.

"Oh, shut up!" Clarann said with fire in her voice. "I've been bedridden for months. My restless slumbers were filled with the sound of wings from the crows that were coming. My dreams were filled with smoking steel dragons in foreign places. I might close my eyes to feel the caress of the sea winds on my face, but I'll be damned if I'm going back to sleep anytime soon. Leodor, why don't you go take a nap? You look like you haven't slept in a year."

Leodor's thinning brows rose and fell.

She turned on the king. "Now, tell me. Who is Abraham?"

"It's a long story and one that might trouble you," Hector said.

Clarann spread her arms out in a showy fashion and asked, "Do I look like anything is going to trouble me? After what I've been through, you no longer need to walk softly around your queen. I'm ready for anything. Please, do not mince words with me."

Hector nodded. "So be it, my love." He pointed at Abraham. "I'll let Ruger explain." He pulled out a chair. "I know that you aren't tired, but I want you to sit down for this."

With a surprised look she said, "As you wish." She sat down beside the king.

Leodor, Lewis, and Abraham joined them at the table.

She eyed Abraham. "Before you begin, first, I want to extend a thank you to your and your Henchmen. Thank you."

"You're welcome, Your Highness," Abraham said. He had to catch his breath for some reason. Finally, his racing heart slowed. "My name is Abraham Jenkins. I'm from another world called Earth. Man, it sounds weird saying that. Anyway, this is my story— this is my song."

He went on for an hour, explaining everything the best that he could. Everyone at the table hung on his every word. Clarann sat upright with her hands on her lap, chin up like a true queen. She hardly batted an eye as he spoke.

He finished up by saying, "And that's how I came to be in Titanuus."

Hector reached over and put his hand on hers and asked, "It's quite a story, isn't it? What are you thinking?"

The beautiful queen arched a brow and said, "It explains many things that we could not otherwise explain. If this... Abraham... truly is who he says that he is, and his essence resides in Ruger, then I wonder what happened to the essence of Ruger?" She seemed sad when she said it, as though truly worried. Her eyes searched Abraham's. "Where is he?"

"So far as I can tell, he's still a part of me, just not all of me. It's his body, my mind. Sometimes I feel it, and sometimes I don't. In his body, I do things that only he would have known to do." Abraham shrugged. "It's possible that his essence might be in the body of someone else."

Queen Clarann looked right at him and said, "Or in your body in your world."

36

ABRAHAM HAD ENOUGH TO WORRY ABOUT REGARDING HIS OWN essence and didn't need to worry about Ruger's too. *Could Ruger be in my body? Back on Earth?* That didn't seem plausible. After all, when he made the transformation into Ruger, Eugene Drisk turned back into what appeared to be his original body and vanished through the portal in the tunnel. *None of this makes any sense. Every day feels more real than the last. But if I'm dreaming, I need to find out how to wake up. Otherwise, I'm in a world where anything can happen.*

"Your Highness," he said, "I sit on this side of the table with little more understanding than you do. It's as new to me as you. But we had a deal. I retrieve the egg, and you help me find a way back to my world. At the same time, I agree to help you with whatever you need."

Hector pulled his shoulders back and said, "I don't need you to remind me to keep my word. My oaths will be kept."

Lewis jabbed a finger at Ruger and said, "You don't have to honor your word with this dog. He claims to be possessed. He has no credibility. He's a madman. You should finish him, Father. Be done with him!"

"No credibility," Hector said. "Son, are you blind? Look at your mother."

"She's not my mother." Lewis folded his hands across his chest. "And there's not so much of a difference that I can see."

Clarann let out a delighted chuckle. "Lewis, as always, your barbs tickle me. And so does your lunacy. You willfully blind yourself to Ruger's value and continue to disappoint."

"Leodor," Hector said. "Draw up papers for Ruger and all of his men that will clear their names under the authority of the king." He landed his gaze on Abraham. "I believe there are some Guardians among you that will be reinstated, if they like."

With an eager nod, Abraham said, "I'll let them know."

"Mother!" Clarice dashed onto the terrace and threw her arms around the queen. Cheek to cheek she hugged her mother tightly. "Oh, Mother, you look so well. So beautiful, like me!"

Clarann squeezed her daughter. "I'll never be so pretty as you."

Abraham rose from his seat and nodded at Clarice. She was a vibrant and beautiful teenager, dressed in a fanciful cotton jerkin and trousers.

Clarice's stare landed on him. "Ruger! So, you are alive!" She turned her glare on Lewis. "That woman Twila said they were dead. And you fell for it, Lewis. You fool. I knew we could not trust that woman."

"You didn't know diddly," Lewis said. "None of us did. The woman deceived all of us." He pointed at Abraham. "Including Ruger. She is his retainer."

"I didn't hire her. Er, well, maybe I did. I don't remember. Perhaps it was Eugene Drisk," Abraham said.

"Who is Eugene Drisk?" Hector asked.

"That was the man that possessed Ruger before me. The man I told you I encountered in the tunnel," he said.

Clarice's eyes moved from person to person. "What in Titanuus are all of you talking about?"

"It's a long story, dear," Clarann said, "I'll explain later."

Abraham's arrival had brought the Henchmen's losing streak to an end, but they still had a problem. Someone wanted their missions sabotaged. They must have planted Twila in the group. Or Eugene knew about it all along and was sabotaging their own missions. Perhaps he didn't share the same interests as the king. Perhaps he secretly served another. He pinched the bridge of his nose. Keeping track of everything made his head ache the more he thought about it.

"Are you well, Ruger?" Clarann asked.

"I have a lot on my mind. I realize that you have much to celebrate, but I need to get back to my men and share the good news. I need to figure out what happened to Twila. She'll have answers. We'll need them. I fear the king has spies in his midst. We have to find out who."

Hector held his emerald stone in his hand and rubbed a finger over the precious gem. "I trust everyone at this table with my life. Including you, Abraham. You've earned it. But if there is a fox in my henhouse, I will reveal them. Go to your men. Share the good news and give them our thanks. I'll summon you soon, and we'll talk in greater detail about your predicament, mine and the Crown of Stones."

Abraham nodded. "Thank you. I'll be at my stronghold, waiting for your call, and I'll probably be bathing the entire time. I apologize, ladies. I probably smell worse than manure. If I'd known you were coming, I'd have at least dunked myself in the ocean before I came."

Clarann made a pleasant smile. "Don't apologize. Every

minute you've spared me from that withering husk means the world to me. Again, you have my thanks and gratitude."

Clarice hugged her mother. "Mine too. But thank you for clarifying what I was smelling. What is that, anyway?"

Abraham shrugged. "A little bit of the worst of everything."

Lewis rose from the table. "I'll escort you out."

With a final nod, Abraham departed with Lewis. The captain of the King's Guardians walked him all the way up to the stables of the House of Steel, near the wall of the main gate. Inside the stables, Lewis led him to the three horses that were taken. All the leftover gear lay on the hay in one of the stables, including his backpack.

Lewis shouted to a pair of stable hands. "Load up this man's beasts and take them to the front gate! He'll meet you there."

Abraham picked up the Pirates backpack and shouldered it, keeping his relief inside. *Ah. I'm not crazy.*

Once they were outside the portcullis, Lewis extended his hand.

With a cocked eye, Abraham shook his hand.

Lewis's iron grip locked on his. He said, "Don't think for a moment that you will be replacing me as captain of the King's Guardians."

"I have more important matters to attend to."

"Good. And tell your dogs that they aren't coming back either. I don't want them."

Abraham looked him dead in the eye and said, "Well, that's not up to you, now is it?" He squeezed Lewis's hand with a crushing grip until the prince paled. He pulled Lewis closer. "That's the king's decision."

Lewis ripped his grip free. "We'll see about that." He stormed away.

37

HIS THREE-STORY STONE STRONGHOLD, WITH ITS RICH FARMLANDS, was a welcome sight. With the day's sun cooling behind the clouds, Abraham gathered all his henchmen inside the Stronghold on the first level. All of them sat at the large oak farm table except for Solomon. He sat on a milking stool beside the front door. The shaggy troglin still sat taller than the rest of them.

Abraham sat at the head of the empty table. Horace sat to his left, followed by Bearclaw, Vern, and Apollo. To his right, Sticks sat on her side with Dominga, Cudgel, and Prospero. Iris sat at the opposite end of the table. All of them had stripped down to normal clothing. The kitchen galley doors swung open. Two haggard-looking bowlegged women wearing off-white aprons teetered out, carrying trays of coffee urns and cups.

"Just leave the trays on the table, ladies."

The rough-looking sisters set down the trays, made unhappy mutterings, and waddled back into the galley out of sight.

"Help yourself," Abraham said.

No one at the table moved. All of them sat as stone-faced as ever. Sweat rolled down from Horace's temple. He had a serious look on his puffy face.

"Or not," Abraham continued. He poured himself a cup of coffee. "I guess I'll get on with it. As you can see, I returned with three horses, our lost gear, and my head. Which all of you should take as a good sign." He paused.

No one blinked.

"And it is. The yolk of the Fenix fully restored Queen Clarann."

Horace gave a short pump of his fist. "That is wonderful, Captain."

All the others at the table started to move. Their heads bobbed as they spoke cheerfully and quietly to one another.

Sticks even poured herself a cup of coffee and said, "So, we aren't going back to Baracha?"

"Nope," he said as he tilted his chair back on two legs. As a matter of fact, I don't know where any of you will go. King Hector is clearing all of our names. You no longer have to be one of his Henchmen."

The group fell silent. They all cast their eyes at Abraham, perplexed looks on their faces. Even Solomon.

Horace clawed at his beard then scratched the back of his head. "Pardon, Captain. We won't be Henchmen anymore?"

"No," Abraham said.

Long looks were exchanged among the company of hard-eyed men and women.

Vern, however, clapped his hands together and said, "That sounds great to me!" He got up from the table. "I'm out of here."

With big smoky eyes, Cudgel said, "So, we will receive the King's Papers? Tark and I are truly free men?"

Abraham shrugged. "The king is a man of his word. But listen, no one needs to run out of here. I have the Stronghold. All of you are always welcome to call this place home."

"Not me. I'm leaving." Vern headed for the door. "With the King's Papers, I assume I can take back my spot with the King's Guardians. You should too, Bearclaw."

"Go ahead," Dominga said. She crossed her arms, looked away from Vern, and frowned. "No one is going to miss you. Especially me."

Horace pulled his jerkin open, revealing the brand on his chest and, asked, "But Captain, what about the mark? We can't so simply be absolved of our duties. We gave our word to serve the king. We are branded for all eternity. To abandon our duty is to die."

"You are released from your duty," Abraham said.

"But how?" Horace asked. "We are still branded."

Vern had stopped by the front door and said, "Yeah, I've never seen a cattle brand go away. Once the king's cattle, always the king's cattle."

"Listen, I don't know all of the details other than what the king said. He's preparing papers. He's..." Abraham's voice trailed off.

The brand of the king's crown on Horace's chest started smoking. Audible gasps filled the room.

Tark jumped up from the table. His chest was smoking too. "I'm on fire!"

The chest of every Henchman in the room was smoking. It wasn't a burning-wood smoke but a misty, oily pink-red vapor. It drifted from their bodies up into the rafters.

"It burns again!" Vern yelled.

"We have betrayed our word!" Horace stammered. "Our treacherous hearts bring death!" He patted at his chest. "May the king forgive me!"

Sticks fanned her hand over the strange smoke coming out from above her breast. "It burns, but hardly like fire." She ran her fingers over the brand on her chest. The inky pink-red smoke dissipated. She pursed her lips and blew downward, and the smoke cleared from her body. The lumpy brand on her chest was gone. Her eyebrows rose. "It's gone."

Bearclaw had ripped his shirt off. The broad-faced warrior lifted his skinned-up hand from his chest and said, "Aye. Mine is gone, too."

One by one, the elated Henchmen looked one another over. All their brands were gone. Each and every one had vanished as if it had never even been there.

"I can't believe it, Captain," Horace said, his hand rubbing his chest. "The King's Brand is indeed powerful magic. Now, it's gone."

Abraham ran his hands over his chest. No smoke came from his body. "Yeah," he said, "everyone's is gone but mine."

38

AT THE BACK END OF THE STRONGHOLD LAY AN INTIMATE CAVERN with pools of hot springs. Abraham sat chest deep in the churning mineral waters. Solomon sat across from him, only waist deep in the steaming waters. They weren't alone, either. Selma, Sophia, and Bridgett, three exotic women with dark hair and eyes, had joined them in the springs. They were lounging in medieval bikinis made from damp cotton that clung to their bodies. Selma wore black, Sophia pink, and Bridgett white. The colors were the only way Abraham could tell them apart. All of them were intoxicating.

Selma slipped over behind him and dipped her perfect legs into the water behind him. She started massaging his shoulders.

"You don't have to do that," he said as her strong fingers penetrated his muscles with a perfect touch. "Really, the water is doing the job."

"But Ruger, you are weary. I see it in your eyes. Let me tend to you," Selma said. She kissed his neck. "I have missed you."

"No more than I," Sophia said as she slipped into the pool.

Bridgett joined them. "None have missed you more than me, Captain."

Abraham didn't want Selma to stop. He didn't want any of them to slow their advances. He lifted up his hands and said, "I'm sorry, but one at a time, girls."

Sophia and Bridgett stuck their bottom lips out.

Solomon lifted his massive hand out of the waters. "I don't have any objections to the extra attention." He winked at Sophia. "If they don't."

"Be my guest," Abraham said. He'd closed his eyes and laid his head back into Selma's lap. "Ah, that feels good. Too good. Help yourself."

"Sure thing," Solomon said.

Abraham opened his eyes. Bridgett and Sophia sat on both sides of the troglin. They ran their long painted fingernails over his hairy chest.

"This isn't right," Abraham said.

"It feels right to me," Solomon said. His smile filled the room, also revealing his canine fangs. "I think your predecessor did things right."

"I don't know about that. You should see the dungeon. That guy was a pervert."

"He clearly had a thing for Spanish and Italians." Solomon brushed the back of his chin over Bridgett's cheek. "What did he look like?"

"He was a flabby older white guy. The bookish type. You were one. You know what I mean," he said.

"I wasn't old, white, and flabby," Solomon said. "I was younger, fit. Well, not fit. I could run a hundred feet if I had to. Smoked too much hash and struggled lifting a bag of potatoes."

"Well you're old looking now."

"True, but stronger than ten hippies." He tossed his head back and laughed. Once he recovered, Solomon said, "Abraham, allow yourself to loosen up. Enjoy what this world offers. You've done well, by what I've seen. You've fared better than me."

"I don't know about that. All of the Henchmen left," he said.

A day after the company had met at the table and their brands dissipated, the King's Papers arrived. The Henchmen, one and all, left him, even Horace and Sticks. That really shocked him.

"I didn't think all of them would go," Abraham said.

"I didn't go."

"And I appreciate that. But it only makes sense because you and I have the same problem. We need to get back to our world."

Selma began massaging his head and asked, "What world are you talking about? The world beyond the sea?"

He turned his head, gave her a curious glance, and said, "No. What world are you talking about?"

"They say that another world lies beyond the Seas of Traversity and Troubles. But the Elders guard it," Selma said. "Is that the world you are from?"

Abraham and Solomon exchanged a look. Solomon shrugged.

Abraham told her, "I don't think so." He wondered if Titanuus might be a lost continent in some earthly place like the Bermuda Triangle or Atlantis. He turned his attention back to Solomon. "You've been here longer than me. Any ideas?"

"I fear that I've wasted valuable time desperately rummaging through the Spine. You're the best hope I've had since I arrived. You have the king's connection. Perhaps that will help."

"Yeah, well, I don't know about that." He rubbed his brand. "I still have to help him if he is going to help me. I'm not sure how I'm going to go about it without the others. I don't know my way around this world. I see things, and sometimes Ruger's memories will fill me in, but other than that, I'm lost."

"You'll just have to learn your way around, like I did. I'm going to help however I can. I have the same stake in our predicament as you do."

"I know. I just wish the others were around. I hate seeing a team break up." Abraham mostly missed Sticks. They'd formed a bond and had been intimate. He hadn't thought she would drop him like that. He even felt guilty being around the triplets. They were his to take, but that didn't seem right. He'd once had a wife and son. He even thought about Mandi. The triplets reminded him most of her. *I'm not sure what is going on, but I have to figure this out. If I'm in some sort of crazy coma, I have to wake up. But if I wake up, what do I wake up to?* "Solomon, do you really think that this is real?"

"A part of me hopes that it is."

"What part?"

"The strange peoples on Titanuus don't appear to judge others by appearances. They judge them by their actions." Solomon kissed Bridgett on the cheek. "That part I enjoy. But there are wicked hearts within—man, myrmidon, troglin, or zillons. The greedy heart of all the races is always the source of trouble. They can all be just as deceptive. I saw that with the troglin. They turned on me. I had to flee. Some are good, some malicious. It never ends, I think, no matter in what world we are."

"Oh, it will end one day," Abraham said. "If I don't believe that, then I might as well not believe anything."

"So, what are you going to do?"

"Await the king's orders and find some new Henchmen."

39

———

LEWIS

In Kingsland's capital city, Burgess, the annual Sea Festival was in full swing. The evening sun had set, and the reveling on the cobblestone streets had begun hours before. Sailors back from long weeks at sea swayed arm in arm, singing in the colorful tongue of sailors. Women blushed as they covered the ears of their children when they walked by. The sailors winked and chuckled. One woman got goosed as she walked by.

Suddenly, scintillating explosions rocked the early night sky. Pyrotechnic after pyrotechnic was launched into the air. Umbrellas of fireworks rained down from the skyline. The children clapped and shouted with glee. Every eye in the streets was up. Hats were waving. Bonfires burned, and the great bells in the towers rang.

Lewis slipped into one of the haunting cathedrals adorned by insect-headed gargoyles with great pincers in their mouths. It was the worship place of the Elder of Insects. He closed the tall wooden door behind him and walked down the center aisle. The numerous bugs beneath his feet crunched underneath his boots.

He sneered. The pews were half circles made from stone. At the end of the aisle, up the steps, on the stage was a twenty-foot-tall praying mantis made of jade.

He looked up at the creepy thing. "Stupid Elders."

"You might find greater favor in this life if you respected your Elders," Leodor said. He was sitting on a pew off to the left. He wore a heavy violet cloak with silver trim. His penetrating eyes were fixed on the mantis. "When is the last time you prayed?"

"Oh, that's easy. It was the last time after I saw an Elder. Never," Lewis said. He stomped more bugs underneath his feet. "There must have been at least one hundred better places that we could meet."

"No one comes here," Leodor said as he brushed some insects from his cloak.

"I can't imagine why. Does anyone even worship this Elder of Insects?"

"Certainly. The Sect controls all of the cathedrals. We have our clerics about this place, too. I cleared it out before you came."

"You cleared out everything but the bugs."

"We don't have control over them. They worship their master." Leodor nodded at the mantis statue. "Even they need a place to give thanks."

"Bugs? Really? Are you a complete fool?" Lewis spat on the floor. "You wonder why I don't worship. I'll tell you why. The Sect has made up an Elder for everything. The Elder of Insects. The Elder of Serpents. The Elder of the Sea. The Elder of Dogs. The Elder of Felines. The Elder of Weeds. The Elder of Gardens." He poked a finger at Leodor. "I have one for you. How about the Elder of Bung Holes?"

"Well, there actually is an Elder of Fools. I'd be happy to obtain a scroll of his prayers for you."

"So smug, aren't you, Leodor? You and the Sect have an Elder for everything and all of the people fooled, don't you? I think the Elder of Fools is fit for everybody."

Leodor hid his hands in the deep sleeves of his robes and replied, "You are the unbelieving fool, not me."

"I let you slide with your first jab, but I am the prince, and I won't let you talk to me like a child." He dropped his hand to his dagger. "I think you need a lesson in regards to your station, Viceroy." He tugged on the dagger, but it didn't come free. His hand was frozen to the weapon's hilt. A chill coursed through his body, like freezing blood in his veins. "What are you doing, snake?"

Leodor's eyes were aglow like silvery shimmering pools. His eyes, now spacey, locked on Lewis. He spoke with a deep hollowness that resonated in the small cathedral's chamber. "You are the one that needs to know his station, you spoiled, infantile child. I can turn your bones brittle as ice with a thought. I can boil your marrow." Through clenched teeth he said, "Respect is given when it is received."

Leodor let out a gasp as a shadowy figure appeared and held a blade against his throat. It was the assassin, Lewis's lover, Raschel.

"I always felt that the members of the Sect were overly chatty. Should I kill him, my love?" Raschel asked Lewis. "He'd make a fine sacrifice to the Elder of Insects. He could feed all of his little worshippers that scurry over the floors." She put her lips to Leodor's ears. "Wouldn't that be nice?"

"It would be," Leodor said in an unwavering tone. "But you would never get away with it."

"I've gotten away with plenty, and that doesn't include all of the dirty little things that you don't know about. The Sect has its people, and I have mine. Now, let me see the whites of your eyes before I nick you."

The silver pools in Leodor's eyes cleared.

Lewis freed his hand from the handle of his dagger and clutched his hand open and closed, frost on his fingernails. "I should behead you, Leodor."

"But you won't." Leodor lifted his chin. "Now, will you call your lady friend off?"

Lewis gave Raschel a nod. She lifted her blade away, spun it in her hand, and sheathed it. She stepped into full view, her eyes shaded by the hood of her cloak. She wore a tight-fitting leather jerkin with a cotton blouse underneath that revealed the womanly curves of her body. "The two of you need to get along better."

"That will be the day," Lewis said. "No more tricks, Leodor."

"Don't draw a weapon on me, Lewis." Leodor rubbed his hands on his knees and said, "Let's start with why we are gathered, shall we? I'll begin. I've reported to the Underlord—"

"What? You contacted the Underlord without me? How dare you?" Lewis said.

Leodor lifted his hands and said, "Don't get puffed up on me. You were tied up with our duties, and I had to report this immediately. If I didn't, my delay, *our delay*, would have drawn his ire. Believe me when I say that you don't want that. Needless to say, he seemed, er, concerned that Ruger completed the quest that should have destroyed him."

"It was your idea. I told you that we should have killed him outright. Instead, you sent him on a mission that not only gained my father's trust but restored the queen."

"Not to mention he killed one Fenix and captured another," Leodor said.

Lewis walked up on Leodor, looked down on him like a vulture, and said, "Are you proud of that notion? Sometimes I wonder whose side you are on."

"Need I remind you that it has been me all along that has been poisoning the queen?"

"Then poison her again," Lewis replied.

"No, that would be obvious. The queen is a strong woman, and she withstood the poison because of a fine constitution. It was a miracle that she hung on so long as she did. You underestimate her vitality."

"No, you underestimated it." Lewis propped his boot up on the bench beside Leodor and said, "So, what did our frightening Underlord say?"

Leodor looked up at Lewis and said, "You get your wish, Prince. He wants you to kill Ruger."

40

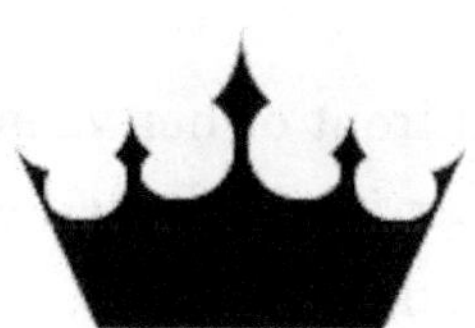

Lewis and Raschel walked the streets of Burgess with their hoods over their heads. He couldn't help but smile. Finally, he could rid himself of Ruger and the Henchmen once and for all.

Raschel grabbed his hand, slowed his pace, and said, "Slow down. You're practically skipping."

"I can't help but feel glee. For years, my father has been tinkering around with the Henchmen, and slowly we've been picking them apart. But now"—he waggled his finger—"we can undo them in a straight-up slaughter."

"I don't think Leodor wants you to be brazen about it. You sound like you are going to fight him yourself," she said.

"Oh, I would love to finish the deed myself. If I could provoke him, perhaps, I could undo him."

"He wields Black Bane. Do you think you can overcome that?" she asked as they slipped into a narrower alley by passing underneath a stone archway that joined the buildings.

"Today, I feel that I can overcome anything."

"Do you believe what they say about Black Bane?" she asked.

"What do you mean? That ridiculous legend that it was forged by the Elders? Pfft. How can I believe that when I don't believe in the Elders?"

They entered Raschel's apartment building and walked up the stairs, two steps at a time, to the third floor, at the top. Using a small key, she opened the door then stepped aside, let Lewis in, and closed them inside. Both of them shed their cloaks and hung them on pegs by the door.

Raschel sat down in front of her vanity and began removing her small golden hoop earrings. "If you don't believe in the Elders, then how do you explain the Fenix?"

Lewis sat down on the bed to remove his boots. "The Fenix is a monster. We all know that there are all sorts of creatures that roam Titanuus. It is just one of them. For all we know, there are flocks of Fenixes elsewhere." He combed his fingers through his feathery black hair and began unbuttoning his shirt. "So, you spent a lot of time with Ruger. Do you know his weakness? After all, you are the one that is going to have to kill him. Thinking about it more thoroughly, I can't afford to get my hands dirty."

She dabbed perfume on her wrists from a glass jar and rubbed them together. "The last Ruger was a very simple animal to conquer. He used all of his physical advantages to his pleasure. He was a womanizer and a coward. He had the Red Tunics do all of the dirty work and shielded himself behind his Henchmen. But even so cowardly, he was naturally formidable and could fight like a lion. No one would cross him or Black Bane."

Lewis lay back on her pillows and said, "So, that straight-arrow became a womanizer. Interesting."

"What do you mean?"

"The Ruger I grew up with would not even look at a lady. He was the epitome of knighthood. Disciplined. Stern. Unwavering in the tenets of the Guardian Order. He trained. He overtrained. I hated him. I should have worshipped him, but I hated him." He turned his head her way. "So, Ruger was a womanizer. Did you have a few tosses with him?"

Raschel turned her head over her shoulder and said, "I wish."

Lewis chuckled. "Oh, you naughty little vixen. You are trying to fire my blood, aren't you?"

"I like seeing you worked up. I've always enjoyed the passion that your hatred brings."

"Nothing works me up more than you do. And when this is all over—and I am the king—we will marry."

"Is that a proposal?"

"Not officially. As for Ruger, you saw the change in him?"

"He told us that he was Abraham. A man from another world. He wanted to earn our trust, I believe. He's genuinely good-natured, unlike the other personality that must have been in him. I think he wants to do right. He's more of a leader." She removed her hairpins, and her brown hair fell down on her shoulders. "He rallied the Henchmen. There is something very different about him. He's... likeable."

"Well, don't go liking him too much. Or at all, for that matter."

She rose from the vanity chair. Tall, dark, and athletic, she stripped off everything but her cotton shirt. With the grace of a panther on the prowl, she crossed the room, climbed onto the bed, and straddled him. "So, how are we going to do this?"

"Did you want to tie me up again?"

"No, that's not what I meant. How do you want me to kill him?"

"Oh." He smiled. "That will make for some exciting pillow talk. Poison that makes him foam at the mouth would be nice. Perhaps an accident where an anvil falls and crushes his skull."

She put two fingers on his lips. "You really don't have a very good imagination when it comes to killing people. I'll handle it, but it's going to cost you because it can't be obvious."

"You are the best at that. You wiped out over half of his Henchmen."

"More like two-thirds. I'll handle this one. It will be interesting."

Lewis reached up, grabbed her locks with both hands, pulled her closer, and said, "Enough talk. Let's make this interesting instead."

41

ABRAHAM'S PAST

Abraham got out of the SUV he'd rented from the airport after the first flight he'd taken since the accident. He'd spent months in recovery and finally gotten himself into good enough shape to walk with a cane. It wasn't easy on his big frame. Now he was in Alabama, miles outside of Birmingham, in the driveway of Buddy Parker's family farm. It was a large ranch house surrounded by miles of split-rail fencing that went on and on. He headed up the walkway. The cane clicked with every step. With a grunt, he stepped out on the porch, faced the door with a brass horse-faced knocker in the middle, and sighed.

Rehabilitation had been hellish. The physical part of it was one thing. The mental and spiritual part was another. His spirit was broken. It was broken like the pieces of airplane he'd crashed all over the woodlands. Maybe worse. Jenny was gone. Jake was gone. Forever. That was only part of the pain. He never would have imagined the tidal wave of heart-twisting pain to come. He remembered when he'd picked up the newspaper in Pittsburgh. They'd thrown him under the bus. The paper said he was reckless and irresponsible. He found a headline on a national paper that read:

HOTSHOT JENKINS FINAL FLIGHT FATAL
JENKIN'S THE JET KILLS FAMILY
BUDDY PARKER GONE
PIRATE'S PENNANT HOPES CRASHED

That was the beginning. The endless stream of reporters, questions, and accusations were more than enough to drive any man insane. They called him arrogant and inexperienced and said he had no business flying the plane. Abraham's father, Earl, tried to keep the press away. Like ravenous wolves, they came. The get-well flowers, balloons, and letters suddenly stopped coming. But the worst thing was the letter that never came. He never got word from Claude and Rose, the parents of Buddy Parker, his best friend and teammate. They were good people who had treated him like a son. But now, nothing. He had to see them. Today was the day he had the strength to face them. It couldn't wait any longer.

He felt a chronic, stabbing pain in his knees and shoulders. After reaching in a pocket and producing a prescription bottle, he fished out a pain pill with his finger, put it in his mouth, and swallowed. He used the knocker on the door.

Claude opened the door. He strongly resembled Buddy. He had dark black skin and graying hair with a matching moustache, and he wore a knit flannel shirt with jeans and a Pirates belt buckle. His eyes widened when he got a full look at Abraham. He closed the door behind himself and asked, "What are you doing here?"

Abraham swallowed. His tongue clove to the roof of his mouth. He could see the anger and pain building in Claude's warm, friendly eyes. With a growing ache in his heart, he said, "Mr. Parker, I came to say I'm sorry. I wanted you to know..." His voiced cracked. Tears started to flow. "It was an accident. I swear I wasn't careless like the papers say. I would never risk your family." He sobbed. "Or mine."

In a rigid tone, Claude said, "Do you think that is going to bring my son back? Do you? I don't care what the papers say or what you say. My son is gone, and he ain't coming back. That's on you!"

The front door opened. It was Rose, dressed in jeans and a nice black polo shirt. She was a pretty lady, but her eyes were tired and heavy. "Claude, do we have a visitor?" she asked in a sweet voice. She looked at Abraham. "Hello. I'm Rose." Rose was looking at Abraham as if she'd never seen him before in her life.

"Uh..." Abraham said. He glanced at Claude.

Claude hustled halfway inside the doorway, gently took his wife by the arm, and yelled, "Veronica! Veronica!"

A woman came running down the stairs. She was a younger white woman, dressed in brown scrubs that matched her short hair. She cradled Rose's elbows and said, "Come with me, Mrs. Parker. It's time for lunch and your medicine."

"But, we have company," Rose said. "Can we feed him too? He looks hungry. Where did you come from, young man?"

When Abraham started to speak, Claude cut him off. "We'll come and eat in a moment, dear. You go with Connie-Sue. Okay." He kissed her cheek. "I'll see you in a bit." He closed the women inside, stood in front of the door, and asked, "Did you see that? The moment Rose found out that Buddy was gone, she just checked out. Have you ever heard a broken-hearted woman wail for her lost son? Have you?" With clenched jaws, he shook his head angrily. "I lost my wife and my son the same day because of you. No apology is going to bring them back, either. This is your fault. It's on you!"

"Mister Parker, I-I swear, if there is anything I can do to make this right, I'll do it."

"Can you bring the dead back to life?" Claude stuck his chin out. "I didn't think so. The Lord might forgive you, Jenkins. But as of now, I can't. Get off of my porch and go." Claude opened the door and slammed it closed behind himself.

Abraham hobbled away with tears streaming down his face. He got in the SUV and drove all the way back to his home in Pittsburgh. His situation became worse after that. He tried to face the media, but the more he fought them, the harder they came. A few teammates and coaches reached out, but that wasn't enough. His downward spiral began, leading to an altercation in a grocery store with angry fans. He spent time in jail three times for fighting and public intoxication and urination. Finally, when he couldn't take it anymore, he moved to West Virginia with his father in Hinton.

Earl protected him as best he could. He kept him away from the articles and newspapers. They fished and went to church. Things seemed to get better, then Earl had a sudden heart attack and died. After that, Abraham wandered for years, deeper into the abyss, until he had next to nothing left. The elevator didn't go down any farther. His life was over.

42

THE PRESENT

ABRAHAM SAT IN THE CORNER OF A SMALL TAVERN LOCATED NEAR the outskirts of Burgess. The local watering hole was filled with laborers from the city and farmers from the country. It smelled of sweat, dirt, and greasy food. He sipped his mug of ale, his second of the day. He wanted to forget the dreams he'd been having about his past. They all seemed very real—to the point that he feared he might not wake up again. *Weird.* He couldn't decide whether he wanted to wake up in Titanuus or wake up living his life over again.

In the meantime, he'd kept himself busy at the Stronghold. He got a feel for the work being done at the unique estate. The hirelings took care of the food and the fields. With the help of Solomon and himself, they fed the baby Fenix, Simon. Abraham wrestled with whether or not to dismiss the triplets, but Solomon talked him into keeping them around. They didn't seem to have anywhere to go, anyway. He tried to avoid them, but they didn't make it easy.

A scrawny young waitress wearing a blue skirt and white

blouse with a matching hat that looked like a shower cap set a plate of food on the table. The portions of ham, bread, potatoes, and greens were generous, almost as generous as the gravy. He took up his three-pronged fork and started digging in.

Abraham missed the Henchmen. He missed Sticks. He couldn't believe they'd abandoned him. The company he'd kept with them was like that of a locker room. He really missed those fun days. They'd filled a void inside him. At the moment, he didn't mind eating alone. He needed the time to himself, and he'd gotten a feel for Burgess. It was a nice city and not very difficult to blend in, either. All sorts of people were coming and going. He even saw myrmidons and troglins, which he was a little bit leery of. The alien-looking zillons—with their big black eyes and white, almost translucent skin—were freaky.

He chewed up his food and took a swig of ale. It was a bitter brew but robust in flavor, which reminded him of a Great Lakes beer he'd once liked. He lifted his mug. "Here's to the *Edmund Fitzgerald*."

The waitress came back with a pitcher and topped his mug off. She gave him a wink. "Let me know if there is anything else that I can serve you."

"I will," he said, without hiding his smile. The waitress had flirted with him a little more and more every time he entered. He liked the tavern. The people were robust and hard working and didn't pay him any mind, and he was supposed to be famous. Slowly, he lowered his hand to his sword.

Two men were snaking their way through the crowd while continuing to cast looks at Abraham. They ordered beers and wove across the floor. They were young, but sword belts were strapped on their hips.

Abraham acted as though he didn't see them. Both men lingered near his table with their backs toward him. They were dressed like commoners, and one of them wore a cowl pulled over his neck. The meatier one with curly brown hair sipped and sipped his brew. The other young man stood loose as a goose, as if he was sleeping while standing. The bigger young man dared a look at Abraham then quickly turned away.

"What do you want?" Abraham growled.

Both men turned around. They both looked the same age but with different builds, and the broader man acted more serious and nervous.

"Excuse me, are you talking to me?" he asked.

"You've been eyeballing me ever since you stepped in this saloon," Abraham said. His grip tightened on his sword, the one he'd sworn had spoken to him once but never again since. "What do you want?"

"What's a saloon?" the other, sleepy-eyed man asked.

"A place where men die when they don't answer my question."

The bigger man elbowed the other man in the side. "Show respect, idgit. Apologies, but let me offer an introduction. I am Skitts, and this is Zann, my brother. Um, may we join you?"

"Sit."

Once the brothers were seated, Skitts continued in a low voice. "We know who you are, and we want to become Henchmen."

Abraham tugged on his ear. He'd spoken to his hirelings about discreetly spreading the word about finding new Red Tunics. That was days before. These men were the first two to show up. This was the main reason he hung around in the tavern. Without saying a word, he sized up the two men. Skitts had some brawn in his shoulders. He was a bit round-faced but a reasonable fit. He carried nervous energy. Zann, on the other hand, looked like he could sleep in the middle of a tornado, but he moved easily and was soft-footed. "Do you have shovels?"

Skitts leaned forward. "Pardon. Why would we need shovels?"

"To make a grave. You might have to make your brother's. He might have to dig yours. I might have to bury the both of you," Abraham said.

Zann's jaw hung low. He looked at Abraham as though he didn't understand what he'd said.

Skitts blinked repeatedly, his fingers fidgeting. "We have one shovel at home. Can we share it?"

Abraham drummed his fingers on the table. "I suppose. Now tell me about those swords you carry. Have you used them?"

"Well, er..." Skitts looked at this brother. "Not in a real battle. But we did our mandatory time in the king's army. We trained with the legions. We guarded the South Tiotan wall for two years. The entire length."

"I shot a Tiotan intruder," Zann mumbled, talking slowly. "Right in the back of the leg. He wailed like a hound and ran and fell and ran and fell."

"Yes, yes! We manned the ballistae and fired many times on the enemy. I'm certain I hit a couple, but the wounds were not fatal." Skitts kept nodding. "We are hard workers."

"You're telling me that your brother is a hard worker? He looked more like a hard sleeper."

"I don't sleep much," Zann said.

"That I believe. You have bags under your eyes like an Elder's grandmother." Abraham wiped his mouth with a cloth napkin. The men across the table eyed his food. Skitts silently smacked his lips. "Why do you want to be Henchmen?"

"We want to serve the king," Skitts said.

"But you did serve the king."

"Well, in a greater capacity. We want adventure. Treasure. See the world," Skitts said.

"Isn't that why you joined the King's Army? To be all that you can be," he said.

"No, I mean, we love our country, but we want more. We want glory. We want to be great swordsmen like you. We want to serve with a legend."

"Yes," Zann murmured in a slow, Southern-like drawl. "A legend."

Abraham leaned back and asked, "You two aren't deserters, are you?"

Skitts swallowed. "Not exactly."

43

Scratching his head, Skitts said, "The colonel commander had it in for us."

"And why would the colonel commander have it in for you?" Abraham asked.

"Zann slept with his daughter," Skitts said.

"I wasn't the only one sleeping around. My genius brother was caught sleeping with the colonel's wife," Zann said. "Skitts takes a shine to the older women like a bear takes to honey."

"I don't have a thing for older women. She pursued me," Skitts said.

"Sure she did. And that's why you were caught slipping out of the colonel's tent." Zann's smile showed his little teeth. "Heh heh."

"Anyway, Captain Ruger, we were both discharged without honor. We'd like to redeem ourselves." Skitts shrugged. "After all, men will be men, and women will be women." He worked up his best smile.

"Boys, you blow a lot of smoke. Everything you said might be a lie. I don't suppose you brought in references?"

The brothers exchanged a look.

"Where do you live?" Abraham asked.

Skitts blurted out directions.

Abraham shoved his plate across the table. "Take this food to another table. Eat and go. I'll think on it."

Skitts grabbed the plate, got up, and eagerly bowed. "Thank you. Thank you."

Zann nodded and slipped away with his brother.

Later in the evening, when the brothers were long gone, Abraham stepped outside to relieve himself by the creek. Once he finished, he sat down on a moss-covered boulder. A nice evening breeze was blowing, with a chill in the air. The clouds moved quickly across the moonless sky. "Plenty of stars, but I don't recognize a single one of them. No Orion, no Big Dipper, not a one of them. Lord, where in the heck am I? I miss my beer truck."

He snaked his sword out of its scabbard and held it up against the sky. Black Bane was a perfectly balanced longsword. He thumbed both of the keen edges. With two fingers, he traced over the runes engraved in the blade. An arcane source of power was within, and the sword had a voice, too. At least he thought it did. The lightning that had killed the Fenix came from somewhere.

"So, do you sing, Black Bane?"

The wind whistled through the trees.

Black Bane didn't say a word.

Abraham turned the blade side to side. It had an extra-long handle, making for a double-handed grip. He swallowed the grip up in his big hands. "Pitching ace to sword master. Incredible."

Back at the Stronghold, he'd come across hundreds of pages of parchment bound with twine. They had images of sword-fighting stances and directions complete with notes. He leafed through half of them in his free time, studying the material with eyes that had seen it before. His memory, or Ruger's, was refreshed. He even took time to practice for a few hours. All the moves came naturally to him.

His eyes studied Black Bane. "If you aren't going to talk, I'm putting you away." He waited a few seconds, slid it back into the scabbard, and headed back into the tavern.

A woman was sitting at his table with her back to him. Her dark hair touched against the cloak on his shoulders. A quiver of arrows hung from her back, and a bow lay across her back. He eased around the corner of the table and slowly sat down. The woman was attractive and dark-eyed and reminded him of Mandi so much that his heart jumped. She filled out her shirt and leather jerkin well.

"Good evening," he said. "Uh, I don't mind the company, but this is my table. You are welcome to join me."

Sitting upright, she said in a soothing but slightly husky voice, "Thank you, but I believe you are the one I am looking for. You are Ruger Slade? Yes?"

"I am, but I don't want to make that public."

His eyes scanned the crowd. No one appeared to be listening. The loud talking carried over their voices. The bawdy drunks throwing darts on the opposite side of the tavern were the loudest ones of all.

"Let me guess. You want to be a Henchman?"

"I know I'm a woman, but I'm very skilled with a bow and my blades." She pulled back her cloak, revealing a pair of short swords strapped against her sides, otherwise well concealed. "I grew up a hunter, and for several years I've worked for the collectors as a bounty hunter. I'd make an excellent Henchman. I want to serve the king."

"There's more to becoming a Henchman than joining. You have to pay your dues as a Red Tunic."

She tilted her head. "A Red Tunic?"

"A retainer. You serve the Henchmen like a squire serves a knight. If you prove your worth, you become a Henchman."

"Oh." She sank down in her chair a little.

The woman's strong resemblance to Mandi got him caught up reflecting on his past. Mandi worked at Woody's Grill, and she had a thing with him. He brushed her off one final time. He wondered what would have happened if he had stayed. *Would I still be here, or would I be with her?* This woman was about his age, had a nice tanned complexion, the tiniest of freckles on the smooth cheeks of her face.

The woman leaned forward and asked, "Were you going to say something else?"

He blinked. "Sorry. I lost my train of thought." He lifted his mug. "Too much ale. Would you like one?"

"No, thank you. But I appreciate the offer. It's a nicer one than those men at the bar offered."

"They hit on you, huh?" he said.

"No, they didn't hit me. They offered to—"

"Never mind. It's just an expression. Do I need to have words with them?"

"Of course not. They are just a bunch of ornery farmers. I can handle myself. Trust me."

Abraham nodded. "Please don't think that woman can't be Henchmen. The ones in my group are as proven as the men. But I have to think about it. You know, I never even asked you what your name was."

"It's Raschel."

44

Later that night, Abraham departed the country tavern and rode back toward the Stronghold. He swayed his shoulders as he sang an old Night Ranger song about rocking in America. Something about his meeting with Raschel got his juices flowing about Mandi. He missed the moderately spoiled woman's warm and friendly face. They both liked Night Ranger, too. It was old school for his age, but he liked it and most classic rock and country, which he'd listened to in his beer truck.

He changed his tune after he forgot the lyrics to the song he was singing and switched to another oldie: "Mandi, you're a fine girl. What a good—"

Out of the darkness, a bolt whistled through the air. Abraham's horse reared and tossed him to the ground. He scrambled back to his horse and hid behind it. The beast lay dead with an arrow in its neck.

"Sorry, fella," he muttered.

A group of men appeared from the surrounding trees and surrounded him. Ten in all were there, a rough-looking bunch in ragged clothing, carrying steel weapons in their hands. One man stood out among the others. He wore a leather overcoat and held a crossbow against one shoulder. His head was big, hair shaggy, and some of his teeth were missing.

He licked his mouth before he spoke and said, "Toss me your purse and your weapons."

"Am I being robbed?"

"No, this is the Burgess escort service," the leader of the highwaymen said. "Don't be stupid. Hand it over."

Abraham took a knee. His fingers loosened his purse away from his belt. "Why did you kill my horse? It was a fine steed, worth more than what I carry. That was stupid."

The highwayman pointed his loaded crossbow at Abraham. "We killed it so you couldn't run away to your mommy. Now, hand over the purse and the steel!"

He tossed his purse at the man's feet and said, "You shouldn't have killed my horse. That was a mistake."

The highwayman kicked the purse over to one of his men, who scooped it up. "Now your weapons," he said to Abraham.

Abraham scanned the crowd. They weren't the durable warriors he was accustomed to keeping with. They were armorless thieves who preyed on the weak.

"I don't think so," Abraham said. "If you want my sword, come and get it."

The highwaymen grunted. "Fool. I was going to slay you either way." He took aim at Abraham's chest. "Let's see if that quick tongue of yours can dodge this."

In that moment, Abraham realized he didn't have his armor on either. And he was too drunk to draw his sword quickly enough to block a crossbow bolt, as he had a bullet. He lifted a finger and asked, "Can I have a moment?"

"No." The highwaymen started to squeeze the trigger.

Out of the woods, an arrow whistled through the air and buried itself in the highwayman's side. The man let out a painful gasp and fired the crossbow at Abraham's head.

Abraham crouched, and the bolt whistled over his head. The money-hungry highwaymen came at him with weapons bared. He drew Black Bane as quickly as a man could bat an eyelash. He took his first attacker's head from his shoulders then sidestepped a downward sword thrust, snaked out his dagger, and pierced the attacker's chest. The man clutched at the bloody wound in his chest while silently screaming.

A second arrow whistled through the air, impaling a man's belly. A third arrow dotted the same man's forehead.

Black Bane rose and fell, hewing one man down after the other with the speed of a striking snake. Abraham lopped off another head and three more arms. The iron in his enemies' spines had turned to water. They fled. They bled. A volley of arrows and thrusts of steel dropped them all dead.

Abraham caught his breath and wiped blood from his eyes. He surveyed the fallen and let out a light chuckle. "I see dead people."

A woman carrying a loaded bow catwalked his way from the darkness. It was Raschel. "Are you harmed?" she asked as her intent eyes swept over the highwaymen.

"I'm fine, but my horse isn't," he said. He wiped his blood-stained sword over the grass and sheathed it. "Where did you come from?"

Raschel eased off her bowstring and dropped her arrow back in its quiver. "I have to apologize, but I was following you. I wanted to show off my skills by tracking you, and well, I needed to know where you lived, too."

"You didn't have to do that." He looked down at the leader of the highwaymen. He was dead with the arrow buried feather deep in his side. "You're a fine shot with that bow. Pretty impressive, given that it's dark outside and people were moving."

"I told you that I was good." She saw his purse on the ground and picked it up. "Is this yours?" She tossed it to him.

"Thanks. A man never goes anywhere without his purse." He took a knee by his horse. He stroked the star stripe on its head. "Sorry, fella."

He started removing the saddle, and Raschel knelt down and helped him. She had quick hands.

"Man, where do you think guys like that came from? Should we tell somebody?"

"Let the sheriff handle it. Men like these are low-end. I don't think he'll care that they are dead. But if he does, he'll probably find us." She smiled. "Well, you anyway. I'll disappear."

"You've come this far. You might as well come to the Stronghold. That's where you were heading, weren't you?"

"I'd like that."

"Consider this your initiation." He laid a hand on her shoulder. "Welcome to the Red Tunics."

45

 Inside Raschel's apartment, Lewis wrung his hands behind his back and paced the floor. "What are you thinking? You joined the Henchmen again? Why didn't you kill him?"

"If you don't like my methods, then why don't you assassinate him yourself?" she said. She sat on the end of her bed, putting her pants on. "I'm glad I didn't tell you this before we slept together. It might have ruined the moment."

"The moment is ruined now!" He clenched his fists. "If you had a shot, you should have killed him, not the highwaymen. Poor saps. You put them in the crosshairs of a death trap."

Twirling her hair on a finger, she said, "Actually, they brought him down well. They just weren't wise enough to finish him. But it served my purpose. I gained his trust."

Lewis stood in front of her, put both his hands on her shoulders, and looked dead in her eyes. "Tell me. At that moment, could you have killed him?"

"I could have hit him. The question is 'Would that have killed

him?' If it didn't, I would have been done in. He'd have killed me."
She laid her warm hands on his. "Believe me when I say that I
have seen him in action. He has instincts, a sixth sense. Ruger
won't be so easy to kill. He has a way of slipping out of danger. No,
let me do what I do. I'll set him up for a fall against a great horde
of enemies. It will happen."

"Well, do it soon. My father is eager to send Ruger on a new
campaign." Lewis started to pace again. "Thanks to my deranged
stepmother, he thinks that Ruger is some sort of savior. Can you
believe that?"

"What sort of campaign?"

"Leodor cooked up some quest about restoring the Crown of
Stones to its full glory. It's nothing short of moronic. It's even a
worse idea than fetching the Fenix egg. Those gems, if they even
existed, could be anywhere in the world. It's madness."

"That will be difficult. Abraham's Henchmen abandoned him
the moment the King's Brand cleared. He's somewhat depressed
about it. The only one left around is the troglin. Hence, he
continues to recruit."

"A troglin. That's three men in one."

"He's old and strange." She came to his side and gently put her
arms around his neck. "Did you ever stop to think that if your
father had the crown, then one day it will be yours to wear?"

"Of course I did. That's the only reason I am going along with
it. But I don't think the Underlord will allow that to happen.
According to Leodor, he wants the mission to fail before it's even
begun." He took her wrists in her hands. "You need end your flir-
tations with Ruger and escort him to the grave. Just poison him
and run. I'll hide you."

"Have faith in me, my love. I know what I'm doing. I've done
this over a hundred times before." She kissed his cheek.

"I want him put in the ground. Next chance you get. Do it."

46

OUTSIDE THE STRONGHOLD, ABRAHAM WORKED WITH SKITTS AND Zann. The brothers were lathered in early-morning sweat. Abraham had been running sword-training drills for days. The brothers stood side by side with their longswords fully extended and pointed up. He kicked at their feet, and they adjusted their stances.

"Good," Abraham said. "Stand still and don't move before I say." He silently counted to thirty. Zann's arms started to shake. Forty-five seconds into it, Skitts's arms shook like leaves. "Fifty-seven... fifty-eight... fifty-nine... sixty. Sheathe your swords."

The brothers puffed for breath and slid their swords into their scabbards with clumsy effort. Skitts wiped his forehead with his sleeve. "I never trained this hard in the army. We just did regular drills."

"And that's why you are horrible swordsmen. Not to take a jab at the King's army, but their foot soldiers need more training." Abraham rubbed his jaw.

Skitts had already lost some of the boyish meat in his cheeks.

Zann had come around and gained some thickness in his shoulders. He moved surprisingly well for a sleepy-eyed goon.

"Okay, high guard on one. One!"

The brothers drew their swords in the high guard and stood with alert eyes.

"Ox guard, two!" he said.

Skitts and Zann lifted their swords over their heads, tip first, blade parallel to the ground, and shifted their feet.

"Wrath guard, three!"

Again, the brothers shifted in their stances as they cocked the weapons back behind their shoulders.

Abraham repeated, "High guard, one! Ox guard, two! Wrath guard, three!"

The brothers stood unquavering.

"Let's go faster," he added. "Keep your feet or lose some meat! High! Ox! Wrath! High! Ox! Wrath! High! Ox! Wrath! High!"

Sweat dripped from Skitts's chin. Zann breathed deeply through his nose.

Abraham stepped between them and said, "I want to see a proper thrust from high guard. Shuffle step forward, plant the back foot, and put some weight down on the swing. You want to end a fight in one blow. Spit a man from skull to chin, the fight is over. It'll send the enemy running. Use your length. Your skill. I don't want to hear a ring of steel. I want to hear steel hitting bone. Thrust!"

The two men lunged forward and stabbed forward and pulled their swords back up.

Abraham backed up with them. "Thrust. Thrust. Thrust. Let's change it up. Switch from the thrust to the chop."

Skitts and Zann nodded.

"Chop! Chop! Chop! Chop! Chop!" Abraham marched them all over the yard, switching from position to position.

The brothers were exhausted.

On a break, Skitts drank from a water skin and asked, "When were you going to teach us any defense?"

"Killing first. That's the best defense," Abraham replied.

Solomon came out of the barn. His gray fur had fluffed up from where he'd cleaned the grime out of it. He wore a blacksmith's apron. "Your bird is becoming difficult."

"Why don't you two take a few laps around the lake," he said to the brothers. When they started to drop their swords, he added, "No, take those with you."

"Yes, Captain." Both of them took off running, shoving back and forth on one another on the way.

Solomon looked down at him and said, "I hate to sound impatient, but you appear to be more focused on the next campaign than getting us out of here. We've been waiting for word for days, and nothing has come."

"I can't really go anywhere with the brand without the king's permission. Besides, you seem to be enjoying your stay here." He passed Solomon on his way into the barn. "I just want to be ready. With only four Henchmen, I think I'm going to be doing much of the heavy lifting."

"If I'm here and you're here, certainly there are others like us. We need to seek them out. Burgess is a large town. Maybe you can look for more answers when you are recruiting."

"You should come with," Abraham said.

"Perhaps. But I'm beginning to feel that you are embracing this world too much. I'm not sure that I want to do that. Look at me. I'm a giant monkey."

"I'm not getting carried away. I promise. I can't help it if I like what I'm doing."

He stood in front of the stable where Simon stood inside. Steel bars went across the top, with wooden walls at the bottom keeping the Fenix inside. The creature walked over to Abraham on his tiny feet and looked right at him.

"Whoa, you're as tall as me. Man, birds grow fast."

"You think that thing is a bird? It's a bat-lizard thing. Perhaps an ugly dragon though the dragons I've seen are fairer."

"Either way, he needs to stretch those wings." Abraham opened the door. "Come on, Simon."

The Fenix followed Abraham out of the barn stride for stride. It swung its leathery winged arms like a man. Outside of the barn, Abraham started to slowly flap is arms like a bird.

Solomon slapped his face. "This is insanity. A man teaching a bird to fly."

"Listen, Winger, you have to jump and flap. Like this. Jump and flap." He did a pair of demonstrations. "Do it with me."

Simon cocked his head.

"I don't know." Abraham scratched his head.

Simon did the same.

"Do you think I can teach him to use a sword?"

"You couldn't do any worse than you are teaching it to fly." Solomon crinkled his nose. "It's a horrid thing. Malodorous. He spooks the horses. I'm sure they know one day he'll eat them. Be done with him. Kill it before it kills us."

"No, I'm not doing that. I don't know why I'm not doing that. Perhaps I should, but I just can't kill the thing in cold blood." He reached out and touched hands with Simon. "It's just a baby."

"True, but at the rate it's growing, it's going to be bigger than this barn before long. What will you do then?" Solomon said.

"I don't know. I'm trying to get it to fly away." Abraham started flapping his arms again. "Fly, Simon, fly."

Simon spread his wings out.

"Man, those things are big. What are they, twelve, fifteen feet?" Abraham started flapping again. "Come on, Simon. You can do it."

Simon batted his wings. His short knees bent. He launched himself into the sky.

"Whoa!" Abraham yelled. "Look at him go!"

Simon circled above them several times and let out a mighty screech. The hirelings who watched jumped out of their sandals. Others dashed into the cover of the barn. The Fenix let out one last squawk and turned north toward the Spine.

Abraham waved. He looked over at Solomon. "See, I'm an amazing teacher."

"Either that or you're really good at running your Henchmen away. I hope it doesn't come back."

"I don't think it is." Dropping his eyes, he saw someone coming toward the Stronghold on foot. At first, he thought it was Raschel, but it wasn't. "I'll be. It's Sticks."

The tomboyish and expressionless woman stopped in front of Abraham and said, "We have to talk."

47

Inside the Stronghold, Abraham sat with Sticks at the farm table. They were alone.

After they both sat down, he asked, "Where have you been?"

"Here and there," she said.

"I'm glad you're back, even it if is only for a little while. You're always welcome, of course."

Her brown eyes drifted toward the ceiling. "I figured you had all of the company that you needed."

"Huh? Oh, you meant the triplets. Listen, Sticks, Solomon is keeping them entertained. I know Ruger's last, er... personality was a freak, but I'm an old-fashioned kind of guy. I hope that makes some sense."

She shrugged.

"So, what did you want to talk about?"

"We've been trying to find Twila. Not much fortune with it. She seems to have disappeared."

"*We've*? We've who?"

"Well, Cudgel and Tark, for one. Did you think they were just going to let that go? Their eyes are filled with blood. Other than them, it's been me and Iris. But Horace checks in."

"What are you doing, forming your own band of Henchmen?"

"No," she said, "we are trying to avenge Cudgel. We can't have Twila running free." Her eyes narrowed. "She must pay."

"She could be anywhere by now. North, perhaps. She could have taken a boat and sailed away."

"We've checked all of the ports. No one has seen her. You do know that we've hunted down and found everything that we've tracked, right?"

"I'll take your word for it. So, what do you want from me? I'm all for finding Twila, but I have to find and ready more Henchmen for the king's quest. All of you left me." He tapped his knuckles on the table. "To be honest, it shocked me. I'm glad you are free, but honestly, I feel lost without the team."

"I don't think that it's you," she said. Her mouth twitched. "They want Twila. I want Twila. You should want Twila. Do you know how many deaths that woman is responsible for? Tark and Cudgel had two more brothers, not to mention the brothers you didn't know."

He knew the number was over one hundred. Whether it was directly or indirectly, he couldn't say. He felt that Eugene Drisk was as responsible as Twila was. "I want to help. You know I do. But isn't it possible that she could have disappeared?"

"What do you mean?"

"There are mages, wizards, you know, people that make portals, that brought people like me here. I think that anything is possible. You might be trying to pick up on a dead trail."

"Or a trail of the dead." Sticks got up from her bench. "That won't stop us. Only death will. Remember, someone put Twila in our midst for the reason. They are behind all of this. No doubt, whatever mission the king put you on, that will happen again. If we find Twila, then we find answers. I wanted to let you know what was going on. The others don't know that I came. They think that I'm beating the bushes."

"You're leaving?"

"I'm not even sure why I came."

Abraham rose. "I'm coming with you."

"No, you stay. Train your *new* Henchmen. Or Red Tunics. Don't let us impede you." She walked out the door.

He stood rubbing his head for a moment and walked outside after her.

Solomon was walking out of the barn with big bales of hay under his long arms. "Hello, Sticks," he said as she walked by.

She didn't reply and kept going until she passed over the slope and dipped and out of sight.

Standing beside Solomon, Abraham said, "Women. I don't even understand why she came."

"You must be daft. Even a troglin can see that," Solomon said.

"Oh, well, why don't you impart some of the divine troglin wisdom on me?"

"Simple. She wants you to chase her. You'd think a jock like you would know that."

Abraham tracked Sticks down to Burgess. She'd entered a tavern with a sign that hung above the door that read The Red Rooster. He walked up on the porch and through the open door. A handful of people were seated at the bar with their noses in their mugs of ale. The tables were empty save for one. Several familiar faces sat behind a medium-sized rectangle table. Horace filled his chair with his big frame. Iris, Cudgel and Tark, and Sticks made up the rest. All their eyes were on Abraham.

Sticks said, "I told you he would come."

He approached with a slight smile on his face and pulled back a chair. "I thought you said that no one knew you came to see me?"

"I lied," Sticks said.

Abraham extended his arm to Horace. They locked hands around each other's thick forearms. He did the same with Cudgel and Tark. "Good to see you. All of you."

"Same here, Captain," Horace said.

"Agreed," Tark and Cudgel replied in unison.

Iris looked at them with dreamy eyes, resting her chin on hands propped on her elbows. "You know I'm happy to see you."

He winked at her. "Ditto." Abraham rested an arm on the back of the chair. "All right, what's really going on? And where is everyone else?"

Horace clawed at his bushy beard and said, "Dominga is about. Haven't heard a word from Bearclaw, Vern, Prospero, or Apollo. They were heading to the House of Steel to be reinstated as the King's Guardians. We don't think that was such a good idea. That's why we hoped you'd come here."

"Why's that?" Abraham said.

Horace looked at Sticks. She gave him a nod.

"We think Prince Lewis is the problem," Horace said.

48

"You know that I'm not going to jump on that wagon without some sort of proof," Abraham said.

A waitress set a mug of ale in front of him. She gave him a smile and walked away.

"I don't care for Lewis any more than you do, so I need to have some proof even though I have my suspicions."

Sticks tossed a skin of black fur and claws on the table. It was the same soft and shiny fur as the Black Growler they'd encountered at the Spine. "That's our physical proof. The rest comes from what I've seen with the naked eye."

He took the pelt in hand. "Where did you get this?"

"The dark markets. I inquired about it," Sticks said. "It was like pulling a tooth out of a live dragon's jaw. I knew that pelt was too valuable for Twila to part with. Only a fool would miss out on that opportunity. Anyway, she slipped."

"Wait a minute. I thought you said that you had no sign of her," Abraham said. As Sticks's mouth opened to speak, he said, "Never mind. You lied."

Sticks nodded. "I'm good at it. Anyway, we tracked the sale back to an apartment complex here in Burgess. There is no sign of Twila coming out, but Dominga stoops on it now. But, at night, we've seen Prince Lewis coming and going."

He leaned over the table. "You saw his face?"

"He was hooded. Same height and build. Same gait. It was him. I saw it myself," Sticks said.

"But—"

"And"—Sticks lifted a finger—"We followed three more similar figures into the Elder of Insects' cathedral. Again, they were cloaked, but we know it was Leodor. He moves like an old spirit. Lewis is more obvious with his natural strut. I didn't know who the woman was, but she wasn't built like Twila. It didn't stop me from following her, either."

Abraham lifted his chin. "And?"

"She went to the same apartments *and* to the Stronghold. It's your new woman."

"Raschel?" He leaned his chair back on two legs. "So, Lewis put a spy in the Henchmen?"

"Lewis and Leodor. That's the theory," Sticks said with a small smile.

"That sucks." Abraham liked Raschel. The thought of her being in cahoots with Lewis and Leodor was nothing short of disturbing. To make matters worse, both men must have been conspiring against King Hector. "His own son. I can't believe that Hector's boy would try to do him in."

"If he is truly behind this, then you need to warn the king," Cudgel said.

"Or we can kill him," Tark said. "A son turning on his own father is sickening."

Abraham dropped all four legs to the floor. "Am I supposed to tell the king? I don't think he'd believe me, an otherworlder, over them. How do I prove they did it?"

Horace leaned on his forearm and said, "You need to watch your back, Captain. This new Henchmen might be another pile of trouble that gets you killed."

"She does appear to be more formidable than Twila did. Maybe Lewis and Leodor want to have an inside source. Perhaps they don't trust us," he said.

"If it smells like a skunk, it's a skunk," Tark said.

Abraham had finally learned to put his faith in the Henchmen. He was better off taking their word for it. After all, they didn't have to be pursing Twila now that they were freed. They were doing it on their own out of honor and vengeance for the fallen.

"I agree," Abraham said. "So, what's the next move? Play along? Imprison Raschel and question her? I'm open to suggestions."

"I say we question her," Cudgel said. He had a bitter sound in his voice and a frown on his face. "I think she'll know what happened to Twila. We need answers. Clearly, they are protecting her."

Abraham sucked on his ale while he mulled it over. He was still the indentured servant of the king. That last thing he needed to do was make accusations and burn bridges. At this point, it was his word against Lewis and Leodor's. That would be a hard sell even if he had proof. He set down his mug. "At least I know there is a snake in the henhouse. For now, let's keep our eyes and ears peeled. Ordinary business. We'll see what reveals itself."

Horace gave a stiff nod, but his eyes were downcast. So were everyone else's.

"What is it?"

Horace spoke up. "Captain, you aren't in command of us now.

We'll do what we want to do. You can't stop us. No disrespect, but what we do, we do for ourselves. And if we choose to pursue it"—he looked Abraham in the eyes—"we'll pursue it."

202

49

Abraham parted his hands and asked, "Then why did you bring me here?"

"Out of respect," Horace said. "You've earned it. We thought you should know in case anything slides back on you." He touched his hand over his heart. "I admit I feel a hollowness within my breast now that the brand is gone. Something is missing. I liked being a Henchman. At least, recently."

Cudgel and Tark nodded. Iris tipped her chin.

Abraham could see some anguish in their faces. They really did want to stay at the Stronghold, but they had to find Twila first. They wouldn't follow him anymore without resolving that matter. He needed them, and he had a feeling that maybe they needed him too. They all gave each other purpose.

He lifted his hands and said, "Listen, I'm not going to get in your way. I appreciate you filling me in, but do what you have to do." He stood up. "If I can help, let me—"

The company's gaze moved past Abraham.

Dominga entered through the tavern's front door. With the grace of a cat, the sensual ebony woman made her way to the table. Her eyes rose when she saw Abraham. She gave him a quick smile and looked at the others.

"It's fine," Sticks said to Dominga. "We are all on board."

"Prince Lewis returned. He's back in the apartments." She grinned. "I finally know what rooms he's in. It's the top floor. I listened to his footsteps from the second."

"Well, who's watching to see if he leaves?" Horace asked.

"I have some reliable urchins keeping eyes on the exits." Dominga picked up Abraham's mug. "Do you mind?"

"Of course not," he said. "It's nice seeing you."

"I know." Dominga looked at Horace and Sticks. "So, what's the move?"

Horace glanced at Abraham and said, "We'll wait until the prince leaves. After that, we snatch this woman and question her. I'm pretty sure it would be a crime to interrogate the prince. That will only get us all back in prison. Was he alone?"

"Same as usual," Dominga said. "I found it odd that he came in the morning, for a change. Usually it's at night."

"I can answer that. Raschel was going to stay at the Stronghold beginning this evening. I was going to start her training tomorrow. Though she doesn't need any help with archery."

"No, she looks really good at handling arrows," Sticks said.

"Listen, maybe you aren't comfortable confronting Prince Lewis, but I am. I say we pay him a visit now. Perhaps we can catch him with his trousers down. Let's get answers. Let's get them today."

Horace nodded. "I support that."

Cudgel and Tark nodded. "Let's do it."

"No time like the present," Iris said.

Sticks shrugged and got up from the table. "So, who's in charge?"

Horace showed his teeth, slapped Abraham on the shoulder, and said, "The Captain is."

50

On cat's feet, Abraham, Dominga, and Sticks crept down the hallway of the apartment building's third floor. The floors were hard wood, and the walls were made from solid stone. No balconies were on the outside, only windows. Dominga pointed out a door at the end of the hall. Sticks put her ear to the door and made a knowing smile.

Dominga mouthed the words "They are having sex" with affirmation.

Now the question was how to get in. Knocking was out of the question. Abraham moved toward the door. A board creaked loudly underneath his foot. He froze. The women looked at him.

He whispered, "So much for surprise. Let's roll." He lowered his shoulder and bashed right through the door.

Prince Lewis and Raschel were coming up out of the bed. Lewis was stripped down to his trousers. His well-built muscles tensed. Raschel had a silk robe on. She went for the dagger on her vanity. Sticks and Dominga cut her off with daggers pointed at her face.

"Ruger! What in blazes are you doing here?" Lewis reached for his sword belt, which hung on the end of the bed's footboard.

Abraham knocked his hand aside with the flat of Black Bane's blade.

Cringing and holding his hand, the prince said, "You dare!"

"I have a strict policy about my Red Tunics fraternizing with the crown. Especially you. Do you care to tell me what is going on?" Abraham said.

"I don't have to tell you anything. You are dead! You drew your weapon on royalty! Every one of you will hang in the gallows!" Lewis shouted.

Dominga pushed Raschel down on the bed. "Sit down. Relax, princess."

"Don't ever touch her again," Lewis said. "You'll regret it."

"Sit down and shut up, Lewis." Abraham held his sword blade on the cheek of the prince, and it drew blood. "I'm not playing around."

Lewis sat. "You are mad."

"You're damn right I am. And don't forget." He got nose to nose with Lewis. "I'm not from your world. I've got nothing to lose."

Lewis's Adam's apple rolled. "You're a dead man."

"Tell me about you and Raschel. Are you putting a spy in my company? Are you the one that put Twila there? Is this her replacement?"

"I don't know what you are talking about. I'm simply sowing my oats by bedding this whore. Who I sleep with is hardly any of your business, now is it?"

"We have an expression where I come from," Abraham said. "I wasn't born yesterday. Now, you tell me what is going on. Where's Twila? We know that she's been here, and you were the last one to see her, that I know of."

The floorboards outside the room creaked as someone big

came down the hall. Horace filled the doorway with his frame. Cudgel and Tark stood behind him. "Do you need me, Captain?" Horace said.

"I might need you to sit on the prince until he cracks like an egg. He's not being very forthcoming."

With his finger, Lewis pushed Abraham's blade aside. "Seeing how you are a dead man, I'll humor you. I've hired Raschel to keep an eye on your mission. I need someone on the inside this time."

"So, you hired Twila."

"No. I don't know anything about that woman. What you are dealing with now is a coincidence. I'm sure many of your hirelings lived in these apartments at one time or another. There isn't anything so special about it."

"He's lying," Horace said.

"You fat oaf. You dare accuse a prince?" Lewis sneered. "I'll have you fed to the hogs."

"Lighten up, Lewis. You won't be feeding anybody to anything. I'm getting to the bottom of this one way or another," Abraham said. "I might not be able to prove you are behind it, but we know that Twila is. Give us her, and we'll part ways with you." He looked at Raschel. "But you're fired."

Raschel shrugged.

"You're a fool, Ruger. Abraham. Whoever you are. After today, you are finished. I don't know this Twila or where she is. You are barking up the wrong tree, and you'll pay dearly for it."

"Maybe not," Sticks said. She was holding something in her hand that she'd picked up from the vanity, a hair comb. "I know this. It was Twila's."

"You lying snake." Abraham locked his fingers around Lewis's throat. "Tell us where she is."

Prince Lewis's body turned ghostly. So did Raschel's. Lewis looked at his translucent hands and laughed. "Huh." As he faded out of Abraham's fingers, he parted with these final words: "I live, but you're a dead man now. You're all dead."

Abraham's hand passed through the vanishing man one last time. Lewis and Raschel were gone.

"What in the world just happened?" Abraham asked.

Sticks looked at him and said, "The snake slipped us. We're doomed, aren't we?"

"They were coming after us anyway. At least me, that is. He doesn't want our mission to succeed. Clearly, someone is helping him." He sniffed. "What is that smell? It's like lilac and spearmint."

Iris entered the room, and her nose crinkled. "They disappeared? Teleported. Whoa. That's thick. I can barely move a candle from one room to another. Someone moved two people. Only the most powerful members of the Sect can do that."

"Leodor. It has to be. We have to warn the king. Iris, how far can someone be teleported like that?"

"My guess, from one building to another. If it's Leodor, he's probably still in the city. In one of the cathedrals," Iris said.

"If that's true, then maybe we can get back to the king first," Abraham said. "Let's go."

"Captain," Horace said. He stood halfway in the doorway and was looking down the hall with Cudgel and Tark. "We might have a problem."

Tark and Cudgel drew their swords.

Abraham peeked around the doorway. Men in dark garb and birdlike black cowls covering their faces and carrying curved, wavy swords filled the hall from one end to the other. Over a score of heads were there.

"Yup," he said. "That is a problem."

51

Lewis was on his hands and knees, spitting bile on the floor. The half-naked man's stomach was twisted in a knot. He was on a floor made of great stone tiles. He looked up and saw the grand support beams of a cathedral ceiling. Leodor stepped into full view.

"What did you do?" Lewis asked. "I feel the flu upon my bowels."

"I yanked you and your clever mistress out of the jaws of stupidity. That's what I did." Leodor hooked Lewis under an arm and helped him to his feet. "You had to take another dip in the pool, didn't you? Couldn't you have left Raschel alone to do her job?"

"What are you talking about now?" Lewis wiped his mouth. "Gack. And get me something to wash this yuck out." He looked side to side. "Where's Raschel?"

Leodor snapped his fingers. "Wine."

A young man wearing robes that were ringed like a racoon's tail appeared from behind the cathedral's stage. He carried a tray with a brass wine carafe and goblets. He poured a goblet full, left the tray on the pew, and vanished back behind the stage.

Lewis drank, swished, and spat.

"Do you mind? This is a sanctuary," Leodor said.

"No, I don't mind. Where is Raschel?"

"She solidified from the vanishing summons faster than you. Her stomach didn't sour like spoiled milk, either. She appears to have the fortitude that you lack. A good thing." Leodor dabbed the top of his sweaty lip with a rag. He sat down on one of the pews. "Now, she goes to finish what you started and finish Ruger Slade, once and for all."

"I don't suppose you brought my sword along? I can help with that." Lewis rubbed the blood on his chest from when Ruger had marked him. "He'll die for this."

"Yes, just like the time when you split your lip. You wanted to take his head then but didn't. Let me give you some advice. Let the assassin handle it."

"She should have done so by now. But she delayed." Lewis guzzled down a big drink. "I think she enjoys the long game too much." He pitched the goblet onto the floor.

"Now we don't have any choice in the matter. We can't let Ruger meet the king. He has Hector's ear. The last thing we need is for doubt and suspicion to be cast our way. We already dance too close to the flame as it is. He can't reach the House of Steel. You need to ride there and rally your men. Just in case. I'll come with. Let us make haste." Leodor rose with a groan. "The Elders really took it out of me when I cast that vanishing spell."

"How did you know where to find us?"

"The Sect has eyes everywhere. I keep eyes on you. They followed you to Raschel's complex. They caught Ruger and his men heading in and notified me. I had to act quickly, and it's a good thing I was in the area." He pointed at a stone pedestal that had two burnt marks on it.

Looking at the marks, Lewis said, "That smells like burnt hair."

"That's yours and Raschel's. It's the only way I could have snared the both of you. A good thing that I had it stored."

"How did you get my hair?"

"Oh, I've had it since you were a boy," he said with a gummy smile. "And I have plenty of it. Remember that."

"You don't think that Raschel can finish the job?" Lewis asked as they were walking out of the cathedral's back door into the alley.

"The man killed a Fenix. I won't believe he's dead until I see it. I would think the complex would be more than enough to handle him, though."

They moved into the alley, where a two-horse chariot waited.

Lewis stepped into the chariot and took the reins. "Complex? What do you mean?"

"Those apartments that you have been fornicating in? They are a front for one of the oldest assassin's guilds. It will be interesting to see how the fastest blade in Titanuus holds up against that."

52

STARING DOWN THAT HALLWAY, WHICH WAS THICK WITH RANKS OF assassins, Abraham said, "Sticks, find us another way out of here and fetch Horace Lewis's sword. He forgot his spear."

The assassins crept closer. They were only four doorways away.

Sticks tossed Lewis's sword belt to Horace then pulled her daggers from her hips. "This building doesn't have any windows. So, jumping or climbing down is out." She climbed onto the bed and poked the roof with her dagger. "We could try the ceiling."

"Better make it quick," he said. He looked at Tark, Cudgel, and Horace. "Gentlemen, we might have to punch a hole right through them. It's gonna be a tough fight in these close quarters. Make sure we don't hit one another."

"They only thing we're going to hit is them." Cudgel stepped beside Abraham. "We have the length. Let's use it."

Shoulder to shoulder, Abraham and Cudgel advanced on the assassins. "Let's go plow guard position." He lowered his sword and got into a fighting stance. The plow guard carried the sword handle down at the hip with the point pointed and angle upward.

Cudgel flashed a white smile. "Let's plow right through them!"

"Come on, dogs! Let's see what you got! Plow one!" Abraham ordered.

As one, he and Cudgel stepped forward and lunged. Two of the charging assassins were impaled by the blades. Their weapons fell free of their grips, and they died, clutching at the wound in their hearts.

"Plow two!" Abraham shouted.

Once again, he and Cudgel lunged forward and thrust with devastating effect.

"Plow three!"

The assassins had come prepared. They wielded shorter weapons, designed for close-quarters fighting, giving them the advantage. What they hadn't counted on was facing skilled swordsmen who had fought in every situation. They were losing.

Like a skilled advancing army, Abraham and Cudgel cut them down. They walked over the carpet of the dead. They plowed though the living. The bodies piled up. The armorless assassins kept coming.

"There is no end in sight of them," Cudgel said as he gored another assassin. "How many can there be?"

"I don't know. But their will should break at some point."

Abraham jammed Black Bane clean through a man's shoulder, just above the heart. The assassin twisted away with the sword still lodged in his body. He pulled against Abraham's grip, causing him to swing to one side. A third assassin slipped in between the two in the front and poked a dagger at Abraham's exposed belly. He jumped back just in time. The assassin's blade nicked his abdomen.

"Down with you!" Tark cried. He cut the assassin's arm off with a quick downward swing then advanced into Abraham's slot. "I'll take this!"

Abraham wrenched his sword free and fell back behind the brothers. He stood by Horace. "Getting bored yet?"

"If I had my spear, this fight would be over. I'd skewer an entire line of them." Horace fanned himself. "It's hot in here, and I'm not even fighting."

"I don't think the air conditioning is working," he said.

"The what?"

"Never mind."

Abraham scanned ahead. The apartment hallway was typical of many hotels he'd been in. Its hallway ran the length of the building with rooms on both sides of the hall. No exits were at the end, however. Instead, the exits were at the intersection in the middle. "We have to carve a path all the way to the middle. We'll make a break from the stairs from there."

In front, Tark and Cudgel continued to hew men down.

"What about Sticks and Dominga?" Horace asked.

Abraham yelled back down the hall. "Did you find a way out?"

Sticks popped her head outside the doorway. "No. Did you?"

"We're working on it!" He turned his attention to the pressing horde, but no end was in sight. "Man, I wish I had a machine gun."

The company had sliced their way within two doors of the intersection, which appeared crammed full of assassins of all shapes and sizes. Each and every one of them wore a black cowl that resembled a raven.

Cudgel and Tark were coated head to toe in splattered blood. Their boots were slick with fresh blood and ankle deep in the fallen dead.

Cudgel shouted the commands. "Plow one! Plow two!"

"There has to be a better way out of here." Abraham heard a click and turned as the doors they'd passed suddenly opened and more assassins poured out. "Horace, watch your back!"

53

AN ASSASSIN FLUNG A BLACK SACK THROUGH THE AIR. IT APPEARED harmless, but when the sack struck Horace in the base of the skull, a tiny thunderclap followed. Horace wobbled on his legs and fell to the ground like a tranquilized moose.

"Hell's bells, what was that?" Abraham asked. His arm hairs prickled from the concussive force that came from the black sack. Another assassin tossed a black sack toward him. "Oh no, you don't." He didn't want it to hit Cudgel or Tark and batted it aside with his blade. Concussive energy exploded up his sword, through his arms and shoulders. The jarring impact knocked him into the wall.

The assassins pounced.

Abraham gored the first attacker in the neck with a quick stab of his sword. He pulled his dagger free from his belt and belly jabbed another. His body stung all over, but he fought the sensation off. The assassins were collapsing on them from both sides.

"Boys, we have a problem!" he yelled. "Girls, find a way out of here now!"

Dominga shouted back at him, "We're working on it! Keep your pants on!"

He eyed the assassins. "That's it. Ruger... Black Bane, show me what you can do!"

The assassins charged at him with swinging swords arcing downward at his head.

Ruger parried both swords. He punched holes in the hearts of both men with his dagger. As the assassins fell, he stepped between them. With dazzling speed, he unleashed Black Bane on the brood. He chopped, sliced, and thrust in blinding strokes. Black Bane turned the lesser men's bodies into chopped salad. The dark blade rose and fell, thrust and pierced. The assassins at the back fell dead.

Dominga stepped into the hall. "Ruger! We found a way out!"

"Brothers, we need to retreat," he said. He saw an unused black sack that had fallen to the floor. He picked it up and hurled it like a baseball between Tark and Cudgel. The sack struck an assassin in the face, and the concussion knocked two rows of the assassins backward.

"Now, that's what I call a fastball."

With a quick look over his shoulder, Cudgel asked, "What's the plan, Captain?"

"We're going backward." Abraham knelt down by Horace and picked the man up in a fireman's carry with a grunt. "Geez, this ox must be three hundred fifty pounds." He backed down the hallway. "Come on, fellas. Attack and retreat! Sticks, you better have a way out ready! We're coming!"

"Hurry up!" Dominga came outside. "Elder's Blood! How many are there?"

"I don't know," he said. "Do you see those black sacks on the dead belts? Grab those, toss them—"

"I know, I know," Dominga said as she hurried into the

hallway and plucked out the black sacks. "I've dealt with the Brotherhood of Ravens' dirty tricks before." She flung two bags over Tark and Cudgel's heads. The concussive blast knocked a wave of assassins backward. "Let's go, boys. I can't bail you out all of the time."

Tark and Cudgel followed Abraham and Dominga into the room.

The bed was moved, revealing a trapdoor in the floor. Iris was in the room. She closed the busted door and circled one hand while chanting. The busted door mended back into place.

Sticks popped her head out of the trapdoor. "You can stare, or you can move. Your choice." She vanished back inside the hole.

Pounding started on the other side of the door. The hinges shook.

"I gave the door more strength with my spell," Iris said, "but it won't hold long."

"All of you go, ladies first," Abraham said as he helped Iris down the hole.

Dominga jumped down through the gap, followed by Tark and Cudgel. Abraham lowered Horace down to them. The big man slipped through the brothers' blood-slick fingers and hit the floor with a thump.

"Nice catch!"

The brothers shrugged at him.

Abraham jumped down through the hole. The room below was empty of furnishings and had a ladder that led down to the first level.

Sticks waved all of them over. "I've scouted this. It leads into the streets. Apparently, Raschel has a formidable station with her secret entrances."

Iris pointed one hand at the trapdoor and rolled the other in a circle. The door closed and sealed shut. Mystical green symbols covered the door all over. She looked at Abraham and shrugged. "Same as the other. It will slow them, but that's about it."

Stomping started on the trapdoor. Abraham shook Horace. The bearish man snored.

"Great." Abraham hefted him back onto his shoulders and started down the ladder. "It's like carrying lumpy keg barrels."

The ladder took them to another room with a secret door that slid open into an alley. On foot, they raced down the channel between the buildings. At the end of the alley, he puffed for breath, set down Horace, and said, "We need to split up. Meet back at the Stronghold. I'll lead them away."

Iris poked a glowing finger into Horace's ribs.

"Eeow!" The big man jumped up. "What? Who?"

"Just shut up and come with me." Iris took him by the hand, and they dashed into the streets.

"Are you sure you want to split up? That's not our way," Sticks said.

"I have a gut feeling they only want me dead. And there's no sense in them catching all of us. I'll be fine. Just meet me at the Stronghold."

Sticks nodded. She and Dominga went one way. Tark and Cudgel went another. The busy streets parted as they passed.

Abraham hung back in the alley and eyed the exit they'd come through. His heart raced. He wanted his friends safe. No sense in them dying on his account. As for him, he needed to lead the assassins off their trail. He needed to find a way to get word to the king. *This is madness. I don't know even know what I'm doing.*

Out of the secret exit, the assassins poured into the alley, their eyes set on him. With deadly weapons in hand, they charged. Abraham ran.

54

The screaming in the streets didn't have anything to do with the battle-splattered warrior shoving through the civilians. It was the wave of black-cowled terror that had the women shrieking. They spilled out of the alley in twos, threes and fours. The Brotherhood of Ravens didn't hesitate to take a poke at anyone who stood in their paths. Word of the Brotherhood spread as quickly as the wind. The people scrambled. The streets cleared. Doors slammed shut, and shutters closed.

Abraham found himself running alone with the fleet feet of assassins hot on his tail.

Maybe this wasn't such a good idea.

He didn't know Burgess as well as he'd thought. He turned down an alley and found more raven-headed assassins barring his path. He jumped onto a storefront porch and tested the door lock of the first one he passed. It didn't budge. He continued down the western-styled porch fronts, jumping to the cobblestones and back onto the wood, pounding on doors that he passed.

"Go away!" someone yelled from inside.

The assassins were gaining ground. On fast feet, they sprinted behind like a silent wind of death. A long-limbed assassin closed the gap on Abraham and took a swipe at him with a wavy-bladed short sword.

Abraham sidestepped the swing, grabbed the man's wrist, and punched the man in the nose. The assassin's nose crunched beneath the power of his fist. He twisted the blade out of the assassin's hand and stabbed the man with it. It was a good move. *One assassin down, countless left to go. Where are all of them coming from?*

The short melee had shortened Abraham's lead. The plague of assassins were cutting off any avenue of escape from the city. Abraham leapt onto the next porch and jumped through the window, and the pane of glass shattered. The store was filled with clothing, dresses, shirts, and fanciful hats. The women in the store screamed.

"Pardon me," he said as he made his way toward the staircase leading up. He noticed a pretty lady in a purple gown and winked. "By the way, that looks great on you. Simply ravishing."

The woman in purple blushed.

He bounded up the steps and burst through the door that led to the balcony over the porch. Below, the Brotherhood of Ravens flocked toward the store. Assassins climbed over the balcony railing and hemmed him in between them. They hurled throwing stars at him.

Abraham ducked and dodged. "Hey! What is this, kung fu theater?" A throwing star lodged itself in his shoulder. He pulled it out and threw it down into the crowd of assassins, braining one assassin in the middle of the forehead. "That's what you get for staring." Black Bane in hand, he advanced with the hunger of a panther. He cut the first assassin down as he half drew his own blade.

Another throwing star whistled behind him and sank into his back. Abraham turned. "Now you're ticking me off!"

The assassin drew two short blades and darted toward Abraham, spinning his blades like a windmill.

Abraham saw a gaping hole in the man's offense and lunged. The tip of his longsword passed through the front side of the man and out the other. The assassin's arms dropped, and his blades clattered on the wood. Abraham shoved the man over the railing into the crowd below him. "How do you like those apples? Who's next?"

Dozens of assassins hurled throwing stars at him with flicks of their wrists. The spinning pinwheels of death whistled right toward him.

Abraham dove to the floor.

The stars thudded into the wooden walls behind him with a cascade of *thunk-thunk-thunk-thunk-thunk*.

"Smack-talking assassins. Maybe a bad idea." Aside from the star still lodged in his back, all the others had missed. He popped up from behind the railing. "Nyah! Nyah! You missed me!"

For the next several minutes, Abraham battled small groups of assassins from balconies, porches, and rooftops. He managed to keep control of the environment by moving. Assassin after assassin fell. They weren't any match for him. They dangled dead over the railings. They crawled in the streets, missing legs from chopped-through knees. Heads rolled down the planks and off the roof tiles, landing in troughs and flower boxes. Nicked up and bleeding, he killed them one after the other.

Facing two more attackers from another balcony, he said, "You guys are terrible." He'd surmised that the black hood didn't make the man. Most of them were novices with some training but far from advanced swordsmen. Compared to him, they seemed to have been dragged off the streets and given weapons. They were sheep for the slaughter. He killed two men in front of him with a single stroke.

He shouted down over the balcony rail at them. "Are you stupid? When you step into my zone, you step into the death zone. Do something else for a living!"

Three more climbed up on the balcony and approached. With sweat and blood dripping from his face, he said, "Great. Hard headed and hard of hearing. Just like I used to be." He motioned them forward with Black Bane. "Well, come on then, dog meat. I think the store owner wanted his walls painted red anyway."

A sharp flutelike whistle cut through the air, and the assassins froze in place. They turned their heads toward the sound of a wagon rumbling down the streets. Black chariots of men pulled by black horses were coming—men the likes of whom Abraham had never seen.

"Who in Sam Hill are they?"

55

FOUR MEN STEPPED OUT OF THE FOUR CHARIOTS. THEIR TALL, WELL-knit bodies were dyed black as coal. White rings were painted around their bodies and appendages. Their heads were sleek, with eye sockets painted white. They strode down the streets like predators. All of them towered over the assassins. They must have stood seven feet tall. The assassins cleared away from the porch. The men in black ringed in white stood in front and looked up at Abraham.

"Nice costumes," Abraham said.

He noted the weapons they carried. Their right hands were missing. Weapons had been grafted onto the metal stumps that replaced their hands. From left to right, one carried a sword blade, the next a hook-nosed axe, followed by a spiked flail then a long chain with a hook on the end. They were wicked-looking devices, nasty, bloodstained, and dully shining.

"Do you have names?" he asked.

The one with the sword hand spoke well. "We are the Siblings of Slaughter. You are our prey." He waved his sword, beckoning him downward. "Come down, Ruger Slade. The time has come for our steel to meet. Let's us dance to the beat that metal reaves."

"That's very poetic, but I prefer the bird's eye view of things. Perhaps—"

"What is all the racket?"

A bitter voice spoke inside Abraham's head. It was the voice he'd heard from the sword when he battled the Fenix. "Black Bane?"

"No, I forget what my name is. All I know is that I'm trapped inside this steel cocoon and you woke me. Again. Keep it down out there, will you?"

The swordsman spoke again. "Are you coming, blade master? We will make it fair. If you find victory, you will no longer be pursued. But if you lose, you lose."

Abraham lifted a finger. "Give me a minute. I'm talking with my sword."

The swordsman continued in a polite accent, "I am Edge. These are my brothers, Axe, Spike, and Hook."

Abraham was about to address his sword when he leaned back over the rail and said, "Seriously, those are your names? You sound more like a garage band or a team of wrestlers." He stepped back and looked at his sword. "Do me a favor and blast these guys with a lightning bolt like you did the Fenix."

"Mmm, hold me where I can see them?"

He held Black Bane out over the railing.

"You can take them," the sword said.

"Can you even see them?"

"Of course I can."

"Then describe them to me."

"Er, well, the enemy is very dark, wiry with sharp little teeth. Is that close?"

"No, I think you just described a black cat." Abraham shook his head. "Who are you?"

"Ruger Slade, come down. The Siblings of Slaughter wait," Edge said.

"I said give me a minute!" Abraham's nostrils flared. "You have me surrounded. It's not as if I can go anywhere."

"I told you I don't remember who I am. The last thing I remember was a great battle. Light against darkness. I was spellcasting. Knocking spider things from grand columns. A world would be crushed beneath my power. I should have died, but I had a spell in my pocket buried in my mind. My essence transported from one body to another. Now I'm in this blade. It's peaceful, aside from the occasional banging of metal. We never stopped fighting where I came from. In this object, I can rest."

"Why don't you write a book about it? Are you going to help me or not?"

"No. Sometimes you have to do things for yourself. Tell me, what do the women look like in your world, are they ample?"

"That's it. I know this world isn't real!" He looked at his sword. "If you aren't going to help, stay out of my way." Abraham looked down at the Siblings of Slaughter. "Make a hole!" He jumped off the balcony into the street and landed in front of the brothers. All of them looked down at him with heavy stares. He walked to the middle of the street, where the Siblings of Slaughter formed a box around him. The Brotherhood of Ravens encircled the four warriors and walled them all in. "So are we going to do this one at a time or all at once?"

With his arms hanging down by his sides, Edge dipped his chin and said, "We are assassins. We don't reveal to the target how we are going to kill them. I will guarantee that it will be only us against you."

"Fair enough." Abraham cut Black Bane back and forth. "I'll be your huckleberry. If you will, give me a moment."

Edge shrugged, the sinewy muscles in his body flexing as he did. "Take all the time that you need. The Siblings of Slaughter have hunted all sorts. We've dethroned masters of all weapons and pierced the hearts of barons and kings. No man can stand against us. You, Ruger Slade, will only be practice. A rat fleeing the cat's claws. A dove that fights against a hawk. Fight with all of your heart and might. We'll appreciate what we learn from you. We'll use it."

"Yeah, yeah. I get it, you're a bunch of bad asses. Now, stop the monologue, and let's get this party started," Abraham said. *All right, Ruger, whatever you got, you better help me use it all now.*

"Are you talking to me?" the essence inside the sword asked.

"No, just shut up."

Abraham readied his sword in the high guard position. He turned slowly in a circle, studying the eyes of his opponents. They were seasoned warriors. Scars showed on their black-dyed skin. They'd been through a scrap or two. Each of them was tall and lengthy. They moved with a dancer's ease for big men, like something spawned from primordial jungles. At he turned, his head moved from side to side. "All right, then. Who wants to die first?"

The Sibling named Hook started swinging his chain over his head. The black links whistled through the air.

Abraham caught himself looking at the links. Behind him, the sibling called Spike bore down on him. The giant man swung his spiked mace in the direction for a collision course for Abraham's head. He chopped at the man. The man slipped to the side with the speed of a cat and rolled away from the sword strike. Links of chain wrapped around Abraham's ankle, and the hook locked into his calf. With a yank, Hook pulled Abraham off his feet. Down to the ground he went in a heap.

56

THE BROTHERHOOD OF RAVENS—NORMALLY SILENT—LET OUT A gusty cheer the moment Abraham went down. Hook pulled on his chain with his free arm and dragged Abraham over the streets. Spike came right at him, swinging his spiked mace at his face. Abraham leaned away, and the mace bit into the stones. Abraham countered with a slice at Spike's feet. The assassin hopped away with a fraction of a second to spare.

"Geez, you freaks are fast!"

Hook towed Abraham over the road. The crowd went with him. Edge had a smirk on his face. Axe showed a white-toothed grin.

"I vaguely remember having a wife. She was built like a chimney stack and was a fine cook too. At night, she gave me the most amazing massages. I can almost feel it when I meditate upon it," the essence in the sword said. *"But for the life of me, I can't see her face or remember her name."*

"Will you shut up?" Abraham said. He hacked at Spike, trying to keep the assassin at bay, while Hook dragged him like a hunk of dead meat. "I don't need stories. I need help!"

"Fine. I'm going back to sleep. Try to keep it quiet out there, will you?"

Abraham managed to dodge another swing from Spike that would have busted into his hip. He used the length of his sword to keep the man at bay while at the same time keeping an eye on the other two Siblings. Their haunting stares soaked in every movement. *Ruger, we have to do something. Soon. Or there won't be anything left of either one of us.*

As Spike attacked with blow after blow, Edge and Axe walked alongside the battle.

Abraham twisted, scooted, parried, and butt hopped away from the heavy-handed blows Spike wrought. His imminent assassination was being put on display for all to see as the citizens of Burgess gathered on the balconies. Clearly, the Siblings of Slaughter wanted to create a moment to remember. He fell backward, feigning exhaustion, and let Hook drag him down the street.

Spike relented in his assault and laughed. Then he asked, "Do you tire so soon, little man?"

"Who, me? No, I'm not tired. I thought you were tired from all of that swinging and missing." He winked at Spike. "Nothing to be ashamed of. Some people just aren't very good at fighting."

Spike's brows knitted together. From a position behind Abraham's head, he brought his axe down with wroth force.

Abraham sat up as quickly as he could.

Spike's mace bit into the street.

In a fluid motion, Abraham leaned backward and thrust his sword back into Spike's neck. As the crowd gasped, Abraham turned his attention to Hook. He sat up fully and hacked into the chain binding him. Black Bane cut through the ebony links.

Hook lost his grip and stumbled.

Abraham bounded to his feet, cocked his sword behind his shoulder, and unleashed. Hook's head leapt from his shoulders and fell among the crowd.

In an instant, Edge and Axe attacked simultaneously. Edge swung his sword high, and Axe aimed low.

With a chain wrapped around his ankle and a hook in his calf, Abraham parried the axe swing and ducked underneath Edge's sword. The resounding blow of sword against axe jarred his arms. The Siblings of Slaughter were as strong as they looked. He jumped back away from both of them and set his feet.

"Two down, and two to go," Abraham said. "The odds are getting better all of the time."

"You need to be more observant," Axe said.

Spike rose from his position on the ground. He had a hole in his neck, but he did not bleed. Hook's head was missing, but he still stood with balance. One of the assassins in a cowl picked up Hook's head and handed it to him. Hook cradled his head with one arm, like a football helmet. His eyes were wide open. He started swinging his severed chain overhead.

An icy caterpillar-like sensation crawled all over Abraham's body, a horrific sensation. His nerves of steel ebbed. "Nice trick. I didn't realize that you were already dead."

"We aren't dead by any means, as you can see. Another power courses through our veins that mortal men can't see." Edge eased toward Abraham. "You will soon know the sting of death, and the grave will hold you until the worms eat your flesh."

"We'll see. I was hoping to be cremated. You know, ashes to ashes, dust to dust. I've never had a fondness for burials." He spun his sword end over end. "Let's do this again."

"Siblings," Edge said, "no mercy."

57

ONCE AGAIN, ABRAHAM FOUND HIMSELF SURROUNDED BY SUPERIOR numbers. He was right back where he'd started, nicked up, sweat drenched, and his calf bleeding into the streets. He shuffled around in the plow guard stance, eyeing the moving enemy. His calf burned like fire. At times like this, he wished he'd worn his armor. *Breastplate. Don't leave home without it.*

Edge made the first strike. With his long half arm and half sword, he attacked with the blinding speed of a boxer's jab.

Abraham parried the strike. Suddenly, a funnel of swordfighting techniques downloaded into his mind. His body immediately went to work. Black Bane came to life. The orange emberlike fire glowed.

The skilled Siblings of Slaughter converged on Abraham. They chopped, thrust, slashed, and jabbed. Hook's chain whistled high and cracked back down. Spike's mace whooshed by. Axe unleashed lethal blow after blow. Edge's sword twisted through air, clipping at Abraham's guts. He might as well have been stuck in a blender.

Body parts and the weapons attached to them started flying. Axe's weapon arm was the first to go. Black Bane chopped it off at the shoulder. Black Bane sliced Spike's arm at the elbow. His axe arm went flying midswing. The Siblings never saw it coming. A storm of blazing steel wrought havoc on their bodies. Hook lost his chain arm and fell to the ground from his leg being severed from the knee.

"Reap the whirlwind!" Abraham shouted with frenzied glee. He drove Edge back on his heels. The assassin's dark face paled as he parried desperately at the devastation being brought upon him. Abraham beat the man's weapon aside with ferocity. The blows would have disarmed the most extraordinary men. But Edge's sword was his arm.

With fire in his eyes, Abraham said, "Ah, screw it." He brought Black Bane down hard.

Edge parried. His blade snapped in two.

Abraham mutilated the weaponless warriors. He took limbs, starting with Spike and ending with Edge. With a single stroke, he removed Edge's head from the shoulders. He held the head up high for all to see. "This is what happens to assassins when they waltz into my world!"

The encircling Brotherhood of the Ravens backpedaled.

"Brotherhood! Cut down this hound!" Edge's head said.

Abraham looked at Edge. "You said I'd be free to go."

"I'm an assassin. I lied. You cannot kill us. You cannot win. We are the Siblings of—"

Abraham hurled the head into the crowd. "Yeah, yeah, I know." He held out Bane Blane. The blade's runes pulsated with angry life. "Who's next?"

A commotion of rumbling of wheels roared nearby. Horse-drawn chariots trampled through the knot of assassins. Three chariots and riders converged on Abraham, plowing through every one of the living.

"Get in, Ruger!" Vern said, his wavy locks waving in the wind.

He was driving a chariot of the Siblings of Slaughter. Bearclaw drove another one of the chariots into the crowd, followed by the third, driven by Apollo and Prospero. "What are you waiting for? I can't stop this thing. Jump in. We have to go!"

As Vern thundered by, Abraham dashed toward the cart and leapt into the back. "Where in Titanuus did you come from?"

"We were trying to have a drink when all the clamor started. Should have known that it was you."

The chariot bumped upward as it ran over two bodies.

"Woo hoo!" Vern said.

The three chariots driven by the Henchmen sent the assassins scattering through the streets. Abraham hung his sword out the window and took the lives of a few more dodging assassins.

"Can you take us to the Stronghold?" he asked.

"So long as the horses hold out, I'll get us there." Vern snapped the reins. "Yah!"

Behind them, Bearclaw, Apollo, and Prospero ran roughshod over the assailing masses. Bodies were crunched underneath horse hooves and hard wheels. Clearing a bloody path through the assassins, all three chariots thundered over the road like a black terror. The Brotherhood of Ravens gave chase, but the horses quickly outdistanced them.

Vern drove the horses through the city like bats out of hell. The chariot slung side to side as it skidded across the road and around the corners. He bellowed at the top of his lungs, "Yeehaw! I love driving these things."

To gasps and cries of alarm from bewildered onlookers, the train of horses broke free and made their way into the rolling countryside.

The runes of Black Bane cooled. Abraham slipped it into his sheath. His bloody hand trembled.

"Thanks for dragging me out of there," he said. "I was beginning to think the fighting wasn't going to end."

Vern showed a twisted smile. "I've seen you handle worse."

"You have?"

The chariot driver chuckled and said, "We better get some bandages. You're bleeding all over my new chariot."

The battle with the Brotherhood of Ravens and the Siblings of Slaughter hadn't come without its toll. He had lacerations and scrapes all over his arms, and that was only what he could see. He looked as though he'd run through a briar bush of razors. "I hope Iris and the others made it."

"What's going on?" Vern asked.

Abraham gave his best attempt at the Cliff Notes version. "Turns out that Twila was the assassin. I don't know if she is dead, gone, or someone else, but she was the saboteur of all our plans. We tracked it all back to Prince Lewis and Leodor. They are behind all of it."

"That explains the frosty reception that we received when we tried to rejoin the King's Guardians," Vern said as he snapped the reins. "That jerk wouldn't have any part of us."

"*Jerk*? Where'd you come up with that?"

"From you. Well, the other you. I can't keep track. Didn't I use it right?"

"No, you used it right. But *jerk* is an understatement."

He looked back at Bearclaw and the brothers, Prospero and Apollo. They raced through the cloud of road dust a few dozen yards behind them. He waved. Bearclaw saluted. Apollo waved, and Prospero appeared to be sleeping standing up. "At least we rooted out the enemy. The problem is how do we get the king to believe us?"

"I wouldn't have any idea." Vern drove mile after mile toward the Stronghold. Nearing the small plantation, he said, "Looks like we're going to have more visitors." He pointed eastward. "Look."

By the score, the King's Guardians were descending a hill less than a mile away. Armored in bright steel from head to toe, they rode on the backs of white horses. At the front, one man led, wearing a great coat. It was Lewis. His fist pumped in the air. A bugler sounded his horn. The flag bearer dropped the guard. In a cloud of thunder, down the hillside they came.

"Faster, Vern!" Abraham yelled. "We can't let them beat us to the Stronghold! We're dead men if they do!"

58

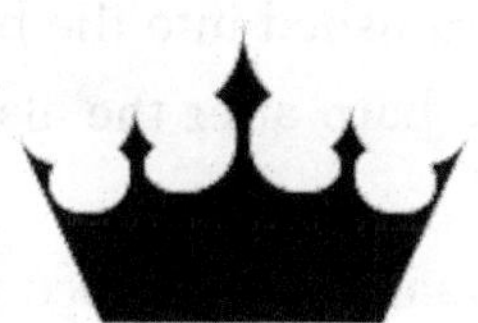

THE HORSE-DRAWN CHARIOTS RACED DOWN THE ROADWAY LEADING to the Stronghold. Ahead, Solomon stood outside, towering over several others, looking to see what all the commotion was all about. Behind the chariots, the Guardians in armor led the charge down the slopes. They were a quarter of a mile away and closing fast.

Abraham shouted at the top of his lungs. "Get inside! Get everyone inside!"

Solomon waved his hands outward. The hirelings dropped what they were doing. With frightened faces, they hurried into the safety of the thick stone walls the Stronghold offered. The livestock scattered throughout the yard.

Twenty yards from the door, Vern brought the chariot to a rumbling halt. Bearclaw, Prospero, and Apollo followed suit. They took a look behind them and hurried inside.

Abraham met Solomon at the door. "Did Sticks and Horace make it? What about Iris?"

"They all are making preparations inside," the old troglin said. "You look like hell."

"You don't know the half of it. Let's get inside," he said.

Solomon shoved him through the door and said, "I'll be back. We need to turn the beasts free of the stables. Those butchers will slaughter them." He rushed toward the barn.

"There's not time, Solomon. Come back!" Abraham watched helplessly as Solomon vanished into the barn. A donkey and two horses bolted out of the barn after the alarming sound of a loud roar. "Hurry up!"

Led by Lewis, the Guardians galloped toward the Stronghold. They would arrive in the next few seconds.

"Solomon! Come on!" Abraham yelled. "Of all the stupid things to do."

Horace hooked Abraham by an arm. "Captain, you need to get inside. There is no time left."

He jerked his arm free. "Solomon! Solomon! Get your hairy butt back here!"

A few more horses bolted out of the barn, followed by cats, dogs, and a slow-moving cow. Solomon didn't emerge.

Lewis and his host of Guardians arrived. The Guardians dismounted in quick military fashion. They slipped their crossbows from hooks, loaded bolts, made a row in front of the horses, faced the Stronghold, and took aim.

Lewis looked right at Abraham and said, "Fire!"

Horace jerked Abraham inside. Bearclaw slammed the door shut. Crossbow bolts peppered the outside of the door with a *thak-thak-thak-thak-thak* sound. Bearclaw barred the door closed.

Abraham limped over to one of the small portals, the chain wrapped around his ankle clinking over the floor. Peering through the portal, he had a full view of the enemy. The King's Guardians were rows deep, showing at least sixty. The barn door was swung wide open, showing no sign of Solomon.

"Stupid hippie!"

Thak! A bolt splintered off the portal's rim. Abraham backed away. He couldn't do anything for Solomon now. All he could do was hope the big man escaped. He faced the crew. All of them were gathered around the room. Of the former Henchmen stood Horace, Sticks, Bearclaw, Vern, Dominga, Cudgel, Tark, Iris, Prospero, and Apollo. The two new Red Tunics, Skitts and Zann, were present, along with a group of hirelings.

"How long can we hold out?" Abraham asked.

"Weeks with food. With the springs in the back caverns, we can water ourselves for a lifetime," Horace said. "We might starve at some point, however."

"I don't think this battle is going to be a matter of weeks. Not even days. Lewis wants this done quick. The question is does he have the means to do it?"

Horace strode to the front and peeked out of one of the other portals without putting his head in it. "I see no wagon for siege. No doubt, they can fetch them. They could try to burn us out using pitch."

Iris stepped forward from the pack. "I can quench the flames to some degree." She studied Abraham with a worried expression. "We need to tend to those wounds."

Abraham peeked out of the wall portal, searching for Solomon. "I hope you headed for the hills."

From outside, Lewis called out. He had a red gash on his cheek where Abraham had marked him. "Ruger Slade! You and your men stand guilty of assaulting the crown! The penalty for that crime is death!" He rode his horse back and forth in front of his men. "However, granted that I am a merciful prince, I will entertain a second option. Ruger the fallen, surrender willfully, and I'll see to it that the sentence of all of your conspirators will be light. However, the penalty for you will be death!"

Ruger yelled out of the portal, "No deal, you lying sack of monkey dung! You are the one that betrays your father's crown, not me! It's you who should surrender to me!"

Lewis looked at his men and rolled his eyes. "A possessed lunatic."

Abraham moved away from the window. "Do we have any allies in the Guardians? Who's the big guy that breaks the horse underneath the saddle?"

"That's Pratt," Horace answered. "He won't bend against the prince. Not unless the king orders it. He never liked you much, either."

"Me? Why didn't he like me?"

"He was the commander of the Guardians until you came along. When you were gone, he took over briefly, but the king gave the command to the prince." Horace nodded his head. "It's called nepotism."

"I know. It's another name for monarchy. So, won't there be bitterness between Pratt and Lewis?"

"Actually, they've always gotten along just fine. Like brothers," Horace said cheerfully.

"You don't have to sound so happy about it."

"Yes, Captain." Horace frowned.

Abraham had hoped to create a seed of doubt and turn the King's Guardians to his side. Realizing that wouldn't happen didn't take him long. The Guardians were fiercely loyal. He knew that himself, or at least Ruger did. They could fight them and hope for the best, but it would be a bloodbath. The King's Guardians wore and wielded the finest steel. They were practically invincible in their armor against lesser-clad men. *Out of the frying pan and into the fire.*

Lewis started up again. "I'm not going to belabor my points, Ruger. Exit or suffer the consequences. I promise I won't leave a single one of you standing."

He shouted out of the portal. "Can I get a count of thirty? I need a little time to think." He ducked back as a crossbow bolt zinged through the portal. "I'll take that as a no. I've got to hand it to you, you're a lot smarter than Khan was when he dealt with Kirk."

"Who?" Lewis gave an irritated shake of his head. "Pratt. Start burning. Begin with the barn and make use of those chariots."

Within a minute, the Guardians had burning torches in hand and took them inside the barn. In seconds, the inside of the barn roared to life in flames.

"No!" Abraham said. "Solomon!"

The Guardians freed the horses from the chariots and rolled one of the chariots to the front door. With the other two they blocked the portals. Using their torches, they set all of them on fire.

"Chariots of fire," Abraham said in a deflating tone. "This isn't the way it is supposed to be." He caught Sticks staring at him, her eyes filled with worry. "Hello," he said.

Sticks rushed to his side and caught him as the floor seemed to bow beneath him.

"Abraham, can you stand? You wobble," Sticks said. "You are as clammy as a fish."

Outside, the flames licked through the portals, and the smoke came rolling in.

Abraham's head rolled from side to side. "Get me some water. I'm only a little dehydrated. And some aspirin too. I'm getting a bad headache." Abraham's knees gave way, and he fell over on Sticks.

59

THE PAST

Back in Hinton, West Virginia, Abraham walked the downtown streets. Years had passed since he'd lost Jenny, Jake, Buddy, and his father, Earl. Now, he strode down the sidewalks, wearing a flannel shirt, with his hands stuck in the pockets of his jeans. He hadn't shaved in months. His hair hung over his eyes. A light snow was falling.

He crossed the street and went into Lowman's Drugstore. A bell rang when he entered. It was an old-school store, complete with a small soda shop and ice-cream parlor. A gift shop and other general goods were there. He walked up two steps and stood behind the counter. A young lady caught his eye. Her eyes grew big when she saw him. Her name was Carly. She turned away, searching for the man working the drug-stocked shelves behind her.

"Mister Lowman, he's here," she said.

The pharmacist, Bill Lowman, was an older gentleman with dark, thinning hair and rectangular glasses on the bridge of his nose. He wore the standard white pharmacist smock with his name embroidered on it. He and the young girl spoke in lowered voices. They glanced at Abraham from time to time. Finally, Bill dabbed his forehead with a handkerchief and came around to the front counter. "Good morning, Abraham. How are you today?"

"I'm getting by. I'll be better if you have my pills ready," he said.

Bill had been a family friend for a long time. He was a soft-spoken fellow too. He ran a finger under his collar. "Uh, listen Abraham, I can't fill this script for five more days. I told you that yesterday."

"I just need a few to hold me over, Bill. Come on. I need them. My back's on fire. I can barely walk or sleep." Abraham arched backward and groaned. "Just give me the pills. No one is going to say anything."

"I-I can't. Abraham, you need to just go. You can't come in here every day, predicting a different outcome." Bill swallowed. "If you are having trouble, go to the emergency room."

Abraham banged his fist on the counter, shaking the counter-top. "I've been there!"

Carly, a raspberry blonde with short hair, yanked the tele-phone off the wall and said, "Mr. Lowman, I'm calling the cops."

Bill lifted a hand and said, "No, no, I'll handle this, Carly. Just let me and Abraham talk this out. Put the phone down, please."

Carly hung the phone back up on the wall. Her blue eyes narrowed on Abraham. "Just say the word."

Carly wasn't the only other person inside the store. A young man, a high-school boy, was working the ice-cream bar. He held a broom across his chest like a weapon. Two other older ladies hurried out of the store.

Bill stepped out from behind the counter. He took Abraham by the arm and said, "Son, I know what you are going through. I know you are in anguish. You're alone."

Abraham opened his mouth to speak.

"But-but-but... hear me out. You think I can't understand. You think none of us can. But we do. Everyone's life is affected by tragedy in one way or another." He turned and faced Abraham. He held his arms at the elbow. "I'd been your father's friend a long time. I've known you since you were a boy. Abraham, you can beat this. I know you can. There are clinics. They can help you. Let them."

Abraham pushed the old man backward. Bill's grip broke from his sleeves. He stumbled over his feet and fell. His head cracked against the counter.

"Mr. Lowman!" Carly cried out. She rushed from behind the counter and came to his aid, kneeling beside Mister Lowman.

His head was bleeding, and he wasn't moving.

Carly laid him out on the floor. "He's not breathing! Joe, call an ambulance!"

The boy behind the counter dropped the broom and rushed to the phone.

Carly started giving Bill mouth-to-mouth resuscitation and giving him chest compressions.

Abraham went numb. Rushing blood filled his ears as he stammered, "It was an accident. I didn't mean to. He tripped and fell."

Carly kept trying to resuscitate the man. She didn't pay Abraham any mind.

Abraham's tongue clove to his mouth. He couldn't breathe. Everything looked and sounded as though it were inside a tunnel. He did the only thing that he could think to do. With a ring of the door's bell, he ran.

60

ABRAHAM SPENT THE NEXT SIX MONTHS IN A STATE CORRECTIONAL facility. Bill Lowman spent weeks in a coma. Not long after Bill Lowman revived, he came to see Abraham. No one else in Bill's family did. Bill, now using a walker, forgave him, but he didn't drop the assault charges. Bill said, "I'm sorry, Abraham, but there are consequences for your actions. I'll pray that you survive this."

Prison wasn't a cake walk. It was miserable. It was worse than anything he'd imagined it to be. They shaved him down and called him "Superstar." There was mockery. There were fights. New wounds were opened. For the first time in his life, Abraham was surrounded by people more miserable than him. It served as a wake-up call, but the healing wasn't easy.

For the next six months, he did his best to be a model prisoner. That garnered his early release from a one-year sentence, but there were stipulations. He had probation. His new probation officer, Mike, was a good man, older and bald with a frosty moustache. He worked for the Mission, a church group that provided housing for young men going through rehabilitation. There were classes, Bible studies, hot meals, and hard work.

Abraham shrugged it all off at first. He still carried so much guilt. Forgiving himself was hard. He blamed himself for the loss of his family. But in truth, the only person he'd hurt was Bill Lowman. That time, he lost control. It was a fatal slip that stuck.

One night, after dinner, Abraham was talking with Mike and Dave, another counselor at the Mission. That was the first time he let it all out—the hurt, the tears, the pain. It kept coming. They counseled him. They prayed for him, and he prayed with them. They tried to teach him to forgive himself and set on a new course in life.

Finally, Abraham finished his course at the Mission. He had nowhere else to go and nothing at all to do. That was when Mike introduced him to one of his friends, Luther Vancross. The old man was seventy-five years old and as feisty as a flea. He owned a microbrewery.

Luther walked him through the brewery, introduced him to the small crew who worked there, and took him back into his office, which had dark wooden paneling, an ugly metal desk, and paperwork stacked everywhere.

"Have a seat," Luther said as he sat down in large green leather chair. Luther was shaved clean from the top of his head to the bottom of his chin. His round face had age spots all over it. He wore a black polo shirt with his brewery logo on it and khaki pants. He was very fit for such an old man.

Abraham sat down in a comfortable matching green leather chair. The leather groaned underneath him.

Luther looked at him with dark, piercing eyes and said, "I'll give you one chance. That's it. Do you want it?"

Abraham hadn't had a real job since he'd started playing baseball. At first, he wasn't sure what to say. After seconds of hesitation, he said, "I'll take it. And… thank you."

"Good." Luther slapped his hands on the desk. "Then let's get you started. There's some paperwork we need to do." He turned around in his chair and looked out the window, which had a view of the outside parking lot. "Say, that's a nice truck you have. Is that a Kodiak turbo diesel?"

"It is."

"You know, you can make some extra money if you want to use your own vehicle. It will save me the expense of buying a new truck."

"It will need some work. Paint and customization."

Luther flung a hand at him. "Ah, I've got a guy for that. He owes me plenty of favors." He turned back toward Abraham. "It's a strange marriage having a fella in rehab driving a beer truck. Do you think you can handle the temptation?"

"I never had an issue with drinking. It was the pills and some other stuff." Abraham shrugged. "I really don't think that will be an issue."

Luther leaned forward on his elbows. "And the other thing? You're truly clean?"

"I am. I don't see myself going down that road again even though my existence at the moment feels meaningless."

Luther leaned back in his chair and nodded. "Good work gives a man purpose and meaning. I think you'll like being a truck driver. I used to be one. It's what led me to all of this." He spread his arms out. "I like the time on the road. I did plenty of soul searching. Enjoyed the music and the news. But I think people don't talk too much anymore." He got up. "Let's get you started on the paperwork. I'll have Janice order you some shirts. Hmph. You're going to be a big one. What size, two X?"

"I wish." Abraham patted his stomach. "It's three X now."

61

ABRAHAM TOOK ON THE MUNDANE TASK OF BEER-DELIVERY MAN THE best he could. The job had its merits. The local bars were always happy to see him. They liked his decked-out truck too. The Chevy Kodiak truck was spit polished black all over with gold lettering and lots of chrome. The job got him around people, but not too much. He had an excuse to skedaddle when the conversations started getting long.

The first couple of weeks kept him plenty busy. He ached all the time from the accident's injuries, but his time in prison had helped him handle it. The hard part was getting in good enough shape to carry the load. Bending over to pick up cases of beer tightened his back up like a drum. He'd be lying to himself if he said he didn't have an urge to take a pain pill, but he fought through it. He even put those round wooden beads on his truck seat. One stop at a time, he started getting better. He even got a call on the road from Mike at the Mission from time to time.

As he drove his route between southern West Virginia and North Carolina, he had plenty of time to think—too much time, perhaps. He became used to the isolation. He preferred the lonely existence—caffeinated drinks and truck-stop fast food for him.

With a picture of Jenny and Jake on his visor, along with Jake's backpack in his seat, he couldn't help but think about them all the time. If he didn't think about them, he felt guilty. Something, somewhere, hurt all the time. That was mostly his heart, however.

Day after day, he kept on trucking until he made a delivery at Woody's Grill and life started to change. He started to feel things.

Abraham pulled his truck underneath the canopy and beside the pumps. The fuel gauge was low. He exited the truck, made his way around to the pump, and unhitched the fuel nozzle. He opened his gas cap and started pumping. He reached into the cab and grabbed his clipboard and delivery docket. He pushed the brim of his ball cap up.

"Twenty-four cases, and I'm done." He tossed the clipboard onto the driver's seat.

He opened the back slat-panel door of the truck and grabbed the dolly from inside. Then he opened the next panel door to the left. Two cases at a time, he loaded the dolly until it was eight cases high. *Three trips to the walk-in. Easy-peasy.* He wheeled the dolly around toward the store and caught his breath.

A woman, about his age, blocked his path. She had straight dark ponytail hanging behind her shoulders. Her pretty face was sun bronzed with small freckles. She wore a hot-pink Woody's Grill T-shirt with black lettering, and her jean miniskirt showed off her great legs. She was tapping her foot and had her arms crossed over her chest. "What do you think you are doing?"

"Uh, making a beer delivery... ma'am," he said.

"Ma'am? That's strike two." She pointed at the truck. "You don't fill up during a delivery, newbie. You're blocking all of the pumps from other customers."

Woody twisted his head around. No other cars were in sight,

aside from the ones passing by on the highway. "I didn't see anyone else around. And this isn't a typical delivery truck. It's not a commercial vehicle."

"It looks commercial to me," she said. "Why do you think they put all of that lettering on it? And that's strike three. If you want to drop that order, load it back up, pump your gas, take your truck over there"—she pointed toward an access parking area—"and then unload it."

Abraham's blood started to stir. His back had already tightened up like a banjo string. The last thing he wanted to do was load up his truck and unload it again. He'd already done over one hundred cases that day, not to mention the pony kegs. He rubbed his bearded mouth, looked down into the fiery woman's eyes, and said something other than what he planned to say. "Yes, ma'am."

Her eyes narrowed. "The name's Mandi." She walked back into the store.

Abraham started slinging the cases of bottled beer back into the truck. After his fuel pumped, he moved the truck and started the unloading process. He wheeled eight cases to the double glass-paned doors and waited. They didn't open automatically like the other stores he entered. Woody's Grill was an older business, off the interstate, beside what used to be the main highway back in the day. It was a quaint red-brick establishment, typical of what would be seen along country roads, but bigger. He turned his back and pushed through.

Mandi stood behind the cashier counter, leaning back and looking through the tabloids. "Figured that out all by yourself, did you?" she said with a smirk.

Abraham felt sweat begin to roll down his back. He was mad, too. "Where's the cooler, Mandi?"

"In the back of the store. You know, where almost every cooler in America is located."

He gritted his teeth, turned the dolly around, and gave her a smile. "Thank you, *ma'am*."

Mandi's cheeks reddened.

Abraham moved on. He loaded the beer cases and the walk-in cooler. On his way out, he smelled fresh pecan pie, hamburger grease, and french fries. His stomach rumbled. That was when he noticed the diner that made up the other side of the general store. It was complete with a checkered floor, red vinyl booths, and spinning bar stools. A venerable man watching one of the televisions that hung from the wall spun around in his stool. He squinted in Abraham's direction and waved him over.

He wheeled the empty dolly into the diner and asked, "Can I help you, sir?"

"Have you seen any UFOs in Wytheville?" the old man asked.

"Pardon?"

The old man cackled loudly. He grabbed a napkin from the bar and wiped the slobber from his mouth. He wore a Woody's Grill sweatshirt and checkered golf pants with white slippers. He hit Abraham on the arm. "I'm just joshing you. They make a big deal about that UFO sighting in Wytheville. You might not know about it." He leaned forward and looked at the brewery logo on Abraham's black shirt. "So, you're the new guy. Luther told me about you. Wow, I can't believe we have Jenkins the Jet in my store. I used to watch you play a lot."

"Luther told you about me?"

"We go way back. He said to keep an eye on you. My name's Herb, by the way. I own this place." He extended a trembling hand.

Abraham shook it. "Nice to meet you, sir."

"Is it true that you could throw a one-hundred-and-three-mile-an-hour fastball? I never believed what they said about that."

"I could throw faster."

Herb cackled. He turned his head toward the kitchen galley doors. "Hey, Martha! Martha! Come and meet the Jet!"

"I don't go by that anymore."

"Martha! Hurry up!" Herb shouted.

Abraham expected to see a venerable woman like Herb come teetering out from behind the double doors. His eyes widened the moment Martha came through. She was an older version of Mandi, pleasantly plump and far younger than Herb. She couldn't have been more than fifty. Abraham's jaw hung a little.

Wringing her hands in her apron, she met both men at the bar and said, "You must be Abraham?"

He swallowed. "Well, yeah, how did you know?"

"Herb's been rambling on about you since Luther mentioned you. And I overheard him say *the Jet*." She shook his hand. "Nice to meet you. Say, I bet a big fella like you could use something to eat. How about I fix you something up?"

"I better be getting a move on," he said even though the food did smell mouthwateringly good.

"Nonsense. This is your last stop, isn't it?" Herb said.

"Yes."

"Well, sit down and eat." Herb hollered across the building. "Hey, Mandi! Get that fancy camera and take our picture. I want to put our picture on the wall."

"I'm not really famous," Abraham said as Martha disappeared into the kitchen.

Herb didn't pay Abraham's comment any mind. He started pointing all over the diner. "That's me and Johnny Cash. Over there is Charlie Daniels. Those are from years ago, some of them, before the interstate took our business away. Lots of famous people came rolling through. Glen Campbell. Hank Williams. Dolly was here twice! Man, you should have seen her. Hey Martha, who else used to come through?"

"Don't ask me," Martha hollered back. "Ask your late wife. I wasn't around back then."

Mandi strolled over with a sucker in her mouth. She held up her iPhone and said, "Say cheese."

Herb grinned so big that his dentures looked as though they'd pop out. Abraham made an uneasy smile.

"One for the ages," Mandi said as she walked way with a nice sway of her hips. She caught Abraham checking her out. "Don't you have some work to finish?"

62

THE PRESENT

ABRAHAM WOKE UP IN FIT OF COUGHING. IRIS HAD A HOLD OF HIM and helped him sit up. The smoky air burned his eyes. They were outside, and people were scrambling over the rooftop. "What happened?"

Sticks stepped into view, her face marred with soot. Without any sign of emotion, she said, "You checked out again. Now we're on the roof, trying our best not to die. Lewis is determined to burn the entire countryside down. He's poured pitch all around the Stronghold."

He looked at Iris and said, "I thought you said you could control the flames."

"I was doing fine up until Leodor showed up. He spoiled my efforts. I can't match his powers," Iris said.

Horace approached and stood over Abraham. "Captain, we are out of options. I think they want to smoke us out. Surrender. But we wouldn't give, not without your awakening first. We'd die first. We're going to die anyway."

Abraham blinked his eyes. He felt as though he'd just relived a big part of his past in his sleep. Coming back to a new reality was jarring. "I'm Ruger Slade, aren't I?"

Sticks's eyelids lifted. She grabbed him by the collar. "Not this again. Are you Ruger or Abraham?"

"Both, I think."

She let out a sigh. "Good. I don't think I could handle a new personality now."

Iris put a flask to his lips. "Drink this elixir. It will help you recuperate on the inside. I've already mended your wounds on the outside." She grabbed his forearm and lifted it for him to see. She'd stitched it up. "See?"

He nodded as he drank. He guzzled the elixir as though it were water, but it was thick like a honey mead, and tasty. With a groan, he reached for Horace's meaty hands. Horace pulled him up to his feet.

The Henchmen were lined around the walls of the top of the Stronghold. They stood between the battlements, looking down.

Fanning the smoke from his face, he asked, "How long have I been out?"

"Since yesterday," Horace replied. "We survived the night only because the Guardians used the time to gather more fire-making supplies. They renewed the flames this morning. They've been piling wood at the bottom, trying to cook us. They keep jamming burning logs through the portal. We jammed that up with stones. We secured the door so they can't burst through. But it's still a smokehouse down there."

Abraham shook his head as though trying to wake from a dream. He had actually been enjoying the reality of getting to know Mandi again. Now, that was gone. He took a smoky breath and asked, "Is anyone hurt?"

"The Guardians have fired several volleys at us, but nothing is sticking," Horace said.

"Did we fire back?"

Horace gave him a funny look and said, "An assault on the King's Guardians is an assault on the king. You don't want us to do that, do you?"

"Right. I guess not." Abraham squeezed between the battlements where Dominga was keeping watch. The smoke obscured his vision, but he could see the barn was burned to the ground. So were the storehouses. Lewis was using the surrounding split-rail fencing for firewood. "Have you seen Solomon?"

With a sorrowful look, Dominga shook her head. "I'm glad you are up and about. Do you feel better?"

"No, I'd rather be sleeping."

Dominga offered a smile. "Me too. Won't be long before we get unlimited rest, it seems."

He laid a hand on her shoulder and said, "Don't give up hope yet." He stepped away from the wall and bumped into Horace, who stood right at his heels. "What's on your mind?"

"It's only a matter of time before the King's Guardians hoist the ladders." Horace walked his fingers through the air. "They'll climb them like metal spiders, and we'll have a full battle on our hands. I just wanted you to know. We spied them building the ladder this morning. And don't forget Leodor aids them as well. We won't be a match for a full regiment of the king's metal. I'd say only the Elders can save us now."

"Have we done anything to get word to the king about this madness?"

It was a hollow question. Convincing King Hector of Lewis and Leodor's treachery would be next to impossible.

"I tried to send some pigeons," Sticks said, tossing a dagger up and down. "Leodor blasted them out of the sky with his magic. We considered trying to slip out of here. At least, that is what myself,

Tark, and Dominga wanted to do. We all agreed that we'd be slaughtered."

She looked at the steep hillside of rock behind the fortress. It was almost as sheer as a cliff. The hillside ran over one hundred feet high and peeled away from the fortress. The other side of the hill was a sheer cliff, making for a strange rock formation that created a massive wall. They called it the Shield.

"I could navigate the Shield at night," she said. "Perhaps I can get word to the king. I could at least notify him that a squadron of his men are assaulting the Stronghold. I bet he'd be curious about that."

"Without a horse, you'll be run down and butchered," Horace said. He tapped his spear butt on the stones. "We're going to have to fight against those soldiers. I never thought I'd see the day when something like this happened, the day I'd fight my own kin. We know those men."

Vern walked by with a sword in hand and said, "They should know better."

"That have to follow orders or lose their honor," Horace said. "But you never understood that, did you?"

"I served as well as any, Horace! So, don't you go barking at me. You are a deserter too," Vern flipped his sword around, sheathed it, and drew it again. "I just want to get it over with. I'm tired of standing around."

Cudgel called out from the battlements. "Captain! Horace!" He waved them over. "The assault begins."

The Guardians marched three massive ladders up to the walls and stopped short of the flames.

"What are they doing?" Abraham said. "They can't climb those ladders with all of those flames beneath them. They'll be burned to a crisp."

Down below, Leodor stepped to the forefront. The bookish

older man lifted his hands to the sky. The air shimmered around him, causing his image to blur. He pushed his hands outward. The flaming wood built up along the wall scooted into separate piles, leaving massive gaps between them.

Leodor gave a shout.

The King's Guardians lifted their ladders up and set them against the Stronghold's walls between the gaps. All three of the ladders were wide. The lion-face-helmed warriors climbed up the rungs side by side, two men at a time. Like great metal beasts they came, cold and fearless.

Abraham's throat tightened. "Looks like it's on like Donkey Kong. Anybody got any barrels?" He pulled Black Bane free of the sheath. He looked at Sticks and said, "You better get some armor on. Horace, ready the Henchmen."

63

Lewis stood beside Pratt, observing Leodor's work. The viceroy commanded powers that he didn't comprehend, nor did he care to. The Elders meant nothing to him. The only thing that mattered was the crown. He'd use Leodor and anyone else he could to get it. Pulling his black leather gloves tighter on his hands, he asked, "Pratt, how long do you think that this battle will take?"

Pratt had removed his helmet. He scratched behind his horse-like neck and spoke poignantly, which was surprising for a brute of a man. "Under normal circumstances, I think this matter would be resolved within an hour. These aren't normal circumstances. Ruger Slade is on that roof, along with some of the finest Guardians from our ranks. This could well go into the night before we overtake them. But we will."

Lewis stiffly shook his head. "It should go a lot faster. I have eighty men. They don't even have twenty."

"They have position, but that will change." Pratt's heavy stare followed the Guardians climbing the ladders with ease and haste in full-plate armor. "They won't be a match for the king's armor. I just wish I had a bird's-eye view of it. Prince, I'll ascend the wall if you order me. It would be my pleasure to clash with Ruger."

"If anyone is going to have that pleasure, it will be me," Lewis said.

Leodor returned from the wall. His fingertips were smoking underneath the cuffs of his loose-fitting robes. He bowed. "The deed is done. Now, we watch."

"Isn't there more that you can do, Leodor?" Lewis asked with impatience and irritation. "Can't you summon lightning from the sky to shatter Ruger's troops? Won't the precious Elder of Light do that for you?"

"You speak as if you believe, O Prince. Have you had a sudden change of heart since I moved the flames and sticks?" Leodor asked with his usual forwardness.

"Don't poke at me, Leodor. Can you unleash something more assaulting or not? Summon a demon, perhaps. Maybe a giant insect."

"Summoning such a creature takes a long preparation. And the arrival of those beings is slow going. It takes planning. It's a shame that isn't one of your strong points," Leodor said.

"One of these days, Leodor... one of these days, I remove that tongue of yours."

Leodor rolled his eyes.

"I worship the Elder of Metal," Pratt stated. "He is strong. He builds well-knit men like me. No stone can crush him. The winds bust against his shield." He knocked on his chest plate. "He is good to those that are good to him."

"Good for you, Pratt. Be sure you don't let your Elder worship interfere with your duty to the king."

"Never, sire." Pratt cracked his neck side to side. "Ruger Slade. I never thought he would be so foolish to assault the crown. I never liked him, but he was loyal. It's almost a shame the madness has stricken him."

"Wild dogs must be put down," Lewis said.

"Agreed."

The first wave of Guardians climbed their way up to the battlements on top of the Stronghold. The clamor of battle begun. At the top of the ladders, the first Guardians forced their way between the battlements with shields. Below, their brethren were pushing at their backs. The Henchmen struck against the shield. Steel banged on steel like a small thunderstorm. Men yelled and cried out. They heaved against one another.

The Guardian at the top of the middle ladder successfully pushed his way between the battlements. Suddenly, his entire body catapulted backward. The Guardian plummeted to the ground with a crash. A bald and beefy warrior filled the gap between the battlements with a big grin on his face. He beat his chest.

"Who in Titanuus is that?" Lewis said.

"That's Horace. Four hundred pounds of horse manure in action. The only one as big as he is I," Pratt stated. "I can push through. Just say the word. I'll toss him off of that wall myself."

Lewis studied the bristling action building at the Stronghold's roof. He needed to get this over with before word got out to the king. "Pratt, you have my word. Finish this."

Pratt picked up his helmet and made a crooked smile and said, "My pleasure."

64

Decked out in their chain mail and black leather tunics, the Henchmen fought valiantly against the forces surging between the battlements. Crossbow bolts whistled between the stones as cover fire came from the forces on the ground, making it impossible for the Henchmen to attack from the side.

Abraham and Bearclaw beat against the shields of a Guardian who'd begun powering his way through the gap. He jammed Black Bane clean through the shield. The man behind the lion-crested shield groaned as his body sagged. Abraham pulled his dark sword free. Fresh blood coated the blade. "Damnation!"

The vigorous Guardians behind their fallen brethren pushed their way between the five-foot-wide battlements standing almost as tall as them.

Bearclaw chopped his two-headed battle axe into their legs with devastating impact. He blasted between a Guardian's shin guard and tore out a knee cap. His second swing blasted into the Guardian's midriff. It dented the metal and sent the hobbled man teetering backward. "Death before failure!" He swung again and again.

A new Guardian climbed over the fallen and hacked away at Bearclaw's exposed head. Abraham stretched out his sword and parried the lethal strike away. Steel rang against steel. He batted the Guardian's weapon aside with a swing of his arms. He pulled back and stabbed the Guardian in the heart. The Guardian flung his arms outward and fell backward, yelling, "For the king!"

"This isn't right. It's twisted. We're supposed to be on the same side," Abraham said.

Bearclaw grunted. "The only thing that matters now is who remains above ground and who goes below."

A lion-face helmet popped up over the wall's rim. He struck it in the face. The helmet went askew, but the Guardian kept coming. Bearclaw chopped again. A second Guardian scaled the ladder and grabbed his arm. They wrestled over the weapon.

Abraham crammed his way onto the battlement. He and Bearclaw wrestled back to back against the Guardians. The King's Guardians fought like the lions that their helmets were fashioned after. The manelike plumes rustled in the wind. Fighting them was a shame, a tragedy to kill them. They were following orders with honor. He kicked one in the face. The man's head snapped backward. Bearclaw cut the man in the neck, and the Guardian stumbled from the ladder.

The last Guardian at the top plowed into Bearclaw. His clutching fingers grabbed a hold of Bearclaw's tunic and jerked him toward the ladder. Both men slid down the top steps. Abraham jumped on Bearclaw, grabbed him by the waist, and started hauling him in. "Get back up here!"

With a heave, Bearclaw pushed the Guardian away. The warrior tumbled down the ladder and took several more to the ground down with him. He pushed the empty ladder away from the wall, and it fell down on the Guardians who stood below, agape. The space between the battlement was cleared.

Abraham helped Bearclaw to his feet. They bumped forearms.

"That rocked!" Abraham said.

He'd bought some time on the left side of the Stronghold for the moment, but trouble was coming up the middle. The huge guardian, Pratt, started making his way up that ladder. It bowed and bent underneath his mighty frame. A train of Guardians fell in behind him.

"We better get over there."

Horace stood between the battlements, shaking his fist downward. "I see you, Pratt! You think you can get through me! Try me!" He thumbed his chest. "I'll flatten you!"

Abraham climbed into the battlement. "I'll lend you a hand."

With nostrils flaring, Horace gave him a hard look that could kill. "I don't need a hand. I want him to myself, Captain."

"We can't afford to let them breach the wall. It's a team effort."

Horace put his hand on Abraham's chest and said, "Don't deny me this, Captain. I want him. He's mine."

He looked over the wall, astonished at how quickly the Guardians moved up the ladder in full-plate armor, as though it was no more than chain mail. "I don't doubt you, Horace. You know that." He held out his hand. "I'll hold your spear."

Horace gave a stern nod and stuffed the spear into Abraham's hand. "Thank you, Captain. Death before failure."

"Aye," Abraham said as though he was one of them. "Death before failure."

Pratt's colossal head crested the wall. In his armor, he had the appearance of two men in one. Penetrating eyes burned behind the visor of the helm. The eyes slid over onto Ruger, narrowed, then found Horace. "Hello, fat man."

"Eat boot, Hog Head!" Horace kicked Pratt in the face.

The Guardian's head snapped back, but only a little. He laughed inside his helmet and forced himself from the ladder onto the battlement. Horace met him head on.

Abraham had never witnessed the likes of the battle he was witnessing. The two burly warriors were locked in a tangle of limbs between the battlements, thrashing back and forth. Pratt's metal glove clung to Horace's beard.

He said, "Smile," and punched Horace in the face.

Blood dripped out of Horace's nose. The burly fighter knocked Pratt's hand aside. He grabbed the Guardian's helmet by the mane, ripped it off, and flung it aside. He smiled with blood on his teeth and headbutted Pratt in the chin.

Pratt's shoulders sagged. His thick neck tilted. His pupils filled his irises.

Seizing the moment, Horace jumped Pratt and put him in a headlock. He ratcheted up the pressure. "I'm gonna pop that pumpkin head of yours like a pimple!"

Abraham exchanged a glance with Bearclaw. "I think he's got it under control."

"I never had a doubt," Bearclaw said.

He moved on to the parapets. The Guardians were still at least eighty men deep and still coming. The ladder they'd knocked over earlier was being lowered back against the wall. The Guardians resumed their ascent.

"Here we go again," Abraham said.

Suddenly, Horace let out an angry cry.

Abraham and Bearclaw turned in the direction of the voice.

Pratt was standing between the battlements. He had Horace hoisted up over his head.

"Impossible," Bearclaw said with awe.

With fire in his eyes, Pratt glared at Ruger and said, "You're next." Then he hurled Horace over the side.

65

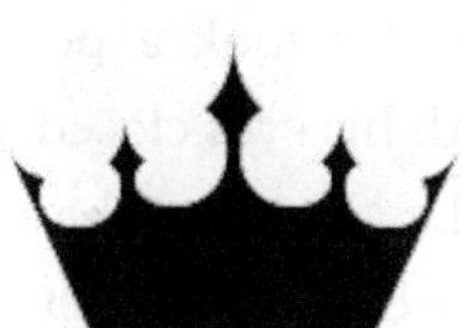

"Nooo!" Abraham screamed. He raced to the wall and looked down where Horace had landed.

The bearish fighter lay face down in the ground. He didn't move. He didn't breathe. A small host of Guardians surrounded Horace. From all appearances, Horace was dead.

"Can he survive a fall like that?" Abraham muttered. He called out, "Horace! Horace!"

Bearclaw hooked his arm and spun him away from the wall. "It doesn't matter. We still have a fight on our hands."

The towering Pratt stood between the battlements. He waved his men through. "For the king, Guardians! Long live the king!"

The Guardians spilled through the gap. Vern, Prospero, and Apollo met them head on with steel banging against steel. The bright steel of swords flashed. Fighters grunted and cursed.

Pratt stepped off the wall and drew his sword out of its sheath, a long handsome blade with an extra-long pommel fit for his hands. He marched right toward Abraham. "It's over. Heh heh.

Much easier than I thought it would be. How disappointing. But I don't want you to surrender. I want you to fight."

With his brows knitted together, Abraham said, "Trust me. You don't want that. I'll down you like a tree."

Pratt smirked, an unnatural fire behind his eyes. He bristled all over with new energy.

The hairs on the nape of Abraham's neck rose. Something was off, something uncanny. He took a peek over the battlements. Leodor was standing with his eyes closed, his thin lips moving like hummingbird wings. Lewis stood beside Leodor. He caught Ruger's eye and made the cut-throat gesture.

Abraham stepped away from the wall. "All right, Pratt. Let's do this."

Pratt's neck muscles flexed. Great veins rose underneath the skin of his neck. He bared his long sword and grinned. "I'm going to enjoy this."

"And I'm going to peel you open like a can of pineapple rings. When you're dying, remember I warned you." Abraham stood in the high point stance. "Show me what you got!"

Pratt cocked his sword back and swung. The metal blades collided with a long ringing effect.

Shockwaves went up Abraham's arms into his shoulders. He shuffled his feet over to the side, fighting to maintain full balance. He'd never been hit by anything so hard before. Pratt struck with the brute animal strength of a bull. His eyes became wild as fire.

Using his superior length, Pratt turned loose a series of one-handed windmill-like chops. The tip of his sword drew sparks from the stone floor he clipped.

Abraham backed away from the deadly windmill of power. He waited for an opening and darted in. He slashed Black Bane across Pratt's abdomen. The tip of his blade skipped off the hardened breast plate.

Pratt backhanded Abraham with a fist, catching Abraham across the cheek. The blow sent him spinning. Pratt followed up with an overhanded chop.

With stars in his eyes, Abraham moved with his momentum, spinning away from the strike and death blow.

"Stand still, you spineless weasel!" Pratt said with a roar. He spat saliva from his lips like a snorting animal. "It's only a matter of time before I finish you off! We'll finish you all off!"

Abraham's battle awareness kicked in. From the corners of his eyes, he could see the Henchmen were fading fast. They were crowded in a corner of the Stronghold's roof, fighting for their very lives, and it was all because of him. "You are a fool, Pratt. You are on the wrong side of right."

"And you are a deserter. I don't care what you say!"

The two warriors thrust and parried against one another with lightning speed. Pratt matched him strike for strike. The ring of steel sang like thunder. Abraham parried the bigger man's attacks and said, "Prince Lewis and Leodor allied against King Hector. If you're a good man, search your heart, and you'll know it's true. Look at you, trying to slaughter your former brethren."

Pratt sliced right over the top of Abraham's ducking head. "You speak the words of a man that is possessed. I don't believe the lies that you spew!"

Abraham stepped up his game. He sent Pratt backward with quick strokes that forced him to parry. He didn't want to kill the man. For the moment, all he wanted to do was talk. "Regardless of what you think, you shall know the truth, and the truth shall set you free."

The rugged-looking Pratt cocked an eye. "I tire of your funny talk. Look around you. All of you are doomed unless you surrender."

Back and forth they went. Sword against sword. Might against might. Skill against superior skill.

"Relent, Pratt, and listen to my words."

"Save them for the afterlife. You're finished, Ruger. The entire kingdom will know that I ended you!" Pratt locked both hands on his sword grip, put his hips into it, and swung.

The blow would have cut a horse in twain. Luckily, Abraham wasn't there to receive it. He leapt high in the air and cracked Pratt between the eyes with the butt of his sword.

Pratt dropped to his knees with a grunt. Blood trickled down into his blinking eyes. "Lucky shot."

Abraham popped him in the jaw. Pratt fell to the ground, his sword slipping free of his fingers.

Abraham kicked Pratt's sword away and said, "Really? I don't feel lucky."

"Ruger!" a woman shrieked.

He turned toward the sound of the voice. Iris was in a choke-hold and being lifted off her feet. The Henchmen were outnumbered three to one. Vern lay bleeding on the ground. Bearclaw's shoulder hung low. Tark limped on a bloody leg. Dominga lay on the ground, not moving, and Sticks was cornered by two Guardians and parrying for her life.

He lifted his arms high and screamed, "I surrender! We surrender!"

66

THE FIGHT WAS OVER. THE BATTLE WAS LOST. ABRAHAM AND HIS henchmen were marched out of the Stronghold, where they kneeled in front of the gloating Prince Lewis and Viceroy Leodor. The only good thing to come out of it was that none of the Henchmen had died, including Horace. The big ox survived the fall. He wasn't moving but lay nearby, stretched out on the ground.

With his usual haughtiness, Prince Lewis said, "You just couldn't die in battle, could you. You had to survive. You had to surrender. Now, I have to do the dirty work."

"Perhaps if Pratt did a better job, you wouldn't have to get your hands even dirtier," Abraham said with a glance at Pratt.

The largest Guardian had blood drying on his face. The bruising over his eyes started to look like a mask.

Abraham looked at Leodor. "What are you smirking at? Even your magic wasn't enough to finish us."

Leodor sank his chin down into his chest. "I wasn't really trying."

Abraham shifted his attention to Lewis. The gloating look in the man's eyes told him that the end of the road was here. "Take me. Leave my men out of it."

Lewis drew his sword and said with an air of authority, "That time has passed. I gave you an opportunity to surrender. Instead, you burrowed. Now, the prince's grace has ended. Now, all of you have assaulted the King's Army. It's an affront to the king himself. The penalty for your reckless incursion is death. Bind him. All of them."

The Guardians bound the Henchmen's ankles together and tied their hands behind their backs. They even did so to the triplets, Selma, Sophia, and Bridgett. The hirelings and Red Tunics were bound up, too. Abraham caught Sticks's gaze, and she didn't have a crease of worry on her countenance.

He mouthed the word "Sorry."

She barely shrugged her brows.

Is this the end of a dream or the beginning of a nightmare? I guess it all has to end one way or the other. What a shame. I was beginning to like this place.

Pratt carried over a large block of wood and dropped it on the ground in front of Abraham.

"You're really good at lifting heavy objects, aren't you? Too bad you suck at swordplay," Abraham said.

"We'll see who sucks when your head hits the ground." Pratt walked away.

Two guardians bent Abraham over the crude chopping block. His head and neck were extended out over the rim. He glanced up at Lewis, who was resting his longsword on his shoulder.

"Don't worry, Ruger. They say the experience is painless," the prince said.

"Oh, I'm not worried about the pain. I'm worried that you'll miss and cut your foot off. You aren't so hot with that steel, either."

"You really know how to piss me off, don't you, Ruger." Lewis stuck his sword point-first in the ground. "How about some poetic justice? Pratt, bring me Black Bane."

67

Lewis ran two fingers down the length of Black Bane's blade and smiled with satisfaction. "I must admit this weapon is quite possibly the finest craftmanship that I've ever seen. I hear that it can cut anything."

"Hand it over, and I'll be happy to show you," Abraham said.

Pratt punched him in the back.

Abraham groaned and said, "Thanks."

Flipping the sword end over end, Lewis said, "Leodor, it is said that the Elders made this sword. If that is true, then why does a man carry it?"

"The Elder's purposes are filled with many mysteries, left to us to figure out for ourselves," the viceroy said. "Then again, perhaps it is a sword made by ordinary men, forged by a craft that was lost ages ago."

Lewis smirked. "I like that answer better."

Abraham didn't care what Lewis thought. *Just keep this blowhard talking. Monologuing always ruins the bad guys. At least it does in my world.* He silently called out to Black Bane. *"Will you do something? Strike down Lewis with lightning. Do something."*

He looked toward the sky. No clouds or birds were there. The chirpings of nature were silent. As in so many fantasy books he'd read before, he hoped to see a dragon or wizard or even the baby Fenix, Simon, swoop down out of the sky and save the day. None of that happened. Not even a wind came. The humidity was stifling.

Abraham took a shot in the dark. "I have no doubt the Elders made it. Only a fool would believe otherwise. I hope you don't think that your feeble hand can wield it. It takes a special person to handle a superior weapon like Black Bane. Strike me down, and you'll only bring the Elders' wrath upon you."

"Your words might frighten the likes of Leodor, but as for me, well"—Lewis thumbed the sword's blade—"I don't believe in the Elders. Now, bite your tongue. It's time to execute your sentence." He lifted the sword over his head with both hands. "Any last words?"

Abraham's heart raced. Blood rushed behind his ears. He strained against his bonds. He tried to think of something riveting to say. Instead, the following words came out: "How much wood could a woodchuck chuck if a woodchuck could chuck wood."

Lewis snorted and said, "Goodbye, Ruger Slade."

"Goodbye, Captain!" Horace bellowed.

Abraham squeezed his eyes shut. With his heart beating in his throat, he managed to say, "Death before failure."

"Absolutely," Lewis said.

The sound of great horns filled the valley.

KAAAAAAH-COOOOOOOOOOO!

KAAAAAAH-COOOOOOOOOOO!

A rustling of armor spread throughout the Guardians' ranks.

"No," Lewis said in a hushed voice.

"The King's Horn!" Horace cried out. "That's the King's Horn!"

Abraham cracked an eye open. The King's Guardians were taking a knee. Lewis's face turned ashen. He stuck Black Bane in the ground, visibly shaken. He seemed to move under a compulsion that was not his own.

Abraham twisted his head around and caught Sticks's eyes. He mouthed the words "What is happening?"

Under her breath, Sticks said, "When the King's Horn sounds, all activity must stop. It's a crime to continue your labors."

Abraham let out a sigh of relief. "That's what I call being saved by the horn." He heard what must have been hundreds of horsemen galloping their way. It sounded like an army. He managed to get a glimpse of the oncoming legion. The soldiers were dressed in the same full-plate armor as the King's Guardians. The only difference was that their helmets were gold plated and the shining steel armor was trimmed in the same gold. They were the king's personal cavalry, known as the Golden Riders. A carriage drawn by a white horse rolled up between the ranks. The carriage was grand, made of polished black oak and painted in gold accents with the crest of the lion face with wings showing on the small flag posts decorating the corners.

Two Golden Riders moved down to the carriage. Someone on the inside pushed the door open, and King Hector poked his head out. He was wearing the small crown on his head. His face showed surprise and frustration, his gentlemanly manner erased from his face. Iron was in his eyes. His forest-green traveling cloak covered him down to his soft leather boots. Everything he wore was finely crafted. He stepped down to the ground and reached his hand into the carriage. Queen Clarann stepped out. The beautiful lioness of a woman wore travel garb similar to the king's. She held her chin high. Her light eyes took in her new surroundings. She looked back as Princess Clarice jumped out of the carriage.

"Oh great," Lewis said underneath his breath. "They even brought the brat with them."

Clarice stood beside her mother, short, young, and vibrant. She was dressed for action in a brown leather tunic. A single rapier hung on her round hips. Her eyes narrowed on Lewis.

King Hector marched right up to his son and looked him dead in the eye.

Lewis swallowed. "Father, what brings you from the House of Steel?"

"What brings me from the House of Steel? You have the gall to ask me that?" King Hector's strong tone carried the weight of a slap in the face. "Am I supposed to recount the running list of transgressions I so recently became aware of?"

Leodor interrupted and said, "Your Majesty, perhaps I can shed some light on the situation."

"You've done enough, Leodor," Hector said without looking at the man. He kept his eyes on Lewis. "You tell me, in your own words, what by the Elders is going on, Son."

Lewis pulled his shoulders back, took a long draw through his nose, cocked his head slightly and said, "It's quite simple. Ruger Slade assaulted me. An assault on the crown means death. I was willing to forgive him, but in his possessed state, well, he rejected my grace with insane and false accusations."

Hector looked down at Abraham and asked, "Is this true? Did you assault my son?"

"I did cut him, your majesty," Abraham said.

"I see many dead," Hector said as he looked at the gash on Lewis's neck. "My Guardians have been downed. Did you attack them as well?"

"We defended ourselves. We didn't want to fight, but we didn't have a choice. King Hector—"

"Silence!" Hector said. "An assault on the crown, its prince, its guards, is an assault on the king himself." He pulled Black Bane from the dirt. "What must be done, must be done."

Lewis's tight expression eased. He smirked at Ruger. "Well said, my king."

Abraham swallowed.

68

"Son, you don't know the half of it," King Hector said. He used the tip of Black Bane and sawed through the cords that bound Abraham.

"Father, what are you doing?" Lewis whined.

"I'm getting to the bottom of this, once and for all." Hector helped Abraham to his feet. He pointed at the Stronghold's front door. "We'll convene in there. Lewis, Leodor, go inside. Clarann and Clarice, follow me. Pratt, you come, along with four of my Golden Riders. Ruger, choose one of your own to enter too."

"Yes, Your Majesty," Abraham said. He wasn't sure what to make of the sudden turn of events, but he felt something big was happening.

He'd never seen much of King Hector before. This time, however, a fire was in him. He stole a glance at Queen Clarann. She was looking right at him and quickly looked away.

He moved over to Sticks and undid the cords that bound her. "You're coming to the last dance with me."

"You're the Captain," Sticks said.

The inside of the Stronghold was mostly intact but smoky. It was stuffy and smelled of burning embers more than anything.

Queen Clarann coughed lightly. King pulled the chair out at the head of the table. "Seal those doors."

With the help of Pratt, two Golden Riders shoved a large slab of stone into the doorway.

"King Hector, shall we bar it?" Pratt asked.

"No, I'm only concerned with prying ears. I don't want the Guardians to see what is about to happen. What happens inside these rooms stays here." He tapped the table then rubbed the soot between his fingers.

Clarann and Clarice sat on his right. Lewis and Leodor took seats on the left. Abraham and Sticks hung at the other end of the table, sitting on the same bench as Lewis and Leodor.

King Hector reached for Clarann's hand and held it tight. He faced his son. "I want you to tell me the truth. What are you into? What is going on?"

"I told you. Ruger assaulted me. I wouldn't tolerate it any more than you would," Lewis replied.

Abraham wanted to object, but he kept his mouth shut.

"Father, you know that he lies," Clarice said. "He's always lied about one thing or another. Every path he takes is full of treachery."

Without taking his eyes off his son, Hector coolly said, "Be silent, Daughter. Lewis, am I supposed to believe that you and your cohort Leodor had nothing to do with the Brotherhood of Ravens overrunning the streets of Burgess? Am I to believe that they acted on their own volition because of him?" He pointed at Ruger. "It sounds preposterous."

Lewis sat with his arms crossed over his chest and said, "I do not keep track of the enemies that Ruger has made. I can imagine that he has many. Look at him. He has the look of a criminal, not to mention that he is a loon."

"So why didn't you notify me, eh?" the king asked. "You used my Guardians in an all-out assault. Now many of them are dead. In the midst of coming war, you treat my soldiers like chaff."

"I could not let this madman escape. He wounded me. He assaulted the crown. Ruger Slade is a wild dog that needs put down." Lewis took his gloves off and fanned himself. "I am the prince. I am trusted with many liberties that do not need your approval. Am I wrong, Father?"

"This is a special circumstance. You know that." King Hector looked down the table at Ruger. "Let's hear your end of it."

"Father, I insist, he's guilty. He's been judged. He is not worthy of your audience," Lewis said.

"This is the man that saved my queen. I will hear him out before I decide what is to be done. You be silent." The King looked at Sticks. "Who is this that you brought with you?"

"This is my second in command. Her name is Sticks," Abraham said.

"Ah, and she is your witness?" the King asked as his gaze gave her further study.

"She is."

"Out with it, then. And make it quick... Abraham," the King said.

Abraham ran through his theory of how Lewis and Leodor were sabotaging the Henchmen's missions. He explained how they'd caught Prince Lewis red-handed with the assassin, Raschel, who Twila either was or worked for. How that happened, he didn't bother to explain. It was still a theory. His story against Lewis and Leodor's. He finished the story by saying, "Prince Lewis and Leodor, I have no doubt, are behind many of your troubles. I don't know who they serve, but I don't believe it's you."

King Hector leaned back in his seat. His eyes looked upward and scanned the ceiling. He took a deep breath, dropped his eyes to Sticks, and asked, "And you verify this account?"

With her head down, Sticks said, "I do, Your Majesty."

"What do you make of this, Leodor? Is it true that my long-time servant is working against the crown?" the king asked.

"Your Majesty, I know that you cannot put your trust in an otherworlder. He is a demon that spews lies and tall tales. He's been desperate ever since he, well, changed." Leodor gave Ruger a sorrowful look. "You cannot trust a word that he says."

Clarice came out of her seat. "Father, they are lying through their rotten teeth!"

Clarann pulled her daughter back down. "Be silent, child."

Clarice grunted and glared at Lewis.

"As you should know, Abraham, it is your word versus the blood of the crown," the king said. "I have no choice but to take my son's word over yours."

Lewis gave Ruger a winning smile.

"However," the king said.

Lewis's head snapped around. His mouth gaped.

King Hector continued as he pulled out the emerald stone from the fold of his cloak. "I didn't bring all of us inside here to have a pissing contest. I brought us all here to find the truth, no matter how much it might hurt." He gripped the emerald pendant in his hand. Green fire illuminated between his fingers and knuckles. His eyes reflected the same mystic fire. "Golden Riders, see to it that Lewis and Leodor remain seated."

The soldiers walked up behind Lewis and Leodor and clamped their metal gauntlets down on their shoulders.

Leodor's jaw hung. His body trembled.

Lewis cried out like a spoiled child, "No, Father, nooo!"

69

KING HECTOR HELD HIS GLOWING FIST IN FRONT OF HIS SON LEWIS'S face and said, "Tell me, are you using the Brotherhood or Ravens to thwart my plans?"

Lewis squirmed. His jaw opened and closed as he stared at the king's hand as if it was a snake about to strike. "Father, you must believe meee!" Sweat beaded his face. His skin became ashen and clammy.

"Answer me!" Hector demanded as he pushed the emerald stone up between his thumb and finger.

The gem floated into the air and hovered at eye level before Lewis. It shone like a brilliant star, lighting the room up with eerie illumination.

Abraham's own stomach twisted. The power of the stone gripped his heart. Something about it made all the darkness he'd buried want to come out. It was cleansing, and the king wasn't even targeting him, but the king had used it on him before. He glanced at Sticks. Her eyes were wide with fascination. She panted and held a hand over her heart. He reached over and held her other hand.

"Out with it, Son," the King said. "Did you hire the Brotherhood of Ravens to sabotage the Henchmen's efforts or not?"

Lewis growled in his throat as if a demon had been trapped inside him and wanted to get out. He rocked stiffly back and forth, but the Golden Riders held him fast. His facial features became a kaleidoscope of twisting emotion. The whites of his eyes cracked with red. With his fingernails digging into the table, he tossed his head back and shouted with unfettered rage, "Fine! I did it! Using the wings of the Ravens, I've sabotaged your stupid, ignorant, hopeless missions, Father!" He was sneering now. "You blind old fool, stuck in your old ways, refusing to budge when the world is changing. Yes, I did it!"

"Who else is behind this?" the King asked.

Lewis's eyebrows clenched together, and he looked at his father as though he was some kind of fool. He sneered and said with disdain, "Well, Leodor, of course. Who do you think made your whore of a queen so sick! Who do you think helped me plan the operations? Hmmm? Do you really think I could have done all of this alone? I had plenty of help."

King's Hector's nostrils flared. He breathed deeply, looked at Leodor and said, "So, Lewis's statement is accurate. You poisoned the queen. You conspire with him, and against the crown."

Leodor's sweaty lips wriggled underneath his nose. His tired eyes held the radiant shine of the stone. Finally, he licked his mouth and said, "I did not make the queen sick. She was diseased. I simply didn't aid her. Need I remind Your Majesty that, as a member of the Sect, I am a neutral party? I serve my order. I serve the Elders. I am washed clean of any crimes."

"Who else is in league with you? Are there more conspirators in my midst?" the king asked. "Tell me how all of this came to be?"

"The only other is Raschel," Lewis said as he tried to stare away from the stone. "She was my spy among the Henchmen. She used her power to steal the identity of a commoner named Twila. Aside from me and Leodor, she is the only one in the kingdom."

Abraham had the explanation he needed. He didn't understand it fully, but clearly, Raschel had become Twila. Given his own situation, anything was possible.

The king wasn't finished. "What drives this conspiracy, Lewis? Hmmm? Why would you turn your back against your own father, who has given you everything, you spoiled son?"

"Clarann. I hate her. She is not my mother. She's a commoner of the streets. No royal blood defines her. She is the scum that coats the bottom of my boots on my feet." Lewis managed to tear his eyes away from the stone to glare at Clarann and her daughter, Clarice. "They are cattle born."

The King grabbed his son's arm and said, "Clarann has been nothing but kind to you. You've had no reason to turn against your father or the crown. There is much more behind this. Perhaps your anger was used to turn your heart against me. Who is behind this attack? Hmmm?" His eyes slid between Lewis and Leodor. "Tell me."

"I'll tell you, Father. I'd be glad to. You don't even need your precious stone, now that the truth is out." Lewis looked his father dead in the eye. "I serve the Underlord. And soon, that crown on your head will be mine."

"No, that's not true, Son." King Hector held his open palm underneath the stone. Its fire went out, and the emerald dropped into his hand. He closed his fingers around it. "Both of you betrayed the crown. There is only death for you."

"FATHER, YOU CAN'T BE SERIOUS," LEWIS SAID WITH GAPING astonishment. "You can't kill your own son. I'm your one and only heir. Your bloodline ends without me."

King Hector looked Lewis dead in the eyes and said, "Under eyewitness testimony, you've given me over a dozen reasons to have you hanged, quartered, guillotined. You've betrayed your king, queen, and country. Worst of all, you turned against your own family." The king let go of his son's forearm and shook his head sadly. "And I had such high hopes for you. No man is greater than his citizens or his country. You've been taught that a hundred times. It is a sad day indeed."

Abraham felt bad for King Hector. His only son had turned against him, for what seemed to be little or no reason at all. Lewis was an even bigger jerk than he'd imagined, a spoiled and pompous brat. He got the feeling that something else was brewing, something much bigger than the situation at hand. *Who in the world is the Underlord?*

King Hector stood up and pulled his dagger out of his belt. It had a razor-sharp edge and a jewel-encrusted handle. "Stand Lewis up, men."

"Wh-what are you doing?" Lewis asked. "You aren't going to kill me here, are you, in cold blood. I-I-I get a trial. I have to have a trial."

"I am the judge! I am the jury! I am the king!" Hector yelled. He pointed the dagger at Leodor. "Stand up that spineless jackal as well!"

As the Golden Riders jerked him up, the smarmy Leodor said, "An assault on me is an assault on the Sect, Your Majesty. You will lose all of their support in the coming wars."

"I reckon I lost it a long time ago," the king said. "Put them on their knees."

Abraham sat on the edge of his seat. *I can't believe the king's going to get blood on his hands.*

Leodor continued his rant. "I've always served you honorably, King Hector. I always will. I was only serving the interest of your son, which you asked me to do. Perhaps I became caught up in it. Spare me, O King. It is what is best for the kingdom. You can't win a war with the Sect against you. I can help."

"You can't be trusted. Neither of you can. As much as it grieves me, I have no other course but to take your lives for those that have been taken." He lifted the dagger before his face. "And I must do this by my own hand."

"Father, no!" Leodor whined. "You can't do this. I-I'll change. I'll make amends. I promise! Father, spare me, please spare me. You are the king. You can do it."

"No man is above the law. Not even me. Kingsland cannot survive on lawlessness. A kingdom without laws is not a kingdom at all." He looked from his son back to his dagger. "This is the Dagger of Death. Its strike is death. This will be the first time in decades I have used it." He looked at Golden Riders holding the two traitors fast. "Hold them still."

"No, no, no, no, no," Lewis pleaded.

Abraham knew the king was a man who would see justice meted out, but this was becoming disturbing. He didn't doubt that Lewis and Leodor had it coming. The number of crimes they had committed would have been countless, but to see the king undertake the execution was another matter. It didn't seem normal for King Hector to execute his own son. *Let Pratt do it or someone else.* He stole a look at Clarann and Clarice. Both of them sat rigid as a ramrod and holding hands with white knuckles. Mercy was in their eyes, in both ladies, but they dared not speak out in defiance of their king.

"It will be quick. It will be painless," the king said. "I'm sorry, Son, that I must do this. May the Elders forgive you." He slowly drew his hand back with the dagger poised to strike.

With his eyes locked on the dagger, Lewis gulped for air like a fish out of water.

Abraham couldn't take it any longer. "No, wait!"

The king froze and slowly turned his head toward Abraham. "Do you have something to say?"

"Brand them," Abraham blurted out. "They can't betray you if you brand them. They'll die if they do, right?"

King Hector lowered the dagger. His hard stare began to soften. "The branded must be a willing participant. I don't think these two are willing."

"I am, Father. I am!" Lewis seemed elated.

"I'd rather not, but I will," Leodor said with the energy of a defeated old man.

King Hector looked back at Queen Clarann and asked, "What do you think?"

"There is no other choice. It is the Brand, or it is death," Clarann said.

"Abraham, or Ruger, where is the Brand?" the king asked.

That was a good question. Abraham hadn't actually seen it before. All he knew was that Ruger's former host, Eugene Drisk, had branded many. Dominga was one of the more recent ones.

"I, uh…" Abraham said.

"I know where it is," Sticks said. "I shall fetch it with your permission. It's inside the Stronghold.

"Then fetch it, young lady," the king ordered. He looked at Lewis and Leodor. "Strip them down to the waist."

Sticks glided over to the right side of the room and stood before the fireplace, a large one made from stone. The hearth and mantle were made of granite. She got down on her knees and pushed the top of the hearth aside. She reached into the raised hearth and produced the Brand. It was a long rod of iron with a crown shape on the end. She walked it over to the king.

With a bow, she said, "Here it is, Your Majesty."

King Hector took the Brand and nodded. "Thank you. Pratt, start a fire. Let the King's Branding commence."

71

Starting the fire didn't take Pratt long. The dried wood burned yellow-orange and started to pop and crackle. Abraham had seen enough fire for the day, but one more wouldn't hurt him. King Hector had given him the King's Brand. He wore a thick leather glove and held it in the flames. The brand wasn't an ordinary length of iron that one stuck to livestock. This one was different. Runes, much like the ones that decorated Black Bane's blade, twisted in rigid patterns all the way along the shaft. The brand itself was an open-faced crown with six horns. It glowed hot blue, not red. Wispy mystic smoke feathered up from the brand into the chimney. Bright bluish and green sparkles went with it.

"Come over here, Abraham. I believe the Brand is ready," King Hector said.

Abraham gave Sticks a long look as he turned away from the flames. Her eyes were fixed on the burning brand. He moved beside King Hector, who faced Lewis and Leodor, down on their knees. Leodor's body trembled as he wobbled in his stance.

King Hector took the brand from Abraham. "This is the King's

Brand, created ages ago, as a seal of honor, to those who would faithfully serve the king. The king of Kingsland, that is. It is not an ordinary brand used for livestock or slaves. With this brand comes power. It grants life. It grants death. The Brand, this crown"—he pointed at the end of the Brand—"is placed over the heart. It will know your intentions. Serve the crown and be blessed. Betray the crown, be cursed and face death."

The well-knit Lewis looked up into his father's eyes and said, "Save the theatrics and get it over with. I don't want to hear some yarn about how Elders crapped it out, either. I'd rather—eee-argh!"

King Hector jammed the brand against Lewis's chest, just above the heart. The stench of frying skin filled the air. He pulled the brand back. It tore from the flesh it had charred. The burned image of the crown ebbed a deep blue. The color faded and reddened like blood.

"Titanuus's crotch, that hurt!" Lewis said.

Beside him, Leodor trembled like a leaf.

Panting, Lewis looked at the viceroy and added, "I can't wait to see how this turns out."

Leodor's sagging skin hung from his scrawny frame in a pathetic display of manliness. He didn't appear fit enough to push an empty wheelbarrow. His tired eyes blinked rapidly, and sweat ran down his temple. "Er, your majesty, this brand is a severe conflict of interest with my contract with the Sect. It cannot be."

King Hector jammed the brand over the frail man's heart.

Leodor flung his arms backward. His mouth dropped open, and black smoke came out.

The queen and princess gasped. The king stepped in front of them and said, "Elders of Light, what is that?"

The black smoke spilled out of Leodor's mouth like lava spewing out of a volcano. It took a humanoid shape and form, made like lumpy clouds. It floated around the room with two glimmering spots for its eyes, showing like bright diamonds. A haunting moaning sound came from its body.

"Begone, wicked spirit," King Hector said. He waved the brand at it.

The black spirit shifted away, floated quickly toward the fireplace, and went into the chimney. A gust of hot wind blasted through the room, and a shrieking moan followed. As quickly as the dark spirit had come, it was gone.

Leodor lay on the floor, hugging the Golden Riders like a baby. Chill bumps were all over his body.

"What happened, Leodor?" King Hector asked. "What was that thing?"

Leodor shook his head. He finally looked at the king and said, "That was the Spirit of the Sect. With it comes power of the order. Elders, no! I've been stripped of my majesty."

"At least you're not dead," Princess Clarice said.

"I might as well be," Leodor replied. He ran his shaking fingers over the burnt flesh on his scrawny chest. "I never saw this coming."

Sticks jumped in front of King Hector and took a knee. She removed her bandoliers of knives and her tunic and pulled her shirt down, exposing her chest. "King Hector, Your Majesty, will you brand me?"

Hector looked down on her and said, "No. I've done my bidding. I am king, not the leader of the Henchmen." He tossed the brand to Abraham. "He's the leader of the Henchmen, and under my authority, all that are branded must follow him, and he must follow me."

Holding the brand in his grip, Abraham looked down into Sticks's eyes and asked, "Are you sure you want this?"

"I never wanted it gone in the first place."

He branded her.

Sticks moaned, but not a tear was shed from her eyes.

Hector fanned his nose. "Good gravy, it's really beginning to stink in here. If we are done, then push away those stones. I want to get some fresh air." He faced Pratt. "You are the commander of the King's Guardians now." He glanced at his grimacing son. "Don't foul it up. There will be no mercy or brand for you."

The broken-nosed Pratt dropped to a knee and bowed. "I will not fail you, my king."

The Golden Riders moved toward the front and started moving the stones from the doorway that closed them in. King Hector started heading that way when Clarice dropped in front of him. "Father, stop. I have a request. You told me yesterday on my sixteenth year of life, that you would grant me anything I wished."

King Hector lifted a brow, gave Queen Clarann a curious look, and said, "Certainly I did, but now is not the proper time to settle the matter."

"But it is. I'm of proper age, an adult, ready for marriage, right?" she said.

"Oh, please don't tell me that you want to marry Ruger."

Clarice made a shocked expression and said, "Well, no. I'm not leaning that way at all. I would like him to train me."

"If that is your request, no doubt it can be arranged, but we have more important matters to attend to. Come, Clarice. Since you are an adult now, exercise the proper time and place to make your conversations. You need to work on that impulsiveness of yours."

From her knees, Clarice grabbed the king's hand. "You misunderstand. I don't want sword lessons as my gift. I want to be a Henchman. I want the King's Brand."

72

"I MUST BE A COMPLETE FOOL. IT'S NO WONDER MY KINGDOM IS IN flux. Look at this place," King Hector said.

Late in the evening of the same day, Abraham discreetly escorted King Hector into the city of Burgess. They made their way into one of the Sect's larger cathedrals. Lewis and Leodor accompanied them along with half a dozen Guardians, led by Pratt, dressed in street clothes. Abraham walked quietly beside the king. That day had been a long one for the old man. He found out his own son and top confidant had betrayed him. To make matters worse, his coming-of-age daughter, Clarice, had been branded. Abraham felt for the man.

Gazing up at the rafters of the gaunt cathedral's ceiling, King Hector said, "This place is vile. There's no light, no hope, no soft burning candles. It was not like this when I was young. What sort of place has this become?"

"It gets worse," Lewis said. "I never cared for these false places of worship to begin with."

Leodor moved to the front of the cathedral as if his legs were made of stone. Since he'd been branded, he acted like a shell of the man he was before. He moved about like a wounded cripple. Leaving the Guardians behind, he led the rest of the group down to the vaults below, not stopping until they passed rows of sarcophagi and faced the great mirror in the back. His natural forwardness was gone, replaced by emptiness. "This is the place you seek."

"Get on with it, Leodor. I don't have time for your stalling," the king said.

The group stood in front of a brown canvas covering something hanging from a black wall. Leodor tugged on the fabric while Lewis lifted three candlestands made of bronze from the ground. Skulls were mounted on the tops of the stands. Candles were held firmly in the tops of the skulls. He made a triangle around the group. Leodor's efforts with the cover revealed a ten-foot-by-ten-foot mirror. The bronze frame was made of demonic images.

"What sort of practices have you embraced, Lewis? What perversion flipped your mind inside out?" the king asked.

Lewis looked away from his father with a deep frown on his face.

"So, this is where you speak to the Underlord," King Hector said.

"Yes, Your Majesty," Leodor replied.

Staring at the mirror, the king said, "Well, I didn't come here to look at myself. Summon this Underlord. I want to get a look at him for myself."

"I will warn Your Majesty that this is very dangerous. The Underlord wields great strength. It is imperative that you stay within the barrier." Leodor stepped inside the triangle.

He stuck his finger on the front candlestand's candle wick. A green flame ignited. A fat little demon like a jack-o'-lantern formed with a grin on his face. It jumped from candlestand to candlestand and merged into the last one with a giggling hiss. All the candles burned brightly. Leodor closed his eyelids and started chanting.

The candle flames quavered. Abraham's skin crawled. Dark, disturbing forces that unsettled his soul were at work. He put a hand on his sword as the air shimmered around him. The old Abraham would have bolted. The new one stood fast, strengthened by the steely resolves of Ruger's fearless body.

Their reflection in the great mirror pinwheeled into black, gray, and white. The tiny demonic eyes that dressed the mirror's edge burned like ruby-red beacons. A new image formed in the mirror as it became crystal clear, like a portal to another room. It was a throne room with black curtains outlining panes of glass filled with pale blue light that made for a dreary setting. A man sat on a king's throne made of ebony marble. His cruel expression was old, smooth, and wizened. With eyes like burning sapphires and skin as pale as stone, the man clad in black leather from wrist to ankle rose to his feet and came forward.

King Hector waited behind Lewis and Leodor. Abraham stood right behind him.

The Underlord came closer. From head to toe, he filled the mirror. "Leodor," he said in a strong voice that was as cold as ice. "What news do you bear? Who are these men that come with you?"

As Lewis and Leodor shrank underneath the Underlord's iron gaze, King Hector pushed between them with his head held high. He spoke with a resounding authority that only the king could manifest. "I am no man. I am the king!"

The Underlord's dark, beady eyes widened as his head recoiled. "What treachery is this?"

"Am I to understand that you don't know treachery when you

see it? That's disappointing to hear from a serpent as vile as you." King Hector pointed at the Underlord. "Wait a moment. You may have changed your image, but I know that face. You can't hide behind those veins of yours. Yes, yes, that build and frame, so womanly, but still a man. Arcayis! Ha, it is you, isn't it, you loathsome swine?"

"Mind your tongue, you spoiled brat," the Underlord said. "This switch I bring on you this time you'll never forget." His bright burning eyes darkened. "It will be fatal next time."

Abraham couldn't help himself and butted in. "You know this man?"

King Hector gave him a quick look and said, "Oh yes, I know this worm. This scum of the sewers. He was my father's right-hand mystic, much like Leodor." He glared at the forward mystic. "And betrayed him. I was a boy, very young, but I was around when this leech was banished. Hmmm." He rubbed his chin. "And now it seems that the crap has finally risen to the surface."

"You are the same fool that your father was, Hector. Except you are still the same naïve, pompous, useless brat." The Underlord spat after he spewed out the last words. "Your kingdom has unraveled beneath you." He spread his arms wide. "I control all of the armies north of you. I manipulate your cities. I am the shadows. I am the wind." He held out a stone the size of his finger. It was a dark-blue sapphire burning with the radiant fire of a star, much like the similar emerald the king held. He smiled like a crocodile. "I am Kingsland's end."

"You are a bag of wind!" Hector said with growing agitation.

"Good-bye, Hector. Enjoy your throne." Arcayis the Underlord walked backward. "And you can have those two stooges. I never really needed them anyway. For every one of them, I have many. And I have weapons the likes of which you've never seen before." With a wave of his hand, the image of the mirror faded.

Abraham stood staring at the reflection in the mirror. The king's eyes were heavy with worry. Lewis and Leodor appeared uncertain. Abraham wanted to return home. Whoever Arcayis was, his reappearance shook the king visibly. Even though the king showed strength in the moment, he seemed to have aged.

"Are you okay?" Abraham asked.

King Hector gave Abraham a blank stare. Then his eyes hardened. He turned on Leodor and grabbed him by the neck. He pushed the former viceroy to his knees. "Leodor, what do you know about him? I want to know everything."

73

EARLY IN THE NIGHT, ABRAHAM AND STICKS SEPARATED FROM THE king and made the long walk on the country roads back to the Stronghold. Some frightening things appeared to be going on in Kingsland. The once-peaceful land by the sea had become a place burdened by mistrust. He needed answers about his predicament. His gut told him that the Underlord might be someone that could help him. *If King Hector couldn't trust his own son, whom could he trust? Whom can I trust?*

Walking side by side with Sticks, he bumped shoulders with her. "How's your brand?"

"I'd be lying if I said it didn't hurt, but it will go away. I've been branded before," she said as she pulled her jerkin open, revealing the puffy pinkish-red wound. "Looks worse than it feels."

"Why did you do it? I mean, you could have started a new life."

"True, but I didn't have much of a life before I was branded, and I like being a Henchman." She gave him the eye. "There isn't anything wrong with that, is there? You almost sound disappointed."

He shook his head. "No, no, not at all. I mean, I don't have anyone else. I just wanted to make sure that you did it for yourself and not me." He gave her a sheepish look and said, "You didn't do it because you're in love with me, did you?"

"Ha ha," she said in a very dry manner. "Just because you're the last man I slept with doesn't mean you're going to be the last man that I sleep with. Don't get me wrong, I enjoy your company, but what I do, I do for me and the king. I like the purpose it gives me."

Sticks was as easy to read as a blank wall. Abraham was pretty sure she could keep her feelings to herself, and only she would know them. If she cared deeply, she wouldn't show it. If she hated him, she wouldn't show that either.

"It's not about me," Abraham said. "I figured it was possible that maybe you and Ruger had a deeper thing that I wouldn't be aware of."

"We didn't. With the last personality, it was only sexual."

Abraham couldn't help but smile. "If you say so, Lilith. That's good to know."

"Who's Lilith?"

"A frosty woman from a TV show. I'm not so sure you'd understand."

"Ah, from your world."

"Yes, a place where everybody knows my name."

They took the rest of the long walk in silence. The road to the Stronghold had become roughshod from all the king's horses and all the king's men. The smell of burning pitch and charred wood lingered heavy in the air. Smoke came out of the chimney's stack. Abraham scanned the area. The barn had burned to the ground, and heat was still rising from the ash. The split-rail fencing, aside from a few posts, was gone, burned with the rest of the wood piles used to smoke them out. It had been one helluva day. He wasn't sure how Ruger's body had held up under the grueling tasks he'd performed, but he felt fine. He stopped in front of the barn's ashes. It was the last place he'd seen Solomon.

"If his bones are in there, I don't want to know," he said.

Together, they went back inside the Stronghold. He expected to see some of the hirelings, but what he didn't expect to see was all the seats at table filled with the Henchmen. All of them turned and looked at him. Horace was in his usual seat, leaning heavily on his forearms. Dominga and Vern leaned against one another, battered from head to toe. Bearclaw had cuts on his arms and face. Cudgel and Tark stopped talking to look in Abraham's direction. Apollo and Prospero looked no different than they normally did, dirty and a little deranged. Iris got up from her seat, shuffled over to Abraham, and gave him a hug.

Slowly, Abraham walked into the room, eyeballing all of them, and said, "So, what's going on?"

"Captain, we've been conversing while we waited for your return," Horace said. He squeezed his eyes shut and grimaced before opening them wide again. "Did matters fare well with the king?"

"I don't think any of the king's business is going well." Feeling uncertain, Abraham pulled back his chair at the head of the table as Sticks took her seat across from Horace. "So, what was it that you were discussing?"

Horace looked down the rows of hardened men and women and said, "We want to be branded again. We want to stay Henchmen."

Abraham's eyebrows lifted. "All of you?" He looked at Vern when he said it.

The swordsman had taken more lumps than the rest of the group. His right eye was black, and he had a gash over the top of his head with a crude white bandage over it.

"Even me," Vern said through split lips.

"You don't want to be a part of the King's Guardians?" Abraham asked.

Bearclaw spoke up and said, "Lewis was such a jerkoff we decided against it. We'd made our minds up even before what happened today. And Pratt, well, horse-neck can have it. There is no sense in working with a man with a grudge against you."

"I don't think his grudge is against me but, rather, the old me." He waved his hands, tilted his head, and said, "Did you say *jerkoff*?"

"Is that not the proper use of it?" Bearclaw said.

"No, that's right, I didn't realize you'd picked that word up from me. It sounded strange coming from you, that's all." Abraham studied their eyes, which were looking right back at him.

The intent they wore on their faces was clear. They wanted to be Henchmen for some crazy reason. Inside his heart, he felt relief. If he was going to get out of this world, he would need help. He couldn't think of any better people than them. "Listen, I want to be clear about something." He touched his chest with his fingers. "I'm not from this world. I want to find my way home. I don't want to use you to do that. And what if Ruger changes again?"

Horace laid a heavy hand on his forearm. "No disrespect, Captain, but we've discussed that. We want to be Henchmen."

At a loss for words, Abraham blinked and managed to say, "None taken." He looked at the fireplace. The King's Brand was propped up against the hearth. The fire logs burned within. Abraham rose from his chair, picked up the brand, and put it in the fire. "I'm not going to mince words. Who's first?"

The branding started with Horace. The bearded and bald warrior stood on a shaky knee. The brand seared his hair and flesh, and he let out a joyous shout. After him went Bearclaw, Vern, Dominga, Tark, Cudgel, Iris, and Prospero. The scruffy-looking

Apollo finished it off, holding his nose and shouting, "Shew! That's a stink you never forget!"

The great room was filled with painful grins as the Henchmen exchanged handshakes with one another. The hireling women brought in pitchers of wine and ale from the cellars and placed them on the table before waddling off again.

Abraham stood with the brand in the fire, scorching off any flecks of hair and flesh. The small chatter in the room quieted. A presence entered the room. He turned. Solomon stood inside of the front doorway.

"You're alive," Abraham said. "I thought you were burned alive. Where have you been?"

The troglin lifted up a long arm and wiggled his fingers. "I've been hiding. This race has a knack for hiding in the woodland." He walked over to Abraham and took a knee. "I've been waiting for your return. I wasn't sure how the others would receive me without you present." He glanced at Horace. "Brand me."

"What?" Abraham said. "Are you sure?"

"You heard me. It's not the hippy thing to do, but I need you, and you need me." He closed his eyes. "Get it over with. Brand me."

Abraham stuck the brand on Solomon's chest. The skin and hair sizzled.

Solomon let out a wild howl. Clutching his chest, he said, "Man, that was a stupid idea!"

"It will pass." Abraham slapped Solomon on the shoulder and extended a hand. "Welcome to the Henchmen."

74

EPILOGUE

ABRAHAM WAS SUMMONED TO THE HOUSE OF STEEL, WHERE HE
alone met with the king, queen, prince, princess, and ex-viceroy
on the terrace that overlooked the Bay of Elders. Long looks were
on the faces of everyone sitting at the long patio table. None was
longer than King Hector's, who sat at the head. He was in a heated
discussion with Clarice.

"Clarice, my daughter, my dearest, just because you have the
King's Brand, it doesn't mean that you are required to go
anywhere. You will stay at the castle, and that is final." King
Hector rubbed his temples and sighed. "Why would you burden
me with such a mad request?"

"Father, I am a woman, free to choose my own future. I don't
want to be pampered and spoiled," Clarice said. She wore a black
leather tunic, and her hair flowed back in a ponytail. "You see how
that turned out with Lewis. This way, I can never betray you or the
kingdom."

"Watch your mouth, you brattish hedgehog," Lewis said. "If
you and your mother weren't in the picture, there wouldn't be an

issue. You should have stayed in the streets where you belong. Instead, you've poisoned the bloodline."

"You are the one that poisoned the bloodline, Son, not Clarice," King Hector said. He noticed Abraham standing away from the table. "Oh, you're here. Good." He cast his glance behind Abraham to where Pratt, the new captain of the King's Guardians, stood. The knight seemed like a giant in his suit of full-plate armor. "Pratt, thank you for bringing him up. See to it that our privacy is maintained." King Hector got up, then reached down and squeezed the queen's hand. "Talk some sense into our daughter."

Queen Clarann gave the king a warm smile and said, "I will." When the king turned away, her beautiful light eyes fixed on Ruger and searched his for a moment.

Abraham nodded and followed after the king to the outer wall. The queen's deep look made the heart inside his body jump. *What was that all about?* Something had told him something more might have existed between Ruger and the Queen—he'd seen those looks before. *But what?* If something was there, only she knew. He looked back, but the queen was in a deep conversation with Lewis and Clarice.

He moved beside the king at the wall, hitched his thumbs inside his sword belt, and asked, "Did Leodor share anything revealing about the Underlord?"

"It appears that the fool is just a pawn. The same as my son was. Disgusting." From a pouch of bird seed and crumbs, he started feeding the sea birds flocking toward him. He flicked crumbs of bread at them. The gray-white birds would dive after what they didn't catch in the air. "I can't have a lineage to my heritage if I don't have a trustworthy son."

"Surely you have other sons and daughters?"

The king gave him a puzzled look and said, "I forget that you don't know things as you did. But Lewis is the one we have to dance with." He reached inside his green raiment and pulled out the colorful cube. "The Cube of Rubix. As you can see, I've completed one side," he said proudly. One side of the cube was green. "Tell me honestly—will it truly grant me a wish if I solve it?"

Abraham struggled between the truth or the lie but chose the truth. "No, I only told you that to save my own skin."

"That's too bad. I could really use a wish right now." King Hector twisted the blocks of the cube around. He looked as if he'd aged ten years in a day. "It is fun. Do me a favor. Don't tell Leodor that it lacks magical properties. It will be another carrot that I dangle before him if the need ever be."

"I won't, and I apologize."

"It is I that should be apologizing to you."

The way the king said that and looked at him made his hairs stand on end. "For what?"

"For using you, a stranger, in this strange world. After my lengthy discussions with Leodor and a thorough search of the library's annals, I've come to the conclusion that the only way to save this kingdom is to complete the Crown of Stones." He pointed at the crown on his head with six empty settings. "I have one stone. I believe that Arcayis has one other. I'm not sure what power it wields, but whoever has them all will have the power to reunite the kingdoms or dismantle them forever." He put the cube away. "You'll lead the Henchmen to find the remaining stones before Arcayis does. When that is complete, I'll see what I can do to help you find a way back to your world. Selfishly, I admit, I need you."

Abraham had hoped he would be given some time to sort through his own dilemma. Now he'd been placed in charge of a grand quest that he didn't want any part of. But he'd promised to help the king, and perhaps helping the king would help himself. Besides, if they found another portal back... *Who could stop me from going home?*

"I'll do my best, but I'm still a fish out of water in this world. Are you sure that you want to put your trust in me?"

"Regrettably, you're the only one proven to be trustworthy so far." The king set down the bag of bird meal and dusted off his hands. He stared down at the ships docked in the Bay of Elders. His eyes searched the skies where flocks of huge birds flew in the distance. "According to Leodor, you will have the better understanding of the artifacts that Arcayis claims to wield. I assume they are objects like the ones that you brought. It will give us an edge, I hope."

"Knowledge can be a dangerous thing. I hope what I have will best serve you." He followed the king's line of sight to the unusual flock of birds flying in wide circles far away. "I'll do my best, but can Leodor be trusted?"

"That's why I branded him. He can't call on the Sect. They'll kill him. And he believes that the Underlord is the head of them. It makes sense. I didn't know Arcayis deeply as a boy, but I know enough to know that he was a worm. How he manipulated my father so long I don't understand."

"Perhaps he turned. People change. It happens all of the time in my world."

Abraham's eyes widened as the great birds flew right toward the castle wall at a high rate of speed. Several of them were flying in a diamond formation. Riders rose up from the back of the birds, but the birds had scales. They weren't birds—they were dragons, with ruddy scales and hard spiny ridges on their bodies the size of horses.

"Your Majesty, those are dragons, aren't they?"

Clarice rushed over to the wall beside her father. "Zillon

dragon riders!" she exclaimed. "I can't believe it!" She started waving.

The king lifted his chin, raised his eyebrows, and made a weak smile. "Long-standing allies," he said to Abraham. "From the Peaks of Little Leg. It seems they come to show support. A good sign from the Elders."

The zillon dragon riders formed a ring and circled about one hundred yards away from the wall. The zillons wore open-faced metal helmets with small purple plumes waving from the tops. They had skull faces and big black eyes, very much like aliens from movies, but they were built like men. They were shirtless and wore leather breeches. The dragons they rode were ugly lizards with wings and a little bigger than horses. They gave Abraham the creeps.

"Uh, are you sure that they are on your side?" he asked.

"They've never not been on the side of the crown," the king said as everyone now stood along the wall. "The zillons are renowned peacekeepers and fighters. That's how they keep the peace. Why?"

Abraham shrugged and said, "Because I feel like fire ants are crawling up my back." He leaned outward and narrowed his eyes. The lead zillon rider unshouldered what looked like a rifle. The zillon rider butted the weapon on his shoulder and pointed it at the king. A red dot brightened on the weapon. The same dot appeared on King Hector's chest.

King Hector looked at the laser dot on his chest and tried to brush it away. "What is this? A glow fly? I've never seen the likes of it before."

Abraham sprang into action. "Everybody, get down!"

He tackled the king just as a hail of gunfire began. The stone wall of the terrace spat chunks of rock as bullets blasted into it. The steady spray of bullets kept coming with a loud popping sound.

"Stay down! Everyone stay down!"

The king started yelling. "Archers! Archers! Pratt, summon the archers!"

A sharp whistle cut through the sound of the advanced weaponry being fired. Archers appeared on top of the castle, wearing acorn-shaped helmets. They drew their bows and fired from the castle roof in kneeling positions. Arrows sailed over the Bay of Elders to the snap of bowstrings.

Abraham dared a peek over the wall. Only one of the six zillons carried a rifle. The other five carried crossbows, and they returned their own volley toward the archers. They unleashed one last hail of crossbow bolts and gunfire. More stones were chipped away. The enemy turned the dragons away and flew back toward the coast of Little Leg.

"What in the Elders was that popping sound?" King Hector asked as he crouched behind the wall.

"That was an assault rifle. It makes a very distinct firing sound," Abraham said as the zillons distanced themselves. "It's a weapon soldiers use in my world. It's like a hundred bows in one." He scanned the group. "Is everyone okay?"

Clarann was covering Clarice with her body, but they seemed fine otherwise. Lewis and Leodor were wide-eyed but fine as well. On top of the castle roof, one of the archers lay over the rim, dangling lifelessly.

Pratt jogged over to the king. His head was bleeding, as though something had grazed his skull. "Sire, I'll send riders to destroy those assassins. Just say the word, Your Majesty."

"Keep your eyes on the skies, Pratt! It seems we have new enemies afoot. How disappointing." The king looked down on his robes and dusted his chest. "Where did that bright mark go?"

"It's gone. With them," Abraham said. "That was a laser

pointer. They use it to aim at a target. I guess they were aiming at you."

The king gave Abraham a dumbfounded look and asked, "Did you say that weapon, eh, assault rifle, was like one hundred bows in one?"

"Sadly, I think that's a fair assessment. It's a good thing that they only had one." Abraham's heart beat in his ears. Something crazy was going on. He searched the skies. "And you better pray that they don't have more of them."

ABOUT THE AUTHOR

Thanks for reading *The King's Assassin*. It's my pleasure to give you the best books that I can write as fast as I can get them out. I know there are some power readers out there devouring books like snack cakes and I want to keep you happy. Hopefully you won't see what I have in store for you coming, but it's going to be fantastic the further that you read. So stay dialed in. The best is yet to come!

Please leave a review. They are a huge help to me! Here is a link.

Book 3 - The King's Prisoner, is now Available. LINK

* Follow me on Bookbub.

* I'd love it if you would subscribe to my mailing list: www.craighalloran.com

* On Facebook, you can find me at The Darkslayer Report or Craig Halloran.

* Twitter, Twitter, Twitter. I am there, too: www.twitter.com/CraigHalloran.

* And of course, you can always email me at craig@thedarkslayer.com. I love to hear from you!

ALSO BY CRAIG HALLORAN

Craig Halloran resides with his family outside his hometown of Charleston, West Virginia. When he isn't entertaining mankind, he is seeking adventure, working out, or watching sports. To learn more about him, go to: www.thedarkslayer.com.

Check out all of my great stories...

Free Books

The Darkslayer: Brutal Beginnings

Nath Dragon—Quest for the Thunderstone

The Red Citadel and the Sorcerer's Power

The Henchmen Chronicles

The King's Henchmen

The King's Assassin

The King's Prisoner

The King's Conjurer

The King's Enemies

The King's Spies

The Odyssey of Nath Dragon Series (New Series) (Prequel to Chronicles of Dragon)

Exiled

Enslaved

Deadly

Hunted

Strife

The Chronicles of Dragon Series 1 (10-book series)

The Hero, the Sword and the Dragons (Book 1)

Dragon Bones and Tombstones (Book 2)

Terror at the Temple (Book 3)

Clutch of the Cleric (Book 4)

Hunt for the Hero (Book 5)

Siege at the Settlements (Book 6)

Strife in the Sky (Book 7)

Fight and the Fury (Book 8)

War in the Winds (Book 9)

Finale (Book 10)

Boxset 1-5

Boxset 6-10

Collector's Edition 1-10

Tail of the Dragon, The Chronicles of Dragon, Series 2 (10-book series)

Tail of the Dragon #1

Claws of the Dragon #2

Battle of the Dragon #3

Eyes of the Dragon #4

Flight of the Dragon #5

Trial of the Dragon #6

Judgement of the Dragon #7

Wrath of the Dragon #8

Power of the Dragon #9

Hour of the Dragon #10

Boxset 1-5

Boxset 6-10

Collector's Edition 1-10

<u>The Darkslayer Series (6-book series)</u>

Wrath of the Royals (Book 1)

Blades in the Night (Book 2)

Underling Revenge (Book 3)

Danger and the Druid (Book 4)

Outrage in the Outlands (Book 5)

Chaos at the Castle (Book 6)

Boxset 1-3

Boxset 4-6

Omnibus 1-6

<u>The Darkslayer: Bish and Bone, Series 2 (10-book series)</u>

Bish and Bone (Book 1)

Black Blood (Book 2)

Red Death (Book 3)

Lethal Liaisons (Book 4)

Torment and Terror (Book 5)

Brigands and Badlands (Book 6)

War in the Wasteland (Book 7)

Slaughter in the Streets (Book 8)

Hunt of the Beast (Book 9)

The Battle for Bone (Book 10)

Boxset 1-5

Boxset 6-10

Bish and Bone Omnibus (Books 1-10)

CLASH OF HEROES: Nath Dragon meets The Darkslayer miniseries

Book 1

Book 2

Book 3

The Gamma Earth Cycle

Escape from the Dominion

Flight from the Dominion

Prison of the Dominion

The Supernatural Bounty Hunter Files (10-book series)

Smoke Rising: Book 1

I Smell Smoke: Book 2

Where There's Smoke: Book 3

Smoke on the Water: Book 4

Smoke and Mirrors: Book 5

Up in Smoke: Book 6

Smoke Signals: Book 7

Holy Smoke: Book 8

Smoke Happens: Book 9

Smoke Out: Book 10

Boxset 1-5

<u>OTHER WORKS & NOVELLAS</u>